THE CREATOR

GUÐRÚN EVA MÍNERVUDÓTTIR, born in 1976, was raised in various villages around Iceland, and spent her youth bartending and studying. A professional writer since the age of twenty-two, she lives in Reykjavik with her husband, filmmaker Marteinn Thorsson, and daughter Mínerva Marteinsdóttir. This is her first book to be translated into English. www.minervudottir.com

# The Creator

## GUÐRÚN EVA
## MÍNERVUDÓTTIR

Translated from the Icelandic by
Sarah Bowen

Portobello

First published by Portobello Books 2012
This paperback edition published 2013

Portobello Books
12 Addison Avenue
London
W11 4QR
United Kingdom

First published in Iceland as *Skaparinn* by JPV, Forlagið,
Reykjavík, in 2008

This book has been published with the financial support of
Bókmenntasjóður/the Icelandic Literature Fund.

Bókmenntasjóður
The Icelandic Literature Fund

A CIP catalogue record for this book is available
from the British Library
9 8 7 6 5 4 3 2 1

ISBN 978 1 84627 252 3

www.portobellobooks.com

Typeset in Bembo by M Rules

Printed and bound by CPI Group (UK) Ltd, Croydon, CR0 4YY

# PART ONE

# I

*Friday Evening*

Sveinn hung the last ones out to dry: the hooks pierced the back of the necks. Fortunately the holes would be hidden by silky soft hair once the heads were added. He placed a ruler between the ankles: it was important that they dried slightly apart, otherwise they might handle awkwardly, like apprehensive virgins. And there they hung, all four of them, all body type number 4. He straightened himself up, eased the small of his back with a damp, aching hand and admired their colouring: golden brown, as though they had wandered naked all summer in the sunshine shielded only by a fine haze of cloud. The colour mix had worked perfectly and he made a mental note to write down the proportions before the numbers faded from memory.

He didn't consider himself an artist, although others sometimes gave him that dubious accolade. He was a craftsman, a master craftsman in his field, yet he didn't puff himself up over it – for what is self-satisfaction other than the flip side of stagnation? He would not be guilty of either. His job was to craft as skilfully as he could, to create an illusion of human consciousness – shining out of blue or hazel eyes, floating behind half-closed red lips, framed in blonde, raven-black or auburn curls – and to let his beautiful girls go into the world, in the hope that they would bring their owners joy.

He took off his rubber apron and hung it on a nail by the door, washed his hands in the cubby-hole off the drying room and put his watch back on. When he saw that it was well after eight he realized his stomach was rumbling, his jaw was stiff and his temples were throbbing unbearably. His finger joints were on fire and pain ricocheted round his wrists and elbows. It was the same every time – when his concentration relaxed his body began to protest.

Leaning heavily against the door frame, he tried to recall what was in the fridge. It would have been quicker to wander into the kitchen, open the fridge and scan the contents, but that was beyond him right then – he needed to let the tiredness ebb away before he did anything, but at the same time he knew he couldn't unwind until he had some food inside him.

What was there? Minced beef nearing its sell-by date, onions, potatoes, flatbread, butter. Anything else? Cheese, tuna in oil, wafer-thin slices of processed smoked lamb in cumbersome packaging. He didn't feel like cooking – he thought the knives and wooden spoons would be so heavy. Heavier than the steel he used in his girls' joints. Heavier than lead. It was a wonder the bases of the boxes he transported them in didn't give way under them.

There were a couple of restaurants nearby, but he wasn't ready to face people after working so many days on end. He could get himself flatbread and coffee, but it went against the grain to let three hundred grams of minced beef go to waste.

No, there was only one thing for it now: to shift himself from the door frame. Although he longed for nothing more than to take it with him into the kitchen and to lean against it while the onions and mince browned in the pan. One foot in front of the other, it could be done. A pleasant problem compared to an empty fridge and having to go out to the shops. Or being broke and needing to borrow cash to go shopping, which had sometimes been the case when he was a student and before the doll-making really got going.

Four medium-sized potatoes in a saucepan; just enough water to cover them. He couldn't help giving a wry smile when he needed both hands to carry the pan from the sink to the stove. If the pain in his joints was anything to go by these working bouts really didn't agree with his body. And the little finger on his right hand had been numb since early January, thanks to a trapped nerve in his arm.

Two red onions, one beginning to sprout. He took one of the heavy knives from the second drawer down and used the point to draw back the kitchen curtains and let in the gleaming-white May sun. At nine in the evening the light was still bright and dazzled him for a few seconds, so he wasn't sure whether there really was a car in the drive or whether it was a trick of the light – a green smudge which danced before his eyes as they grew accustomed to the brightness. He would put butter and salt on the potatoes. The very thought of butter jolted his stomach like a hearty dig in the ribs. Yes, it was a car, a bright-green Renault, and a woman with long, wavy blonde hair was getting out. He automatically thought, *Honey-Golden Susie*, but her hair was perhaps the only doll-like thing about her.

What was she doing there?

Whatever it was, she would have to wait while he ate. The mince was in the pan, the pan on the hob. He tasted some of the raw meat – it got his stomach juices going. He concentrated on the feeling of hunger, which left him little attention to give to the woman hunched over the open boot of the car. Perhaps she wanted to sell him something. Or talk to him about Jesus. He would soon shut the door in her face.

A jack. A wheel brace. Only then did he notice that one of the tyres was completely flat.

The woman dragged the spare tyre out of the boot and rolled it along to the front of the car, leant it up against the grill and attempted, rather comically, to get the dirt off her hands by shaking them and patting her palms.

'Good girl,' he muttered, with tears in his eyes from the onions, when he saw her sure movements. She seemed to know what she was doing, even if she was wearing a pure-white woollen coat and fancy shoes. Off with the hubcap in one swift movement. *That's it, take up the wheel brace and loosen the locking wheel-nut.*

The last time he'd had to do that he'd begun by jacking up the car and then had to jack it back down so he could loosen the nuts. The shame of it hadn't run very deep, it hadn't wounded his male pride – he hadn't been quite with it, that was all.

The woman pushed the wheel brace with her foot, but the nut didn't budge. She stood on it as though it was the edge of a step, held onto the car roof with both hands and bounced up and down in a determined fashion, but nothing happened. She tried the nut above, but to no avail, then flung the brace onto the gravel, flopped her elbows down on the roof and buried her face in her hands.

She looked like she was about to burst into tears and, without thinking, he turned off the heat before heading for the door, rather too quickly as he then came over dizzy. On the way out, he determined to be friendly.

'Is it stuck solid?' he asked, and despite his voice sounding harsher than he'd intended she gave a lopsided smile.

'Yes,' she sighed, and judging from the sigh and the stoop of her shoulders she was almost as tired as he was. Her eyes were edged with crow's feet, her eyebrows drawn as if she was permanently worried, and she had a sensitive mouth with a dimple on one side. 'I thought breaking down outside a garage was too good to be true, but I see it's not a garage any more,' she said, and looked over at the neat almost weed-free lawn, with its newly sprouting grass which looked even greener than the surrounding vegetation.

'They moved to bigger premises down the road ten years ago,' he said, and bent down for the wheel brace, slotted it over the nut and applied his full weight. But nothing happened. He laughed in disbelief. 'Who on earth can have done these up?' he muttered.

'Dad!' she replied, the dimple becoming more pronounced as a shadow passed across her face. 'He was a taxi driver and the European Seniors Bench Press Champion.'

'I can well believe it,' he said, and ran his eyes over her ample frame. There was certainly no shortage of flesh on the bones of this statuesque family. He looked back at her face again to contemplate her sorrowful smile, but it had already disappeared and her face was expressionless.

He couldn't keep his eyes off her hands, without registering what was different about them. And her wrists; they were complex, alive. You could say they were practical. He recalled the blind musician – what was his name? Ray Charles, wasn't it? – who would feel the wrists of women to see if they were beautiful. Clever of him. It wouldn't have been very gentlemanly to run his fingers straight over their faces before asking their name. What would Ray have felt if he had slid his hands over those strong wrists?

She stuck her hands into her coat pockets and watched him, her face displaying expressions he could in no way decipher.

'What?' she asked.

'Nothing,' he said, and stared at his feet, which seemed far away, covered in mist. The very presence of the woman in the white coat made him tired. He was in no state to deal with this. 'I have a small sledgehammer in the shed,' he said. 'I'll fix this for you when I've had something to eat. I haven't had anything since this time yesterday evening.'

She raised her eyebrows and glanced around as though searching for some alternative. At that, his head cleared and, with all the warmth he could muster, although he feared it sounded more like sarcasm or outright impatience, he added, 'If you wouldn't mind sitting with me in the kitchen in the meantime I guarantee you will be ready to go in an hour and a half.'

She followed him hesitantly, and he was grateful to her for sparing him the 'Oh, I really shouldn'ts' and other insincere protestations. It was best that way. He didn't want her to leave immediately, for although he needed to unwind he was keenly aware that he hadn't seen another human face for days. He wanted to look at a face that moved. It didn't matter if she had nothing to say or was full of empty chatter – he didn't have the energy to listen or make intelligent comments in any case.

The woman laid her coat over the back of a chair and flopped down on the one next to it. She glanced around with little sign of interest, didn't say much and barely moved, evidently because she understood that he was hungry and tired. He didn't want her to be understanding; the thought of understanding women made him shudder. Millions upon millions of understanding women throughout the world, who thought little and said even less.

He was taken aback by this thought, which had come to him unbidden and was so unlike him or, at least, so unlike the image he had of himself. It was as if he had a radio transmitter in his head and some unscrupulous type was dictating what was going on up there. He turned the heat back on under the pan, tossed some spices in and set the table for two, without bothering to say that his visitor was welcome to join him. He didn't believe in wordy explanations, they always became nonsensical, and he didn't believe in helping people to make decisions either. If a person was too reserved to help themselves, or so polite they left the food untouched, then that was their affair.

The mince was cooked through, but the onions were still half raw. It didn't matter much. Sveinn opened the glass cabinet and, after a moment's hesitation, decided not to bother with the wine glasses and to use small tumblers for the wine instead. Otherwise she might think he had unrealistic romantic ideas about the meal. He picked up a half-full bottle of red wine and said, 'I hope you don't think this is inappropriate, but I like a glass of wine with my meal.'

She shook her head and her eyes lit up a little. It was obviously all right for him to unwind: she was clearly not the type to read something into every single action. She didn't even seem to properly take in what was going on around her.

What was she thinking anyway? He was well aware that fatigue made him appear drunk. Didn't she hesitate before following a drinker into his house?

She poured out two glasses of wine, and helped herself from the pan. That was the last thing he noticed for a while. He almost forgot she was there, because it took all his exhausted attention to slice his potatoes in half and smear a dollop of butter over the smooth surfaces. Salt. Oh, God! Tears came to his eyes at the very thought of the taste of buttered potatoes with salt.

When he next looked up she had finished her glass and was refilling it. *Well, now!* he thought and must have relaxed slightly, because he was genuinely delighted that a strange woman was sitting down to eat with him, even if they were both rather uncommunicative.

'I knew I wouldn't be able to undo the bolts,' she said, and glanced quickly at him before turning her attention to the fork in his hand. 'That's why I was hoping the garage would still be here and the guys wouldn't have all gone home.'

She shook her head and added, 'When Dad changed a light bulb he often broke the bulb and the fixing, and sometimes he pulled knobs off doors. I think he did it deliberately so that we would tell these stories about him.' She laughed, and he couldn't help laughing with her. Mainly because the wine had made her ears red.

'Is he still alive?' he asked.

'We buried him last week,' she replied. 'It was a heart attack. He had stopped driving but carried on lifting weights even though the doctor and I had both begged him to ease off.'

An unpleasant feeling, which Sveinn had been trying for days to keep at bay, settled heavily upon him. He couldn't help thinking about the fellow who had killed himself a few days before. And now when a strange woman talked about her father's death he had the feeling that men were dropping all around him like flies. As though the hand of death were caressing him, poking his ribs to see if he was fat enough for slaughter. Which was rather extreme, considering both men had been old enough to be his father.

That suicide case had managed to force its way into Sveinn's life. Sveinn had refused to be interviewed by the journalist, but nevertheless she had printed a photo of him next to her article which somehow implied that he was indirectly responsible for the tragedy.

What about the guys who'd sold him his television? Weren't they equally to blame? If the old man had been soft in the head and muddled fantasy with reality that wasn't Sveinn's fault, and it certainly wasn't the fault of the doll who, the tabloid said, had accompanied him in his death. Although, yes, the man had torn off her head, sliced off her breasts and ripped her skin to shreds before he shot himself with an old farm rifle.

Sveinn had done his best to make the journalist see how lacking in taste it would be to cover this story at all. That the self-destruction of an old man was not newsworthy, no matter how many sex aids he had in his cupboard, or if he had chosen to destroy some of his possessions before he looked down the barrel. But she'd refused to listen, keen to prove herself in her new job and as fascinated by his girls as everyone else was. And just as most people felt obliged to veil their interest with moralizing, she justified her inquisitiveness by making out that this was something she, as a journalist, had a duty to expose.

He observed the woman sitting opposite him at the table more carefully. She resembled typical drawings of the first women settlers: large, round eyes and big, shapely bosoms that rested firmly on a sturdy, solid torso, and legs like two magnificent pillars. Without getting up, he reached across for another bottle and opened it discreetly. He wanted to see her drunk. If she chose to drive home in that condition it wouldn't really be his fault.

On the other hand, it wasn't right. He had some responsibility towards her while she was not quite herself.

Unbalanced in a beautiful, peaceful way, not at all hysterical, there she was sitting in his home, and he wanted to top her up with wine, even though she was driving and had almost been shedding tears onto the roof of her car a little earlier. He wanted to know more about her loss and the pain it had clearly left her with. He wanted her to say something crass, to make a fool of herself, to be degraded by sentimentality. There was something inside him which he couldn't understand, and this was the only way he could give vent to it.

Later that evening, she sat in the living room – though it barely deserved the title; it was a small room off the kitchen with three comfy chairs and a little table. She sat there sleeping, her mouth half open, covered with the coat and blanket he had put over her. Her face looked childlike and peaceful in sleep, and with her lips parted like that she reminded him of the face design he called *Lovely*, a design that didn't have the popularity he felt it deserved. She would be far from pleased when she woke up, but there was no point in waking her – she was in no fit state to drive home anyway.

He had changed the wheel. When he had succeeded in getting the thing off there were dents in the steel rim from the nuts – this father of hers must have been a giant of a man – and while he had been abusing the sledgehammer and applying his full body weight to the wheel brace, she had worked her way down the second bottle of wine. Even so, it wasn't as if she'd got wildly drunk. She'd just succumbed further and further to the tiredness until he'd offered her a more comfortable seat and almost at once she had nodded off. But this was not before he had discovered that the reason for her trip had been to seek psychological help for her two daughters. What else could her mysterious confession have meant?

'Both my daughters have lost their grip, although they've barely started out on life, and I have to do something,' she had replied, with an inebriated shake of the head, her downturned mouth quivering slightly, when he'd asked her why she was there.

That had been the only time she had really seemed vulnerable and the only vulgarity she had treated him to all evening. She was clearly one of those who can drink themselves into a stupor without losing self-control.

He sat down in front of her at the table, felt for her right hand under the blanket and found it on her thigh, the palm facing upwards and the fingers in a relaxed curve. He slid her hand out from under the blanket and examined it; the woman who called herself Lóa did not flutter an eyelid. She might as well have been on drugs. One could be forgiven for thinking he had knocked her unconscious with the wheel brace, not offered her food and wine.

Transparent nail varnish, beginning to flake slightly. A partially healed cut on her index finger. *That must have bled a lot*, he thought. Her hand was warm and he turned it over and looked at the bones showing through the skin.

Her hands were not remarkable, quite the opposite, they were quite ordinary. He had been mulling this over earlier in the evening, when he was out in the covered driveway, and had realized that the hands were the main thing that stopped his girls looking like people. Their fingers bent in odd directions, their wrists were stiff and, on the back of their hands, no bones could be seen gliding under the skin. He had no idea how he could design something similar to what he was now holding in his hand and admiring.

He had almost forgotten his weariness, but now it swept over him inexorably and he laid Lóa's hand on the arm of the chair, pulled a corner of the blanket over this work of art and unbuttoned his shirt on his way to bed.

# 2

*Saturday Morning*

Lóa's eyelids were glued together from yesterday's make-up. The clatter of the letterbox had woken her and, as she heard the postman's footsteps fading, she became aware of a raft of discomforts pressing in on her. She was so desperate to pee that she doubted she could even stand up. Her slumped position filled her with alarm because, instead of lying on her front as she usually did when sleeping, she was sitting half upright with her chin on her chest, and it felt as if her right hand was floating in mid-air. She pulled it towards her and placed it on her cheek, then used two fingers, stiff with cold, to prize open one eye and then the other, only to find herself staring at a blank wall covered in pale-green wallpaper with a dark-green pattern on it. Although her body felt sweaty, her feet were cold and heavy, and she looked down to see that someone had covered her with a coarse checked blanket, which she didn't remember seeing before. She was still wearing her shoes, and her coat was in a pile on the floor.

Of course. She wasn't at home but at the house of the man who had offered to help her change the tyre. Her tongue was dry in her mouth. Margrét. Ína. Her heart pounded as she thought of everything which could have happened to her daughters left alone that night.

The cold hit her as she threw off the blanket. Still, she didn't dare bend over to pick up her coat and just eased herself carefully to her feet; she felt pins and needles spread out from

15

her groin, as the blood began to circulate freely round her legs once more, and she set off in search of the bathroom. She passed through the kitchen, which bore no traces of last night's meal, and the morning sun which flooded the room made her eyes fill with tears for the second time since her arrival there. There were cobwebs in the corners, but otherwise the kitchen was neat and tidy – much tidier than her kitchen had ever been. Except perhaps when she and the girls had just moved out and left the girls' father seven years before and she'd tried to compensate for the upheaval by having everything just so.

Knives clung to the magnetic strip along the wall and kitchen utensils hung from iron hooks: pans, wooden spoons, ladles, whisks and forks. The oak cupboards were old and small. The work surfaces were low, the drawers shallow and the doors of the eye-level cupboards had been removed so that the crockery was on view – white and stacked as if in a guest house.

The kitchen table was covered with a yellow cloth, and in the middle lay her car keys and mobile. The clock on the mobile said 6:47. Hopefully the girls had not noticed her absence. She was particularly anxious about Margrét, who often took a while to calm down if there was no-one around when she woke. She was fifteen, going on sixteen, but really needed an eye kept on her day and night.

Leading from the kitchen was a hallway with three closed doors. There were two large strip lights in the ceiling, but no switch to be seen and she couldn't find one even though she patted the walls around the doorway in case it was hidden from view in the half-dark. A tiled floor stretched before her in the gloom and her footsteps resounded from it, despite her efforts to tread softly.

She felt uncomfortable nosing round a strange house, but

there was nothing else for it as the pressure on her bladder impelled her forwards. And if the owner woke up and found her he would surely understand that there was no way she could wait to relieve herself of the whole bottle of red wine she'd drunk the previous evening.

She opened the first door very carefully to reveal a small room facing south like the kitchen. Her eyes quickly became accustomed to the light, and when she saw the man lying there in a single bed against the wall under the window she was so taken aback that she trod on her own toes in her haste to back hurriedly out of the room. But he was sleeping so soundly it was hard to imagine that he would ever wake again, and she allowed herself to pause a moment. Mainly to take a deep breath so she didn't knock into something or inadvertently make a noise shutting the door.

There were no curtains at the window so the sun was visible in the blue sky and she saw that her car stood waiting for her. It was no longer standing askew from the puncture, thanks to the man who lay sleeping with his arms around the duvet. He had old-fashioned black underpants on – no boxers or designer labels on the waistband – and she remembered that he had a name. Half-naked men were rarely nameless and this one, with the back of his dark head resting against the hard headboard and his face hidden in the fold of his duvet, was called Sveinn.

He had folded his clothes over the back of a chair before going to bed. She also noticed a large wicker basket next to the wardrobe, obviously used for dirty laundry, and next to that a little shoe-cleaning box with brushes and cloths. This touched her in a way she couldn't quite fathom and mustn't dwell on now. She shut the door silently and fumbled her way further down the hallway. She found a doorknob and tried it, but the door was locked.

Behind the third door was an empty room, streaked with light which forced its way in through the greyish blinds. Lóa screwed up her eyes to see through the dust motes, making everything look fuzzy round the edges. The rug was dirty and the smell of lubricating oil reminded her of those hours she had spent in her youth waiting aimlessly for her father at the garage. Because taxis need to be polished regularly, as he never tired of telling her. His taxi had been a top-of-the-range West German model and looked almost brand new when it had a good coat of polish. At the funeral she had had the irrational feeling that she was waiting for him.

Ína had sat by her side in her best dress, which was slightly too tight, and swung her feet, which didn't quite reach the floor. Lóa had sat there with tears in her eyes, her head drooping as she clutched tightly onto Ína's coat, looking round now and then as if she was a child again, waiting in a dirty tea room where there was nothing to do except suck on a sugar cube and look at the pictures of bikini-clad girls on the walls.

As she was closing the third and final door, she saw from the way the faint streaks of light fell on the floor that the hallway carried on, that there was not a wall at the end of it, but more darkness from which came a slightly sharp smell, reminiscent of varnish and vinegar. She fumbled around in the darkness until she found a switch. Row after row of strip lights sputtered into life with buzzing and flickering noises and a large, windowless room appeared. This was the section of the house which, from the outside, had looked like a small Nissen hut attached to the main building, and the fluorescent lights were suspended on cables from the convex ceiling.

Female torsos hung in the corner furthest from the door, their feet held apart with rulers. There were four of them, all exactly the same design, with breasts so pert that the skin-coloured nipples pointed straight up in the air. Their arms hung slightly away from their bodies, not by their sides, in the way people stand to keep their balance on board a ship. The way they held their arms made them look alive even without their heads, and Lóa felt surrounded. Her shoulders tensed and the pressure on her bladder became almost unbearable.

She longed to escape, but an ominous fear overwhelmed her and she stood frozen in the doorway. She exhaled quickly, took a deep breath and looked carefully around her. Not a sound. No movements other than her own. She was alone there, no-one was watching and she had nothing to fear. Now she had to think clearly, reassure herself that she was indeed awake and try to come up with a convincing explanation for this grotesque scene.

The previous evening, just before she had nodded off in the armchair, Sveinn had told her he made dolls, but she hadn't exactly been paying attention and maybe she had imagined something romantic: puppets with extraordinary nobility in the lines of their carved faces, or pale china dolls in creamy white silk dresses. It was hardly possible to dream up something more unromantic than this.

As she took a long, comforting breath to rid herself of the final remnants of fear, the doorway to her memory opened a crack wider. Their skin was silicone – hence the smell. She had smelled this sharp, vinegary smell of drying silicone before, and now she wanted to examine the dolls more carefully, to see if the texture was as close to human skin as it appeared.

No, it was more important to find the bathroom and hurry back home before the girls woke. Besides, maybe this Sveinn had a screw loose and would go berserk if he found her there.

That's right. Hadn't he behaved rather oddly the evening before? The man had been gruff one minute and gentle the next, at times attentive and at others totally blank.

She was just about to turn off the lights and leave, when she noticed another door inside the room. The thought that this could be the door she was looking for drew her towards it, despite her discomfort at being in there. Windowless rooms were unpleasant, headless torsos were unpleasant and the same was true of sleeping men one barely knew. The shame of having babbled on with grape-stained lips and then nodded off was also unpleasant, and too alien for Lóa to admit even to herself.

The room off the workshop turned out to be some sort of storeroom for bodies and heads wrapped in polythene, wigs, large canisters full of liquid, bags of silicone powder, boxes of all different sizes, waterproof paints and brushes. There was also a sink, spotlessly clean yet giving the impression that many hands had been washed there over the years – the white enamel was beginning to wear away revealing the shining steel underneath. She simply stared at the plughole and then it was as though all thoughts were suspended and something else took over. She pulled up a little stool covered in paint splashes, climbed up onto it, undid her trousers, felt carefully behind her to support her hands and let it flow. It took a moment or two because her muscles were so tensed from holding it all in, but finally she managed to aim a fountain of pee fit for a horse directly down the plughole and let out an anguished sound of pained relief.

She felt almost weightless when she'd climbed down from the stool and zipped herself back up. *Empty like those dolls out there*, she thought, and laughed out loud as she washed her hands and splashed water all around the sink to remove any evidence.

She hadn't felt so light-hearted in a long while, not since long before her father died, perhaps not since before Margrét became ill. It was a physical joy which sprang from physical relief, but the mind makes little distinction between physical and more sublime joy. An exaggerated sense of courage and curiosity accompanied this particular feeling. Even though she was first and foremost an anxious mother and a grieving daughter, she was still a person in her own right.

It was the labels on the crates and sacks which aroused her curiosity: *Plaster, Alginade, Skinflex*. And the wigs: *Candy-Pink Lisa, Red-Hot Daisy, Raven-Black Lola, Honey-Golden Susie*.

As she came out of the storeroom, the first thing that met her eye was a huge poster of Da Vinci's Vitruvian Man, except it wasn't a man but a woman whose outstretched limbs were marked by circles which focussed attention on the perfection of her proportions in ideal ratio. There were also drawings of models, photographs of various parts of the body, sketches and models for the dolls' skeletons. And in one corner stood a small, battered desk with a computer and printer.

It felt like she was snooping round an elderly watchmaker's workshop – everything in there seemed to point to an ongoing uplifting endeavour. The roof of the Nissen hut rose over her like the vaulted ceiling of a church and, despite the brilliant fluorescent lighting, she felt she was in the presence of an overwhelming holiness and that she was actually breaking an ancient covenant simply by being there.

She was hardly aware of her footsteps as she walked over to the corner where the dolls were hanging, and with each step the floor seemed to become more distant and insubstantial. There was something forbidden and voyeuristic about seeing them half formed like that, irrespective of whether she had permission to be there or not. Yes, they were naked, but that was not the issue, it was rather that they had no faces, no eyes, and that gave Lóa the feeling that she was staring at people who didn't know they were being watched. It was as though their sanctity was being violated, as though they were not just objects.

They were beautiful, without blemish, apart from barely noticeable joins on their sides and the outsides of their legs. They had not yet been given nails, but from the shape of their fingertips and toes it was obvious they would have them.

Cautiously, Lóa touched the seam on one of the dolls' thighs. The fact that they were hanging there could mean that they were still hardening. But the silicone skin was stretched tight and firm to the touch, and left no mark when she gently prodded it.

The ball of the foot felt as smooth as a pebble from the beach. She ran her finger under the arch of the foot, and her own feet, which were still numbed from sitting all night in tight trousers, tingled in response. It was obvious what the dolls were intended for and Lóa felt compelled to slip two fingers into the doll's private parts: it felt firm but soft and rather cold.

She wanted to see the dolls in their finished state, to touch their hair and see how realistic they could appear. She glanced around and noticed an oblong wooden box by the wall. From the position of the two metal strips, one on the lid and one on the chest itself, it was evident that a padlock was meant to secure them together. But there wasn't one.

She crept towards the chest and opened it slightly. Her heart was thumping again and her blood pulsated down to her fingers. She wasn't sure how she would feel about meeting the eye of a finished doll and considered closing the box before she'd properly looked inside. Of course she shouldn't delay any further but just get herself out to the car and drive home to Margrét. And to Ína, who was not at all happy to be left alone with her sister. Lóa vowed this would not happen again. But she couldn't resist opening the chest wider. She might not get another chance and five minutes or so would hardly make any difference to the girls.

The chest could have held at least three of the dolls, but there was only one, floating in white styrofoam. A sea of little white balls which looked like freshly fallen hailstones settled around her dress and reached up to where her hands were resting. Her skin was almost as pale as the foam balls, her hair was smooth and jet-black, her pink lips were slightly parted and her face was oddly familiar.

Even though her hand looked steady enough, Lóa was sure she could feel it tremble as she reached forward to touch one of the doll's eyes. It was made of glass and cold to the touch, but the expression was not at all cold or dead. She'd dreaded seeing this dull, glassy stare and now couldn't help shuddering at how life-like it was, how the eyes seemed to move and the eyelids flutter with their dark, sweeping lashes.

She touched the doll's mouth and saw that she didn't have any teeth, that the silicone on the inside was soft and yielding, like the vaginas of the ones hanging from the ceiling, although somehow 'vagina' didn't feel like the right word. It was strange to think that she was toothless, for the pubescent plumpness of her face certainly didn't give that impression.

The dress, which was made from semi-transparent pink silk with narrow shoulder straps, fell in soft folds over her breasts, which quivered at the touch of a hand and felt slightly firmer than their living counterparts. Under the silk was a hint of black pubic hair and pink nipples unlike the skin-coloured ones of her unfinished sisters.

Lóa was amazed at how plump her backside was and how solid her thighs. The doll in the box was more curvaceous and feminine than most bodies of flesh and blood.

Her thoughts turned to Margrét, and a lump rose to her throat. Tears distorted her vision and her eyes felt like the doll's – made of thick glass.

If Margrét had a doll for company perhaps her loneliness wouldn't be so painful. A doll might help her break out of her isolation and find her way back into the world.

Indeed, wasn't that how phobias were treated? People who were chronically afraid of spiders were introduced to plastic spiders before they came near living ones which run quickly in all manner of directions. What was troubling Margrét but an irrational aversion to her own body or a dread of life? A deep-seated distrust of anything and everything? It wasn't exactly possible to put your trust in a doll, but equally, it wasn't possible to distrust her either. She would always be waiting for you wherever you'd put her last and would never catch you unawares.

Margrét had turned her back on life because she didn't want to be caught off guard. No-one had managed to make her see that her response was illogical and simply wrong. But you never knew, the doll might just succeed where everyone else had failed. Even if it was only due to the doll's life-affirming sexual charisma: *Look at me, I am the very embodiment of the ideal, healthy woman.*

Something unravelled in Lóa, as if a coil had snapped or a shoelace broken. She became oblivious to everything except the tender lives of Ína and Margrét. She didn't even stop to consider how much the things cost, brand new and all dolled up in pink silk, lying in twenty litres of styrofoam which looked as though it had fallen from heaven in a cold snap in January. Sveinn could make a new doll. Lots of new ones, exactly like that one.

The rustling of the styrofoam balls was like whispering voices which gave no hint of warning or moralizing when Lóa eased one arm under the doll's knees and the other behind her back. Lóa was going to pick her up, but couldn't budge her because she was much heavier than she had anticipated, as if she was filled with sand, and Lóa could feel the jerk in her back. She rubbed the small of her back where the pain seemed to originate, and again moved towards the doll's head, put her arm round her shoulders and drew her half up out of the chest. By curling her fingers under the doll's breast, she got a better grip and raised her up into a sitting position.

A shiver went down Lóa's aching back, because handling the doll reminded her so much of handling a real person. She stayed sitting up, like a sick girl who had been helped to sit up in her bed.

Then she noticed the case at the back of the chest: a black, velvet-lined box, half hidden under the foam balls. It was unlocked and in it was a tube of viscous fluid, some pink nail varnish and a folded sheet of paper. She smoothed out the paper and read:

| | |
|---|---|
| Hair: | Raven–Black Lola |
| Face: | Lovely |
| Body Type: | 1 |
| Pubic Hair: | Black, Whole |
| Lips: | Natural Pink |

She folded it back up, left the box as she had found it and looked at the doll, who was still sitting upright, as though she were waiting for someone to pick her up and take her away. But of course she was incapable of waiting for anything or wanting anything, and even up close her expression was eternally blank. It occurred to Lóa that what she was planning was not only wrong but also foolish. It wasn't like slipping a cigarette lighter into your pocket or a ball-point pen, this was more along the lines of stealing a valuable painting or the family cat.

But stolen paintings and cats do not stop the world from turning.

*I'll return her later,* she thought. *I'll return her when Margrét is on the mend. And this Sveinn chap doesn't know my name or where I live. He'll fuss and fume, draw harsh conclusions about the drunken woman who was too weak to change her own tyre – and then he'll forget all about it.*

She looked around for something to protect the doll with, and saw some clear-plastic sheeting spattered with transparent white and skin-coloured splashes on the floor under the drying torsos. She spread it out behind the doll, then wiped her finger over the splashes to make sure they were completely dry, but didn't bother about the cloud of white dust which billowed up each time she moved the plastic. She grasped the doll's arm and lifted her in one swift movement over the side of the chest and laid her on her back on the plastic sheet. Her legs remained pointing up into the air. That was better than dragging her heels across the floor and getting wedged in the doorway. But her dress slithered up around her in an undignified fashion and she slipped onto one side because of the weight of her legs.

The doll slid across the concrete floor like a sledge over crisp snow. Lóa strained to listen and her tensed shoulders ached as the swishing and rustling plucked at her taut nerves.

The hallway was dark and too narrow to absorb the noise. If this didn't wake the doll's owner up then he was either ill or on medication. Still, there was nothing for it but to carry on.

'I don't give a damn,' she thought out loud, over and over, as though the words provided the impetus she needed to drag the doll that final stretch, through the kitchen, over the doorstep to the porch and across the paving stones to the covered driveway.

Next to her car was a dark-red pickup truck which must belong to the doll-maker. A Dodge Ram. A make her father had either deeply admired or intensely disliked. She couldn't remember which, just that such cars had aroused some kind of feeling in the old man.

Lóa straightened up, relieved to be in the daylight, which was beautifully golden in comparison with the white-blue of the fluorescent lights, and leant against the car while the fatigue drained from her back. The damned keys were still on the kitchen table. And her mobile. Which at that moment started ringing. Ína must have woken up and now she was about to wake the doll-maker too.

She shoved the doll's feet down onto the gravel, hastily covered her over and ran back towards the door. But she had forgotten to check whether it was on the latch, and held her breath as she tried the handle.

It didn't open.

Lóa's heart sank and she could feel hot tears burning her throat and the backs of her eyes, blurring her vision. She tried the handle again and gave the door a hard shove. It creaked open softly and she half stumbled into the kitchen, grabbed her keys and phone, which was as silent as a spring morning and in fact hadn't been ringing at all. The screen showed 7:09.

She ran back out, this time not even shutting the door, opened the boot and, with hands shaking so much that her keys jangled, she wrapped the plastic more evenly round the doll, eased her with difficulty into the boot and spent a mentally gruelling eternity getting her into the right position: curled up and more or less covered with the plastic. Each time she looked up, she thought she spotted a shadow appear in the doorway. And she kept looking up because her imagination had gone into overdrive, turning every heartbeat in her ears into approaching footsteps.

When she had carefully closed the lid of the boot, pushing it down with both hands till she heard it click shut, she got into the driver's seat and tried to quieten her ragged breathing. But then she remembered, and it was like a blow to her chest, that her coat was still indoors on the living room floor.

For a long while, she stared at the open back door, and a few times made as if to get out of the car, but stopped each time. She tried to recall whether there had been anything in the pockets, and convinced herself that there had just been her phone and the bunch of house and car keys which now swayed gently in the ignition – gently but enough to intensify her nausea. All the strength had drained out of her fingers as she turned the ignition with difficulty, put the engine in reverse and pressed hard on the accelerator. Too hard. The car gave a lurch and stalled.

Tears streamed down her face and, with a loud sobbing, she turned the key again. She longed just to lean on the steering wheel and sob her heart out until someone found her and took her somewhere she could rest, preferably somewhere protected by a tall hedge of thorns, or in a glass case with a heavy lock.

She backed out onto the road and was off, amazed that the car held steadily to the road, that it didn't career into a ditch or explode into the air. She couldn't remember ever having stolen anything in her life before – not since she was a youngster and stole cigarettes and small change from her parents' pockets and wallets – and the terror of committing such an anti-social act was greater than she could ever have imagined. She glanced back quickly – the back door was still ajar and the doll's owner was nowhere to be seen. She could hardly believe that she had done it, but instead of feeling relief she was overtaken by such anxiety that her surroundings seemed to glow white with danger. It was as if the aim had not been to steal and get away with it, but to be caught and taken out of action, the freedom and responsibility removed from her shoulders and given to a better and more competent person, who could take Ína and Margrét into their arms and help them. As for her, she was on the verge of collapse and in no position to help anyone, least of all herself.

The blue of the sky was so intense that she could almost taste it, and she took in the colours and shapes as she drove by: Akrafjall mountain, the fence posts, the hayfield just recovering after the winter. When she handed her credit card shakily to the lad in the booth at the mouth of the Hvalfjörður Tunnel she only needed to glance at his eyes to catch the distant cry of his hopes and desires.

She kept her eyes on the road and yet it was as if she was looking down on everything from above: trawlers in the estuary of the fjord, rippling glittering waves, speckled hayfields and crooked fences, a sleepy young lad in the tollbooth. She saw down into the sea and through the carved-out slab of rock below it; and the green Renault in the badly lit tunnel, herself at the wheel with the silk-clad evidence of her crime in the boot. The phantasm was bathed in light, full of reflections dancing off the surface of the sea, but still the sunlight dazzled her as she drove out of the tunnel and the soft, smooth sky took over from the coarse-hewn rock. Occasionally she looked in the rear-view mirror, half expecting to see a red Dodge Ram speeding out of the tunnel or appearing up on the slopes ahead.

The front door opened seconds after she turned off the engine outside her home in Framnesvegur, and Ína came running towards her in her short-sleeved pyjamas with the word *Curious* and a picture of Britney Spears across the front.

Lóa got out of the car, took Ína in her arms and laughed with relief as she felt four robust limbs wrap around her and took in the familiar smell of peanut butter and jam on her little girl's breath. Faint reddish lights glinted here and there in her ash-blonde hair, which she liked to colour with felt-tip pens, even though she had been strictly forbidden to do so.

'You're like an octopus,' laughed Lóa, disentangling a chubby arm so she could make Ína more comfortable on her hip. Silently she swore to herself that nothing like this would ever happen again.

Anyway, it wasn't necessary to make such solemn oaths, because it had been nothing more than a bizarre accident or some kind of strange breakdown. She couldn't remember ever having been knocked out like that from drinking before, let alone in a stranger's house.

'Where were you?' Ína cried. 'I was so scared. Why didn't you come home?'

'I did come home!' Lóa said, with such conviction that she

almost believed herself. 'I came home when you and Margrét had both just fallen asleep, and then I had to go out first thing this morning to buy a few things for Margrét. What are you doing up and about so early? I thought you liked having a lie-in on Saturdays.'

'I woke up because I heard you weren't home,' answered Ína, tensing up to slip off her mother's hip and wiping the tears from her face. 'What did you buy for me?'

'I didn't buy anything for you, but tomorrow we'll go together and buy you a bike as a present for the summer,' said Lóa. 'But now you must help me with Margrét's summer present. Run in and put on your shoes and anorak.'

'No, it's *summerrr*,' Ína said. 'And you're not wearing a coat.'

'It's not quite summer yet,' replied Lóa, stroking Ína's arm with her finger as she blocked out the thought of her coat's whereabouts. 'Just look at those goosebumps on your arm, my love. Now, go and put on your shoes and anorak.'

When she opened the boot a ghastly sight met her eyes, nothing like the beauty she'd seen when she opened the chest at the doll-maker's house about an hour earlier. The doll lay there all curled up, with a dirty bit of plastic half-covering her and her dress crumpled up around her chest. Her hair was tangled and full of static and dotted with styrofoam balls. Her eyes, which before had appeared so warm and alive, now just looked open and staring.

For a few moments, she bitterly regretted what she had done, but it was too late now to do anything about it. She lacked the courage to face a man who had just woken up and return his lawful property, crumpled and grubby after a pointless journey.

She pulled herself together, for Ína's sake – Ína would be

terrified if she realized the apprehensiveness and indecision which plagued her mother – and pushed the plastic sheet to one side. She rearranged the dress as best she could and attempt-ed, with little success, to brush the foam balls off the silky, black hair. She inched the doll up out of the boot, laid her on her back on the tarmac and was just straightening her up when Ína came running out in unlaced trainers and with her pink quilted anorak flapping open.

'Wow!' she exclaimed. 'Is it a mannequin? Why is she so dirty?'

'Because she should have been in a box, but there wasn't enough room for it in the car, my poppet. Mind your fingers,' said Lóa, and banged the boot shut. 'We'll just shower her down. Lift up her feet. No, don't hold her knees, that'll be too heavy for you. Hold her by the heels so that they don't get dragged along the ground.'

They made their way slowly up the steps with the doll. Much to Lóa's relief, there was not a soul in sight.

When they got indoors the stairs were much steeper and Ína frequently lost her grip. Halfway up, she plumped down and pretended to be much more out of breath than she was. 'Hold on, Mum, it's so heavy,' she puffed dramatically.

'There are only ten steps to go,' said Lóa. 'Let's count them together: One . . . two . . .'

The dress was a size too big and had a zip down the back, so it was a simple enough task to undress the doll. Lóa propped her up in the shower and let Ína rinse out the dress in cold water in the washbasin. She took the shower head from its holder and aimed the lukewarm jet at the doll's face and hair. The water merged with the dust, which had spread all over her from the plastic, and ran down her body in greyish rivulets. Lóa's conscience seemed to clear as easily as the dirt lifted from the doll's skin. The cold shiver of trepidation at having stolen such a valuable item quickly washed away in the water and Ína's chattering.

'Victoria's Secret!' squealed Ína, over the noise of water. 'It's a Victoria's Secret dress, Mum. May I have it?'

Lóa was about to say that it would be too big for her and not right for the doll to be naked. But she stopped herself because the dress wouldn't look as good as new once it had been washed and so was not worth returning with the doll, if it came to it. There was also no point in having her dressed up like a tart until then. She turned the tap off, put her arm round Ína as she stood on a little, pink step-up stool at the basin and kissed her silky soft rounded cheek. 'If you promise to go in the shower yourself afterwards and rinse your hair thoroughly then you may have it,' she said. 'Pass me a large towel and then fetch my checked pyjamas – they're in the cupboard behind the door in my room.'

'I can't find them,' yelled Ína from Lóa's bedroom.

'Have another look,' Lóa called back, as she carefully dried the doll's hair. 'And don't shout like that. Margrét may still be asleep.'

Shortly afterwards, Ína appeared in the doorway next to the shower clutching the pyjamas and said, 'Margrét isn't sleeping. She's always awake.'

'I know, my darling,' said Lóa. 'But sometimes she likes to make out she's asleep, and you know she can't stand noise. You'll have to be the big sister until she gets better. Do you think you can do that?'

'Yes,' replied Ína sulkily, as she put the pyjamas on the edge of the washbasin. Then she began picking up the foam balls from the floor.

'Don't worry about that,' said Lóa. 'I'll do it with the Hoover later.'

'No, don't do that. I'll pick them all up. Then can I have them? Let me, Mum. I'm going to make a Christmas card. Well no, not a Christmas card, I'm going to do a picture.'

'Of course you can have them,' said Lóa, and spread the towel out on the floor. It was enormous, with pictures of parasols and beach balls. She placed the pyjama top in the middle of the towel, laid the doll on top of it, with some difficulty, and slipped her arms into the sleeves.

'Why has the mannequin got hair down there?' asked Ína, pointing to the doll's pubic hair.

'Just because,' answered Lóa, and pulled the pyjama bottoms up her legs. 'You can button her top up.'

Lóa swayed gently from side to side to ease her back, stroked Ína's hair – damp after her enthusiastic dress-washing – and said, 'Shall we go and say good morning to Margrét?'

# 3

It was already late when Sveinn awoke in a room full of sunlight and warmth. Although his muscles were still aching with fatigue and his thighs damp with sweat around the crumpled duvet, he luxuriated in the feeling of being rested like longed-for sunshine behind his eyes and forehead.

He sat up in bed and ran his fingers through his hair, greasy and spiky with dirt. Where did this unexpected sense of anticipation spring from? What did he have to do that was such fun? Take a long shower. Make himself coffee and toast. Read the paper. Focus on completing the few remaining tasks to get the girls ready to go: glue on their nails, attach their heads to their bodies, slip them into their dresses and secure the lids on their boxes.

Then he must deliver the dark-haired one – *Raven-Black Lola*. She had been ready to take to Kjartan for a while, but Sveinn hadn't made the time. Or perhaps he had just been putting off the test of his patience which seeing Kjartan entailed.

Kjartan had already bought one doll and was now going to buy another. He just about earned a living wage at the recycling plant, and it had taken him many months to save up for this second doll. He had used all his savings to buy the first one shortly after Sveinn moved to Akranes, and Sveinn had the feeling the purpose had been to buy Sveinn's companionship as much as the doll's. And Kjartan had succeeded. Not because Sveinn needed Kjartan's money, but because Kjartan's desperation

35

touched him and sometimes he too was relieved to have someone to talk to. Kjartan had taken to trawling the Internet and gathering all the information that was to be found on doll-making. It was sometimes a relief for Sveinn to talk out loud about his work, which he thought about most days of the week, and Kjartan was undoubtedly the only one who was willing to listen.

But each time they met it was as though some of Kjartan's unhappiness seeped into Sveinn's being. The thought of spending yet another evening sitting on Kjartan's expensive, urine-yellow leather sofa, drinking beer from the bottle rather pricked the bubble of anticipation which had been growing in Sveinn as he slept.

He took off his underpants as he got out of bed, using them to wipe most of the sweat from his back before dropping them in the laundry basket. But he stopped dead in the middle of the hallway as he remembered the woman he'd left sleeping in the armchair the evening before. He could not be sure that she had gone. Perhaps she was still sleeping. Or busy in the kitchen making fresh bread and coffee. There was no way of knowing what people might take it upon themselves to do and he didn't want to meet her there in the hallway with his bits dangling.

Back in the bedroom, he fished out a pair of crumpled trousers from the laundry basket, put them on, sighed, chose a pair of clean underpants, trousers and a shirt from the cupboard and made his way out to the bathroom.

The water refreshed and awoke something in him which the daylight had only half-managed to reach, and when he stepped out of the bathroom – barefoot, clean-shaven and in fresh clothes – he realized he was hoping that this Lóa was still in the house. Mostly hoping that she would come on to him with her compassion and needs, like women sometimes did in films. Eventually she would succeed in moving his hardened and rusty heart, he would become a better person and for the rest of her life she would sing with delight at her achievement. *The End*. He laughed, or rather snorted softly. But when he went into the living room no-one was there. The blanket lay on the floor and when he picked it up to fold it he found her coat underneath: a white woollen coat with a pale-green lining.

'Hello!' he called, carrying the coat through into the kitchen, where he absent-mindedly put it down over the back of a chair. He looked out of the window. Her car wasn't there. She'd gone and left the coat behind.

She would probably come back. Perhaps he would manage to ply her with drink again and maybe she wouldn't nod off next time. The previous day, he'd had the feeling there was more to her than met the eye. They had both been utterly exhausted.

How long had it actually been since he slept with a woman? Months and months. More than a year. Well, if they didn't feel like taking their clothes off perhaps he could just talk to her. He had nothing in common with the few friends he had. Lóa was probably quite good company. At least she hadn't filled all the silences with endless chatter, as women tend to do in the belief that they are sharing something of themselves and lightening the atmosphere.

He put the coffee on and got out flatbread, cheese and slices of smoked lamb, cut thick slices off the cheese with the serrated bread knife and piled the meat between two halves of flatbread.

He ought to go to the shops later. Try to appear oblivious to the staring eyes of the locals. The article in the local rag must be adding fuel to the fire of any gossip. In small communities, people might remain indifferent to world issues and the ultimate meaning of life, but they kept a close eye on what went on locally and if someone known to them ended up in the papers they followed the news with interest.

There wasn't any milk, so he put four sugar cubes in his coffee instead. After taking several bites of the flatbread, he happened to notice that one sleeve of Lóa's coat was brushing the floor. He reached over to set it straight, and a lined, green pocket caught his eye. There was nothing for it but to slip his hand inside.

Both pockets were empty.

He left his half-finished coffee and carried the coat into the porch. The outside door was open. He closed it and hung the coat up on a hook. The faint trace of perfume that rose from it reminded him more of incense than of a fragrant meadow. He couldn't remember when he had made up his mind that all perfumes smelled unpleasant. This one wasn't exactly unpleasant. It was different and added to the tension deep in his gut, giving him the feeling that Lóa was more beautiful than he remembered, that perhaps he had missed something right before his very eyes.

Weariness and discontent could wear away at the faces of women over thirty, making their beauty unrecognizable. He'd not thought about that the previous evening. He had been too much in need of company to be able to accept anything more than the limited gratification an unknown woman could offer him just then. He had expected her to be shallow, or at least sufficiently lacking in confidence to appear shallow – it amounted to the same thing – and when she had met neither of those expectations he had all but forgotten that she was there. Two glasses of wine later, and he had wanted her to satisfy some suppressed and boorish aspect of his nature by losing her self-control. But she hadn't done that either, except for a brief moment after he had subjected her to some rough questioning about her daughters, and then it had been done in an understated manner. A quivering chin hardly counted as dramatics or a gross lack of control.

He let go of the coat and it seemed to him that the scent clung to his hands. He was looking down at them, as if he thought they had suddenly changed shape, when out of the corner of his eye he noticed that the morning paper lay on the floor by the porch door. It was thoroughly trampled, as though a whole army regiment had used it to wipe their boots. Next to it, a pristine envelope seemed to mock the wrecked newspaper. There was no window in the envelope and the sender's handwriting was neat and feminine.

He dusted the worst of the dirt from the paper and flicked through it while finishing his coffee.

The envelope lay untouched next to the coffee mug, a white rectangle someone had bothered to glue down and address. Yes, of course he was curious, but also slightly anxious. Was he in the right frame of mind for the unexpected, or would the peace of mind he had known in recent months in some mysterious and fateful way be destroyed like some remote fort, hit by neglect and the ravages of time?

Finally he broke the seal with the tip of his knife, slit open the envelope and took out a card with a newspaper cutting glued to it. It was an obituary. There was a small, black cross above a picture of a man aged between sixty and seventy. The words below read:

*Our beloved father and brother, Hans Sigurjónsson from Hlíð in Svarfaðardalur, died at his home on the first of May. The funeral will be held privately, at the request of the deceased. No flowers, please. Donations may be made to the Red Cross.*

He put the card down. He had no doubt this was the chap who had ended his life with an old farm rifle. He was probably a farmer, or had been a farmer. The newspaper article hadn't made that clear, nor did the obituary. Protect the deceased but disgrace the living – wasn't that the press's questionable code of ethics?

But wait a moment. Wasn't it customary to sign obituaries? He looked at the card again. The names of the relatives had been cut out, so the sender must be one of them. A sister? A daughter?

It would be best to do nothing – he mustn't let himself get obsessed with this. But there was that pile of old papers stacked up in one corner of the kitchen. He couldn't stop himself flicking through a few to find this same obituary.

It wasn't there. He tended to spread newspapers out around the tub when he stirred the silicone mixture and then throw them away once he'd finished mixing. It would be out with the rubbish by now.

He examined the card. White, ordinary, the clipping glued to it with unnatural precision. He turned it over and saw that a computer-printed note had been fixed to the reverse. His own obituary, with the picture that had been published in the paper. In place of the cross was the Devil's star.

*Our creator and father in crime, Sveinn Guðmundsson, who died suddenly at his home on Friday 13th June.*

*The Used Innocents*

Rising slowly to his feet, Sveinn stretched, breathed in deeply, then tried to breathe out the cold shivers and weariness he felt. He tossed the card in the rubbish bin, then, thinking better of it, dug it out again and put it in a drawer where he kept his screwdriver, pliers and Allen keys. He resolved to put this sick person's death threat out of his mind and clear his head. He wandered down the hallway, his feet seeming to move of their own accord in the direction of the workshop.

He had received a few strange calls recently and sensed something in his gut as he listened to the angry silence on the line. Perhaps they too meant that someone was out to get him.

It might do him good to have a few beers with Kjartan that evening after all. The alcohol would help him to relax. He seemed to be always buzzing with restlessness except when he was engrossed in his work. How he relished the feeling of emptiness in his head when he was entirely focussed.

Ingunn, his ex, had left him a year and a half before, saying that there were many different kinds of affair and workaholism was one of them.

He had asked her whether it was because he did this particular job and not some other work, whether she would have been equally determined to end the relationship if he was always out teaching disabled children or trading on the stock market.

It wouldn't make a damned bit of difference, she'd said. She simply didn't want to witness the torment in his eyes when he was forced to talk with, or even be with, her.

He had believed Ingunn. She had never shown any sign of jealousy, even though he'd been running his hands over these perfect, plastic, feminine forms all day long. Maybe she'd thought herself above it and hid her hurt.

Perhaps he shouldn't have taken her at her word. Perhaps she'd kept other things hidden from him.

Being with her hadn't been pure torment – that wasn't true. He didn't know how to love anyone else and had been meaning to suggest that they start living together, to promise her for the umpteenth time that he wouldn't let his work smother their relationship. But she had been more realistic and quicker to understand that he wouldn't be able to keep such a promise.

Perhaps he needed a woman who could accept him with all his qualities and quirks, who would even share his interest in making dolls. A partner in crime who would sit with him in the evenings in the pool of light from a powerful work lamp, sewing dresses, varnishing nails and attaching wigs. She would calm him with her gentle smile and well-chosen words when he was upset or his nerves were on edge. She would have no doubt that a woman and a doll are two entirely different entities and know that to draw any comparison between the two was ridiculous; like a man who compares himself with the statue of the Icelandic outlaw – staggering around with his family and all his worldly goods on his back – and then suffers from an inferiority complex.

When he was younger he had put considerable effort into convincing himself that he didn't need a woman in his life. But he had long since accepted that he was no different from anyone else and that man is governed by his needs and longings, rather than the other way round. *Age has the effect of keelhauling a man, flaying and humbling him*, he thought, and laughed at the idea; only just turned forty and already resigning himself to a bent back and arthritis.

The laughter was still on his lips, a half-laugh which some-times slipped out in the solitude, when he stopped in his tracks in the middle of the floor. The workshop wasn't how he had left it. The lights were on and styrofoam balls were scattered everywhere, as though they had been tipped up from the box where the dark-haired doll was kept. And the plastic sheet wasn't on the floor under the dolls that were hanging up. A nasty suspicion began to form in his mind, and he couldn't help holding his breath as he rushed over to the box and snatched up the lid.

When he'd laid the doll in the box the styrofoam balls had formed a surface almost as smooth as Lake Bingvallavatn on a beautiful day; now they lay bulging in peaks and troughs – in one place the bottom of the box showed through. The velvet lining was still in place, but the dark-haired doll was gone. Sveinn glanced around sharply, peered into every corner. He was sure she must be there somewhere and was filled with a sense of unease at the thought that someone had been rummaging round in his workshop while he slept like a babe, wrapped in false security.

When he had finished looking in every room of the house to confirm his suspicions, he ran out into the yard. He stood on the spot where he had knelt down the evening before to change the tyre, shielded his eyes with his hand and stared down the road, as though he imagined the thief might be disappearing over the horizon at that very moment with a dark-haired doll in tow.

Tyre tracks in the gravel by his feet showed she had been in some hurry, the little darling, when she left without saying goodbye, without saying thank you. What kind of behaviour was that, to repay a favour by stealing the most expensive item in the house?

There again, how could he be sure it had been her? He

often forgot to lock the outside door before he went to bed and everyone knew that he had valuable things in his workshop.

No, it was too much of a coincidence. A stranger falls asleep in his living room and the next day one of his dolls is missing – the first and only doll to be stolen from him. She must have taken it. He would go after her and if he found her he wouldn't hesitate to ring the police. There was nothing illegal about his girls, even if some people might find them indecent and lacking in taste.

His thoughts drifted to the deranged contents of the white envelope and it all came to him in a flash. Hadn't Lóa referred to her father's death? *We buried him last week*, she'd said. She'd also said that it had been a heart attack, but she could have been lying. Lóa must be Hans's daughter, the one who wrote his obituary. What other reason could she have had to steal the dark-haired doll?

Without quite realizing what he was doing, he rushed to the outside door on the west side of the Nissen hut and opened it. The layer of dust under his feet showed, beyond a shadow of a doubt, that no-one had gone that way, probably since he moved into the house. Why hadn't she gone out of this door? Clearly she hadn't noticed it. It blended in with the cladding anyway – the door panels looked exactly like those on the walls.

He closed the door again, went into the storage room and ran his eyes over the shelves. He didn't know the exact number of bags, cans and buckets he'd had of plaster, silicone powder, binding agent, colour and paint, but it certainly looked as though everything was in its place. Everything apart from the little wooden stool, which wasn't up against the wall behind the door, but under the sink. What was that supposed to mean? Unless he had put the stool there himself and forgotten.

At a loss, he couldn't decide what his next move should be. He sat down on the wooden stool, rested his arm on the edge of the sink and, for the first time since he moved in, he noticed that there wasn't a window anywhere, not in the storeroom or in the workshop. He looked at the watch which his father had given him for his fortieth birthday. It was a solid, old-fashioned and reassuring object.

It was twenty past two. Kjartan often went to his mother's for lunch on Saturdays, but he would surely be home by now and sitting in front of his computer. Sveinn had to admit to himself that Kjartan was the only person he could look to in a situation like this. He needed to have someone on his side. Someone he could think out loud to and assess the situation. Someone who would laugh at the ridiculousness of it all, then take his mind off it by talking about something else entirely.

Why was he so despondent? He wasn't afraid. He had looked Lóa in the eyes and seen that she wasn't a threat to his life any more than was the dark-haired doll or he himself; he trusted his instincts in such matters. And God alone knew he had no emotional ties to the doll, whatever people might think about a loner like him. If the doll was anything more than a beautiful object to him he would never let Kjartan have her.

It wasn't the financial loss he was worried about either. A few orders would be delayed, but that was only to be expected. His customers would understand. Kjartan would take things in his stride. It was always important to Kjartan to come across as an easy-going country type who didn't let the world's hustle and bustle bother him.

There must be a grain of truth in what many people believed: that threats are unnerving, even when one chooses to ignore them. And the loss aside, a theft was always an unpleasant assault on one's private life.

He put on his Barbour despite the warmth and the sunshine – as though he thought it would shield him from reality and further unjust attacks – and went over to Kjartan's on foot.

# 4

Lóa knocked on Margrét's door, her arms full of clean laundry. It was with a sense of relief that she felt the familiar old flutter of anxiety after this morning's agitation. She felt apprehensive about entering her daughter's spartan bedroom and looking into her pained eyes – eyes which had become strangely bright and protruding, as if about to burst out of her head.

'Come in,' said Margrét's voice.

Ína was nowhere to be seen. She'd obviously gone berry-picking in the bathroom – gathering up all the styrofoam balls, which seemed to have totally captured her imagination.

Lóa walked into the room aiming to exude an air of love and redemption, like the Holy Mother of Jesus. The psychiatrist who was treating Margrét had explained to Lóa that anger was natural, nothing more than an aggressive expression of fear, but that, whilst being angry might not be harmful to Margrét, Lóa should refrain from using guilt to control her daughter.

The desk beneath the window was littered with pens, books and printed notes, and crowning the pile was a humming laptop. The royal-blue curtains, which Margrét had never much cared for, were drawn open. Either she had got up earlier that morning and opened them or, which was probably more likely, she hadn't bothered to close them when she went to bed. The jet blackout blinds, which she disliked about as much as the curtains, were also untouched.

The window had been their battleground until Lóa won the

skirmish over the curtains. Margrét did not want a carpet, cushions, or anything which could liven up the whitewashed walls and give the room a cosier feel. However, Lóa had made it clear that in this house there would be no gaping windows which gave the wrong impression, from the outside, that Margrét's bedroom was standing empty.

Lóa put the pile of clothes down on the old oak chest of drawers, which had come from Margrét's grandma. Socks and underwear went in the bottom drawer, trousers in the middle and cotton T-shirts in the top. Dresses and skirts were hung in the large built-in corner cupboard next to the chest of drawers.

Margrét kept her eye on her mother, as if she were committing some dastardly deed. When Lóa had put everything away she sat down carefully at the end of the bed, as though she feared breaking something. In the past she had sometimes lost her self-control and snapped at Margrét, tried to shake her out of this illness. Now treating her harshly had become unthinkable and yet unavoidable at the same time, because every word uttered to her, every breath or glance, seemed to abuse her.

She was sitting bolt upright in bed, a heavy tome on the history of mankind open on her gaunt chest. Lóa simply couldn't get used to her appearance: her lifeless hair, her stick-thin arms, her sharp cheekbones which towered over her sunken cheeks and the fine, blonde hairs which now covered her whole body like soft down. The child was nothing but skin and bones. She was like a chick just hatched from an egg. The yellow cardigan, which had once stretched indecently over her bust, now hung like a rag from her protruding collarbones.

'Don't you know these schoolbooks inside out, my little

star?' asked Lóa. 'Do you remember what we discussed? That you would get dressed and have some breakfast before you began studying?'

'I'm getting up,' said Margarét. 'It's not even nine yet.'

She was just about polite, but couldn't conceal the bitterness. Her voice rasped like that of a very old woman.

*She doesn't hate me,* thought Lóa. *Not really. I mustn't take this too personally.*

'I've got something for you,' Loa said. 'Don't make up your mind about it straight away. Do something for me: try it first to see if you get used to it or not. It's just something to help you feel better in yourself. It'll ease the hunger pangs,' she added, even though she was against people lying to their children. But all is fair in love and war, and this was both. War against death, waged in the name of love.

'I'm not hungry,' said Margrét.

'Don't worry, it's not edible, but it is beautiful,' said Lóa. 'Wait a minute while I fetch it.'

There was no point in disturbing Ína while she was quietly amusing herself and there was no other way of fetching the doll in a dignified manner. There was nothing for it but to carry the doll on her own, even though it would offend Margrét to witness her mother's unseemly wrestling with an inanimate object. Perhaps it would even do her good!

After several attempts, Lóa decided that the best way was to clasp her arms round the doll's waist from behind. The breasts prevented the doll from slipping from her grasp. She must weigh about fifty kilos. It reminded her of the sacks of fertilizer and bags of animal feed which she had never managed to lift without help when she was a young childminder and cowherd over in Landey. At the touch of the doll's silky soft, jet-black hair flowing over her arm, Lóa felt a strange peace bubbling under her skin, right down to her bones.

Sometimes she had seen Ína pull off her T-shirt, tilt her face upwards and waggle her head from side to side so that her hair swayed to and fro over her back. Now she thought she understood why Ína did that. She was capturing the contentment which came from gentle caresses over eternally hungry skin.

'Yuk, Mum, it's repulsive,' whined Margrét, without looking properly at the pyjama-clad present in front of her. There didn't seem to be any curiosity in her any more, no amazement at unusual things.

'She's not repulsive, darling,' said Lóa, out of breath from the exertion of getting the doll to sit down in the dark-red armchair next to the bed.

'I think it's repulsive. What do you want to have it here for? I don't even want that old chair,' she said, and gestured towards the richly upholstered armchair beneath the doll. 'It smells musty.'

'I just want you to have someone by you all the time,' said Lóa, trying to make her voice sound authoritative rather than pleading.

'That isn't *someone*. Have you gone mad? Take it away. What do you think people will think of me if they see that thing here? I'm not retarded.'

'No-one comes in apart from me,' responded Lóa, and as the words slipped out of her mouth she felt she was on dangerous ground. Until then she had had the sense to keep quiet about Margrét's sudden lack of friends. She didn't know whether she had said it out of bitchiness or because she wanted Margrét to understand something. She so wanted to help her.

Tears streamed involuntarily down Margrét's cheeks; she

seemed too weak to cry properly. Her mouth quivered and turned down in a toddler-like grimace. Old-woman's wrinkles formed on her dry, paper-thin skin. She had a scar in the corner of her mouth from a sore which had only just healed after her last stay in hospital.

Seeing something spilling from Margrét's body, even though it was only water, was like witnessing an accident. Tears held important minerals and salts which Margrét needed to retain to stay alive.

'I feel awful, Mummy,' said Margrét in a choked voice. 'I feel so ghastly.'

'I know,' said Lóa, and sat back down on the bed next to her. She tried to embrace this human skeleton who had one foot in this world and the other in an alien realm, as if suffering under some unbearable curse. Margrét looked away for a moment but then pushed her mother from her. She could not conceal the hostility she felt at her touch.

'I'm sorry,' Margrét cried into the pink pillowcase.

There it was in all its power: she felt that empty feeling of victory which always flared and then waned in Lóa's mind when she had succeeded in forcing closeness between herself and this semi-hostaged daughter of hers.

Now at least she would be more tractable for a short while. Crying was a release for her anger. A release uniquely suited to those who were either too discreet or too feeble to scream and throw things.

Lóa gently pulled the feather duvet off Margrét, folded it up and laid it at the end of the bed. She could do nothing but look blankly at Margrét's pelvis, which protruded like two mountain peaks under her blue, stripy, flannel pyjamas.

'Now let's go into the kitchen,' she said.

Margrét sat up in bed and held her forehead. She looked as though she were seeing some indescribable horror way off in the distance. 'I feel faint,' she said.

'It's no wonder,' responded Lóa, and offered her arm for support.

As they went past the bathroom, they heard Ína talking and singing to herself behind the closed door. A freewheeling medley of all her favourites. 'They're called Barbapapa and Barbamama and Barbabelle and Barbalib and m m m ... Little mice all around the world, now must go to bed ...You're toxic, na nana na na.'

Margrét sat at the kitchen table like one condemned, and sulkily flicked through the previous day's paper, running her eyes over the headlines and the pictures. Lóa meanwhile poured milk into the blender, peeled a banana and reached for the powdered nutrition supplement. She kept it at the back of the top shelf in the cupboard so that Ína wouldn't find it.

Margrét's silence was loaded with pain. She had stopped complaining that the drink was horrible since Lóa made it clear that grumbling would achieve nothing. A deal was a deal. So she sat there and forced it down in minute sips, painfully slowly, with a touching expression of martyrdom on her face. It made no difference how long she dragged this out. Lóa barely took her eyes off her and never turned her back or went out of the kitchen.

The doctor who discharged her from hospital, a weary woman with close-cropped hair and nails bitten to the quick, had stressed the importance of this: she must never take her eyes off Margrét while she was eating. She had gone on and on about it until Lóa had lost patience and retorted brusquely, 'Do you think I don't know that?'

They had faced each other in hostile silence until Lóa thought she detected an apology in the doctor's expression, but then she had quickly lost heart and said goodbye. She had half run to Margrét, who was sitting on her suitcase by the lift. Lóa had kept pushing the lift button, as Margrét watched her uneasily from under her long, lifeless fringe.

It had been a joint agreement between them all – Lóa, Margrét and the doctor – to allow Margrét home while she was revising for her exams. However, Lóa often felt that now she had sole responsibility and that this had been a mistake. She feared that she wasn't up to the challenge and that Margrét would go downhill in her care.

Lóa wasn't bothered about Margrét's grades. However, Margrét clearly preferred death to poor or even average marks.

When Margrét had emptied the glass Lóa rinsed it out, filled it with water and took out two enormous capsules of omega fatty acids.

Margrét's eyes filled with tears. 'I can't do it,' she said. 'My stomach is stuffed full. There isn't even room for the water.'

Lóa felt for her, but she mustn't show any leniency. 'My darling,' she said, and the liquid splashed over the edges as she banged the glass onto the table. 'We have to make sure you don't damage your brain. If you look after yourself you'll only have to spend a few more days at the hospital.'

'They're so difficult to swallow,' said Margrét.

'You can swallow them; they won't get stuck in your throat even though they're big,' Lóa reassured her. 'Look, they're slippery smooth.'

'I can't be doing with this; I have to revise for the exam.'

'Then get them down you.'

Eventually Margrét staggered back to her room with the

omega capsules safely inside her, and only then did Lóa's hang-over creep up on her. She could hardly keep her eyes open she was so tired, and the muscles in her throat and shoulders ached.

She couldn't be bothered to get undressed before she crawled under the duvet. She didn't intend to fall asleep, just to rest her eyes a while.

She woke to find Ína clambering round her. When she managed to open her eyes she noticed that the light had altered since she laid her head on the pillow. The afternoon had engulfed the morning like an invisible avalanche of snow. Sweat held her hair fast to her neck, hunger rumbled round her belly and an uneasy memory of the morning's events lay in ambush behind every thought.

A sudden fear gripped her, her heart thumped and her mouth went dry. She imagined she was being pursued by the police, Margrét's doctor, the doll-maker with murder on his mind and an enraged rabble with guns and cudgels. A crimson Dodge Ram came shooting over one hill after another.

'Look what I made,' said Ína, waving something in front of her mother's nose.

Lóa took hold of Ína's fist, which clutched a piece of A4 card. She held it out at arm's length so her eyes could focus on it. It was a picture of a green car with blue windows on a black road. The sky was smeared with dry glue and there were foam balls scattered all over, creating a snowstorm which would have looked quite convincing had it come all the way down to the car and the road.

'That's brilliant, sweetie-pie,' said Lóa. 'Did Margrét get herself anything for lunch?'

'I don't know,' replied Ína, and brushed a felt-tipped curl

from her forehead. She suddenly looked like she wanted to slip away – perhaps she had just remembered that she'd promised to wash the colour out of her hair – and quickly added, 'Björg has arrived.'

'Björg?'

'Yes, she's just cooking.'

'Why didn't either of you wake me?' asked Lóa.

'Björg said I shouldn't,' said Ína, and stared entranced at her brand new work of art. 'Don't you think it's wonderful, Mum?'

'Yes, I do.'

'Are you going to hang it up on the wall?'

'May I, darling?'

Ína nodded. A deep dimple formed a hollow in her chubby cheek. She had a dimple on just one side, like her mother.

'I'll do that,' promised Lóa, and lifted herself up onto her elbows. She felt bewildered by the rapid change from the unconscious state of sleep to this conscious state, where her mind raced from one thing to the next, worrying about every single thing. 'Why are there never people in your pictures?' she asked.

'There are often people in them,' said Ína, and looked hurt. This was not a fair criticism – to require a picture to be something it wasn't.

'Only when I especially ask you to draw people,' said Lóa. 'But it doesn't matter. Move now; I need to get up.'

But it did matter. Girls of Ína's age usually drew little else but people: themselves, their families, princesses, pop stars and other celebrities.

Lóa went straight into the bathroom without greeting Björg. She needed to wake up properly and collect her thoughts before she could look another adult in the eye or make intelligent conversation.

There was a quivering restlessness about her, a late-afternoon unease in the pit of her stomach. She shed a few tears in the shower as she acknowledged it, and the tears merged with the almost scalding water.

What made her tearful was the compelling thought of the bottle of wine. It lay on its side on the top shelf of the cupboard, next to that damned supplement powder of Margrét's, a powder intended for sick children and old people who had lost their appetite for life.

She wouldn't be able to resist having a glass, even though Björg was there and Ína was awake and would be sure to tell her father.

She wouldn't get really tipsy until Ína had gone to bed. Four or five glasses were just enough to soften her pain, without her becoming rowdy or her speech slurred. You couldn't call her pain grief, because that would mean she had already given up on Margrét.

'God, I wish she was out doing drugs and stealing rather than putting herself through this living hell,' she hissed under her breath, as tears and hot water stung her eyes. She cleared her throat and tried to stop the tears. She wouldn't get away with lingering endlessly in the limited safety of the glass cubicle of the shower unit.

Fortunately she only had this one bottle, but it would be empty by midnight or soon after. Tomorrow, of course, she would have to try and find an off-licence that was open on a Sunday.

This was a new experience for her. She had rarely drunk before, unless actually pressured to, and even then only on special occasions. Very few people would consider her an alcoholic, but she was well on the way to becoming what people call a lush. That might perhaps be acceptable if she was an artist or a fading pop star, but she wasn't either. She just worked in advertising and was a single mother with two children. One and a half children, to be more precise. She had to be OK.

She was slightly ashamed of her petty bourgeois habit of being concerned about the opinions of others when there was something else so much more pressing. She was turning into a lush full of self-pity. She was worried what other people might think even when her child was at death's door.

She turned off the tap and smiled wryly at the thought that she could be described in such pitiful terms.

It was important to be able to laugh at everything – especially the most harrowing things. She had learnt that from her mother. This was something her mother had relentlessly maintained through the years, to the bewilderment of her husband. He had been a kind, reasonably intelligent man, but oddly lacking in humour. In fact, this was the only decisive opinion Lóa's mother held. In other respects, her life had been characterized by a gentle compliancy.

What would happen to her mother now that her husband was dead? Would the role of ordering her around now fall to Lóa? Or would she transform into an energetic independent woman? She was pushing sixty and there was no knowing what fate had in store for her. But that didn't matter. The most important thing was to carry on laughing at circumstances, regardless.

Such as at a wake.

Lóa had been in her parents' bathroom washing her face and touching up her mascara, which had run during the funeral, when someone started hammering at the door. She had just managed to unlock the door before her mother barged in, red in the face. She had sunk down on the side of the bath, grabbed a large towel, which she crumpled up, and howled with laughter.

At first, Lóa thought she was having some kind of breakdown and went to comfort her and to ask someone to ring for an ambulance, but her mother stopped her. Eventually she had managed to stammer out that Gugga, her sister, had embraced her warmly and, with tears in her eyes and genuine empathy in her voice, had said: 'Congratulations.'

As far as Lóa was concerned, the only thing to do was to laugh with her, because if this was a nervous breakdown then it was the best possible kind.

Later, she had gone out and cheered up Aunt Gugga by saying that she had released the grieving widow's laughter from two weeks' hibernation.

She quickly combed her hair, brushed her teeth and tongue, moisturized and put on deodorant and flung her clothes into the dirty laundry basket. They were all creased and crumpled from having been slept in – not only once, but twice. She wrapped herself in a bath towel and went out into the kitchen.

'Oh lá lá,' said Björg, and gave a sideways look at Lóa's bare thigh. 'I hope you don't expect us all to dress up for dinner too.'

'You can have a larger towel if your embarrassment gets the better of you,' said Lóa, and smiled contentedly at the serving dish. She pictured herself getting up, casually reaching over for the bottle and opening it. But in her mind the bath towel got in her way and ended up slipping down over her breasts. No, it was too much of a challenge and too early to start drinking. It was too desperate.

'Is the emaciated seal pup in her bedroom?' asked Björg.

Lóa nodded. Her thighs and buttocks were sticking to the

seat cover as rapidly cooling water dripped from her hair onto her shoulders. She knew that her awareness of everything was heightened. She sensed her own being far too acutely.

'Goulash and mashed potatoes, that should put her in a good mood,' said Björg, humming as she worked the potato masher vigorously, then added, 'Ína says you were out all night.'

'Does she indeed?' said Lóa, trying to sound amused.

'I hope you were doing something exciting,' said Björg, and hit the masher firmly against the edge of the bowl a few times. 'You never go anywhere. I don't know why I take it upon myself to do the shopping and run errands for you. It's not healthy to hang about the house like this.'

'Heaven help me if you're always going to take what Ína comes up with literally,' said Lóa. 'I just had to nip out this morning and poor Ína got a shock when she woke up and couldn't find me anywhere.'

'Nip out?' said Björg. 'Where does one nip out to on a Saturday morning?'

'Some people nip out to the bakers and others go to visit their grandma or go for a swim,' said Lóa. She was finding it difficult to hide her impatience. She wouldn't get away with concealing the doll and making out she had slipped out to the bakers. It wouldn't be long before Ína put such inaccuracies straight. 'I'll tell you later,' she said and stood up with difficulty. 'I need to get dressed.'

'Do, for goodness' sake,' said Björg. 'I don't fancy finding your short and curlies in the sauce.'

Lóa stood in front of the wardrobe for a long while, and ran her hands over her clothes until she picked out a lime-green skirt with brightly coloured flowers. The cut didn't do anything for her, but she needed the freshness of the colours. She found a black jumper on the floor which she had only worn once. However, she decided against it, shook imagined dust from it and laid it over the back of a chair. She couldn't imagine putting anything on unless it had just been laundered. Clean and fresh, come what may. She needed that to make up for something. She felt there was something unclean within her and had an ever-growing feeling that the world was filthy. More than that, that the world's filth was wrapping itself around her, grasping the chance to spread over her, her daughters and her home.

It was warm in the flat so she stayed barefoot. Ína always turned the radiators up when no-one was looking. She was not the chilly type, but tropical temperatures at home seemed to give her a sense of security. She would lie on the floor by a blisteringly hot radiator, in her underwear or nightie, drawing pictures of snowstorms.

Lóa turned the radiator down in the bedroom and called to Ína, who came clattering in noisily on her kitten-heeled sandals. She had begged to be bought these in Hagkaup department store. Her friends had them and Lóa didn't have the heart to refuse her, despite the fact it was not exactly healthy for a young, developing spine to be in such an unnatural curve. She was relying on this being a short-lived fad and that Ína would soon look for the comfort of her old trainers.

'Whaaaat?' said Ína impatiently. She had evidently been absorbed in helping Björg in the kitchen.

'You can turn up the radiator in your own bedroom, but not in mine and not in the living room, as I have told you many times. Is that understood?'

'Yeah.'

'And you can set the table now if you want.'

'That's what I was doing.'

'Well done, darling. You're such a good girl,' said Lóa. Putting her arm tightly round Ína's soft, plump shoulder, she bent down and kissed her on the head. She smelled of the cheap, strawberry scent of the felt-tip pens. Ína's pens were special perfume pens – a present from her guilt-ridden father.

Ína squirmed free and ran off. When Lóa came into the kitchen she was rummaging in the cutlery drawer. Björg had opened the window a crack and was sitting on a kitchen stool, leaning precariously out of the window, smoking. For a moment she looked sheepish as she met Lóa's eye, but Lóa tossed her damp hair and laughed to herself. Björg's failings paled into insignificance next to her own shortcomings. And Ína wouldn't come to any harm from the smell of Salem Lights.

Lóa leant up against the fridge, peeled the foil off the neck of the bottle and sank the corkscrew into the cork. Her stomach tensed with anticipation as the wine flowed into the glass, and relaxed slightly after the first sip. She noticed that Björg never looked directly at the bottle or the glass.

Neither woman spoke while Ína clattered about in the dining room with the cutlery. The smoke from Björg's cigarette swirled into nothingness outside the open window. Lóa tried to swallow silently, but couldn't. It seemed that the wine objected to being consumed in such a shamefaced manner.

Ína appeared in the doorway and, swinging on the door knobs, announced that she'd finished setting the table.

'Well done,' said Lóa. Her mind was elsewhere as she turned from Ína and counted the sachets in the box. There were four sachets of food supplement – the same number as that morning. Margrét hadn't had any lunch. But she hadn't made it

look as though she had eaten. It would have been easy enough
for her to mix the powder with water, pour it down the sink or
the toilet and casually leave the empty sachet sitting on top of
the rubbish in the bin. She wasn't as deceitful as the doctor had
maintained. Perhaps she was getting a tiny bit better. A baby
step. Thank God.

She opened a new packet, vanilla flavoured, and mixed the
drink without adding a banana, or anything else Margrét could
use as an excuse for refusing to drink it with the meal.

Of course, Lóa could have blamed herself for oversleeping
and missing Margrét's meal time, but it was Margrét who
would have to pay dearly for that oversight. She was used to
drinking water with the evening meal, but now she would have
to work her way through her lunch along with the goulash and
mashed potatoes. No matter what.

Björg finished dishing up and Ína was sent to fetch her
sister.

Lóa served Margrét about half a normal adult's portion and
Margrét immediately began to protest, raising her new whin-
ing-old-lady voice as best she could. 'I can't do both; I can only
manage one or the other. I'll eat this meal, but I just want water
with it. Why do you have to be so horrible?'

'You should have had something for lunch; you know that
very well. I can't think for you all the time,' said Lóa, and leant
forward across the table threateningly. The hangover had faded
and she felt up to any conflict.

'I was studying. I just forgot – it wasn't my fault,' said
Margrét.

'No-one's to blame,' said Lóa. 'But I have to tell the doctors
at the hospital the truth, and if I tell them that you've skipped a
meal you'll be forced to stay there until you're old and grey.

Don't be silly – it's just one glass and it doesn't taste of anything.'

'You can't drink this with food,' said Margrét.

'Lots of people have a vanilla milkshake with their meal,' said Björg. 'With a hamburger and chips, for example.'

'I think people like that are revolting,' said Margrét, glowering. 'Revolting, greedy pigs.'

Lóa's heart sank as it always did when Margrét opened a chink and revealed the murderous depths of her rage.

Björg gave a slightly forced laugh and said, 'Then that makes me a revolting, greedy pig.'

To make the point, she took a mouthful of salad and chewed noisily with her mouth open. A bit went down the wrong way and she choked and laughed with tears in her eyes.

Margrét did not smile and avoided looking at Björg, who was sitting next to her.

'Can I have a vanilla milkshake with my meal too?' asked Ína.

'You can have yours for dessert,' answered Lóa. She looked around, overcome by the feeling that she was very tiny and everything around her was very tiny. She was a little woman in a little house and her heart was full of small, insignificant drama. Björg and the girls were very tiny, sitting at a very tiny dining table set with dining things a normal person would have to handle very delicately. The doll in Margrét's room was no more than a feather you could barely feel in the palm of your hand. The pattern on the wallpaper seemed so finely wrought that you needed a magnifying glass to see it properly. The sofa in the living room was the size of a matchbox and the embroidered cushions were like Oriental works of art. Withered pot plants appeared finer than the most delicate wildflowers, and even though the daisies in the tiny vase were beginning to rot, it made no difference: they were too small for anyone to detect the smell of decay.

All that was needed now was for a child's hands to come squeezing in through the windows and knock everything over, crushing and smashing it all to pieces.

# 5

*Saturday Afternoon*

Sveinn knocked sharply on the door. He waited awkwardly, not really knowing whether he wanted Kjartan to answer the door or not. He didn't want to be on his own, but neither did he want to be subjected to Kjartan's rambling, esoteric conversation.

*There are some days when you are only sure of what you don't want,* he thought, as the sun warmed the back of his neck and one of the first bees of spring buzzed around a weather-beaten, green-hatted garden gnome.

Kjartan's house was a corrugated-iron-clad timber house in good condition with a large garden. Kjartan had moved in some years previously when his mother had moved into sheltered accommodation nearby, and he showed his respect for her by keeping the garden in a reasonable state.

The door opened and Kjartan looked at Sveinn good-naturedly from under his greying brows, and held out a stout hand in greeting. A barrel-chested man with unkempt hair, he was dressed in a white shirt, neatly creased trousers, woollen socks and Jesus sandals.

'Well, hello, my friend,' he said, shaking Sveinn's work-worn hand. 'Come on in out of that terrible sunshine.' He shuddered then gave a loud guffaw.

Sveinn smiled politely and followed him in. He sat himself down on the leather sofa and felt mildly claustrophobic when Kjartan came scurrying in from the kitchen with two opened bottles of beer.

'No, I . . . Oh, do you have black coffee?' he asked, and was relieved to see Kjartan go back into the kitchen.

He returned quickly with a large pot of instant coffee and two sugar cubes. 'Here you are, mate,' he said. 'Get this down you, if it's not too strong for you.'

He sat down in an armchair which matched the sofa and gulped down half his bottle in one, as if drinking for both of them. He was probably just covering his embarrassment, as with just about everything he said and did.

Sveinn felt ashamed, yet again, of the harsh way he judged his only friend.

'Did you go to your mum's for lunch?' he asked.

'Yes, I did,' said Kjartan, with a sensitivity and warmth in his voice. 'And what do you think the old girl came up with? She said that the leg of lamb had just gone in the oven and asked if I wanted a bowl of Cocoa Puffs to keep me going till the meal. I just said to her, "Mum, I don't eat rubble, not even the finest pumice stones."'

'Rubble?' repeated Sveinn.

Kjartan put on a pompous face and stretched in his seat, pausing to make the most of the moment before he said, 'There are only two types of men in this world: those who wash their hands after they pee and those who wash their hands before they pee.'

'What are you talking about?' said Sveinn sensing his claustrophobia forcing its way deeper and deeper into his lungs.

'Self-respect, man,' said Kjartan. 'You don't get your dick out with dirty hands and you don't eat American junk food from a packet.'

Sveinn knew he should have started laughing by now, slapping his thigh and joining in the tomfoolery, thereby accepting the camaraderie being offered him – *us two, we know what life is about, we have our code*, and so on – but he couldn't do it, just couldn't.

'How about you cook her a meal for once?' he said, unnecessarily gruffly, knowing full well that Kjartan adored his mother and would do anything for her, even wipe the salt and grime off the garden gnomes with a damp cloth when the weather had taken its toll on them.

Kjartan's usual look of amiability and cheeriness slipped from his face and he put his bottle down so he could use both hands for emphasis. 'Do you think I haven't offered time and again? She is so ancient she can barely lift an empty saucepan.'

He scratched his side and looked pleadingly at Sveinn. His eyes spoke for him: *Don't mistreat me: I'm not a bad person.*

Sveinn thawed under his gaze. It always moved him to witness Kjartan's submissiveness. He felt a compassion that was at once full of pain and triumph.

He dipped a sugar cube in his coffee and slipped it into his mouth before pulling out the card with the obituary notice and passing it to Kjartan. 'Is this him?'

'Yes, that's him,' replied Kjartan. 'Hans Sigurjónsson from Hlíð. Poor old boy. What the devil could have got into the man?'

'Turn the card over,' said Sveinn.

Kjartan looked in silence at the announcement of Sveinn's impending death. Then he gave a shout of laughter, rubbed his forehead and looked over at Sveinn as if he wasn't sure whether he was winding him up.

'This was sent to me in the post,' said Sveinn. 'Some woman sent me this.'

'Really? Did the sender sign her name?'

'No, I could tell from the handwriting on the envelope. There's no doubt about it. I'm absolutely certain.'

Kjartan shook his head, without taking his eyes off the card in his hand. 'You'll take this to the police, of course,' he said. 'This is nothing less than a threat.'

'Well, maybe I shouldn't let it get to me too much,' said Sveinn.

'Because it's some woman, you mean?' said Kjartan, and the laughter welled up in him again. 'Never underestimate the enemy. Women kill as well, you know. Men shoot, women poison. According to tradition. You should at least keep your eyes open and never turn your back on them.'

Sveinn dismissed this, although his stomach lurched and his throat knotted. 'Stop talking rubbish,' he said. 'And anyway, I've got some bad news for you. Your new girlfriend has been stolen.'

Kjartan looked in disbelief towards the bedroom. 'What do you mean?' he asked.

'Exactly what I said. The new one, the one with dark hair – Raven-Black Lola. She was all ready. There in the box and everything. I just had to stick her into the back of the truck and run her round to you. I'll make you another, of course, and you'll get a fifty per cent discount because of the delay.' Sveinn realized as he spoke how relieved he was to have this excuse to cut the price.

Kjartan stared at him, his biceps tensed and shoulders raised as if preparing himself for an attack. 'Was there a break-in at your place then? On top of everything else you've had to put up with?' he asked.

Sveinn shook his head, drummed his fingers on the edge of the table, his anger simmering under the surface as he carefully chose his words.

'I had an unexpected guest last night,' he said. 'Some woman I've never seen before. Actually it was rather like the story of "Goldilocks and the Three Bears". She ate my food, sat in my armchair, took advantage of my amazing masculine prowess when I changed her tyre, but instead of repaying me by scrubbing the floor or becoming my girlfriend, or whatever Goldilocks did, she decided to steal your Raven-Black Lola from me.'

'Ah well, you do someone a favour and look what you get,' said Kjartan, and laughed.

'Not that I have the faintest notion what she intends to do with her,' added Sveinn.

'Ha, ha, ha,' chuckled Kjartan, probably thinking up something predictable to say about two women fondling each other.

'Don't say what you're thinking,' said Sveinn. 'I really don't want to hear it.'

'Who's ultra-sensitive then?' said Kjartan. 'Are you jealous of Raven-Black Lola? Would you rather have been shut in Goldilocks' boot yourself and had a taste of her golden pussy? I think that might be less fun than you think. Raven-Black Lola shouldn't be in her clutches, and neither should you. Isn't she the same person who sent you this charming postcard?' he added waving the card like a fan.

Sveinn got to his feet impatiently and looked around. 'Where's your old girlfriend?' he asked, and looked straight at Kjartan.

'In the bedroom,' replied Kjartan, looking back at him challengingly.

'Have you finally finished test-driving her?'

'Well, I'm in no hurry,' replied Kjartan. 'She's so young, poor thing, and always looks at me so shyly when I suggest the idea.'

'She's so young?' said Sveinn, and burst out laughing. 'She's body type 3, with breasts like watermelons. I don't understand why you waste all your money on something you don't use. Why don't you just get yourself a dog?'

'Why don't you focus your efforts on dog-breeding?' retorted Kjartan. 'You don't shag them either.'

'Only in the beginning, when I was developing the landing mechanism,' said Sveinn. 'And I can certainly vouch for it. Nothing to worry about there, no serrated edges in the vagina.'

'Sit down,' said Kjartan. 'Sit down and relax. It's the coffee making you so uptight. You know I don't mean it literally. Why shouldn't I enjoy collecting these beauties just because I don't shag them all day long? Are you sure you don't want a cold drink?'

Sveinn shook his head, but Kjartan was already on his way into the kitchen and didn't notice.

'What's this woman called?' Kjartan asked, when he had placed the two open bottles on the table and propped himself up in the armchair. 'How old is she? What does she look like? Where does she live? Did you look at her number plate when you were changing her tyre? We'll find her and ask her nicely to return the goods. I'll buy the doll from you afterwards, just as we'd agreed. She'll just be a bit more experienced by the time I get her, that's all.' He gave a contented grunt, took off one sandal, scratched his heel and then slid it back on without taking his eyes off Sveinn.

'She's called Lóa, she's blonde and she lives in Vesturbær,' said Sveinn. 'She's about thirty-five and, no, obviously I didn't commit her number plate to memory. I was dog-tired and saw no reason to be suspicious of her. Besides, she didn't show any particular interest in my things.'

He suddenly felt constricted in his jacket, but as he took it off, his own indecisiveness annoyed him. But perhaps it was nothing more than tiredness. His limbs still felt heavy despite a good night's sleep and he was feeling hungry again.

'Of course, the first thing that occurred to me was to look her up,' he added. 'I didn't realize straightaway what a hopeless idea that was. What am I supposed to do? Walk round Vesturbær in Reykjavík with a knife, hammer on all the doors and put a cross on the doorpost when I've ascertained that no-one called Lóa lives there?'

'That's a possibility,' said Kjartan. 'There's no question that it's feasible. It's not like we live in a vast metropolis; everyone helps out here. There must be someone who's seen her.'

It was crystal clear that Kjartan was going to force his good offices on Sveinn whether he wanted them or not. For his part, he didn't know whether to be glad or to despair.

'She forgot her coat,' he said, and massaged his numb finger. It was like rubbing an inanimate object or someone else's finger.

Kjartan sat bolt upright. 'Did you look in her pockets?' he asked.

'Of course I did, but they were as empty as the bubbles in my beer, which was only to be expected. Thieves don't often leave their calling card when they steal something.'

'It's only to be expected if they leave their clothes behind,' said Kjartan. 'It's not as though this particular thief was masked and wearing gloves. What sort of a coat was it, anyway?'

'A white woollen coat with a light-green lining, and what on earth does it matter?' said Sveinn.

And suddenly, more than anything else, he felt empathy for this Lóa, who he could hardly picture now, except her hair, which was *Honey-Golden Susie*, and her face, which reminded him slightly of the dark-haired doll she had stolen. Perhaps that was exactly why she had stolen her. Did she identify with the doll in some way? God alone knew how women's minds work when they were on the verge of a nervous breakdown.

He shook his head and added, 'The poor woman was going through some kind of breakdown. It could well be that she returns the doll in a few days, when she's feeling a bit better, and who knows, she might even offer an apology as well.'

'Well, you should at least talk to the police and get a crime reference number so you can get something off the insurance,' said Kjartan. 'And see what they say about the threatening letter.'

'I'm not insured and I don't want to make a mountain out of a molehill with this pathetic prank,' said Sveinn.

Kjartan stared at Sveinn, a disapproving frown creasing his brow. 'You are more of a fool than I took you for.'

'Well, at least my brain isn't steeped in cheap TV programmes, like some people,' said Sveinn, as he got to his feet, then promptly attempted to take the sting out of his words with a clumsy smile. Kjartan had an uncommon tolerance for barbed comments, but this was definitely not what he wanted to hear.

He set off home with his Barbour under his arm. The warmth, the light, the buds on the trees, a jet which chalked a streak across the blue expanse of the sky: everything conspired against him and sent his thoughts spiralling off their usual course. Something was missing from his life, and he didn't even know what it was. It wasn't more of these gleaming rooftops dancing in the sunlight or the glittering ocean, which he'd seen enough of, but something else. Not more coffee, or more beer, not more of anything he knew, either real or imagined, but something he had never experienced. Perhaps something which didn't even exist.

The sure-fire solution to such an unfamiliar state of mind was to work more. But today he was too tired to do anything. He knew that if he didn't rest for a few days he would go crazy.

He had been on the brink the evening before without even realizing it. Looking back, it now seemed it had been some brute and not a man who had invited a disturbed woman into his home and thought solely about what satisfaction he could get from her.

Yes, he had changed her rock solid tyre, but not before she'd had to wait for a few hours, and all the time he'd let her know what a major hassle it was. The decent thing would have been to ring Kjartan and ask him to help her. Kjartan would have revelled in the story for days afterwards and the woman would have got home to her children at a reasonable hour, instead of waking, stiff and anxious, perhaps in the middle of the night, in a stranger's armchair which was far from comfortable to sit in, much less sleep in.

In many ways, he'd got what he deserved when she made off with the wretched doll. Was there any chance of her returning it? It was unlikely that she would have the courage to look him in the eye, but she could just leave the thing outside, lying on the lawn with her hair flowing over the grass.

It would be a far from ugly sight. Raven-Black Lola was one of the most beautiful compositions he had put together – she was as good as perfect. His own role in the final design had been considerable. Kjartan had asked for his advice when he commissioned the doll and in the end had accepted all his proposals with a dignified reluctance.

He stopped in the middle of the street and took stock of the house where he lived. A windowless Nissen hut with a concrete walled extension. Tomato-red window frames, which he had whiled the time away painting, one miserable, grey day the month before, hoping all the time that it wouldn't start to rain. And it hadn't rained.

He was fond of this house, but did not want to go inside. Not quite yet. He wanted to be out of doors, walking, and to feel his chest expand with a vernal and primeval shout that was building up inside him. All he needed was a good reason. Walking without a purpose was for poets and people who needed to lose weight.

He stepped onto the pavement when he heard a car approaching from behind, and then remembered that he needed light bulbs, washing-up liquid and various items of food. He turned around and set off in the direction of Einar's corner shop. It didn't matter that he didn't have his wallet; they would put it on his tab until his next visit.

The sea breeze ruffled his hair and whistled in his ears, yet the temperature was quite mild. Spring had crept into the town while he was shut indoors with the sour stench of silicone and not a single intelligent thought in his head. When working, he could only focus on his next hand movement and the next and the next. The number of moulds of this type he would need. So many kilos of silicone powder, so many litres of drying agent, a tiny touch of colour in the first mix, stir it well, but gently. The skeleton made of steel and fibreglass finally laid to rest within a flawless covering of skin, the front and back glued together before it was painted over with the final coat. Always the same steps, and in the same order. Admirable or demeaning, depending on how you looked at it.

He pushed open the door to Einar's shop and nearly

stumbled over a small child on a trike, who stared up at him. He had green knee-length trousers and a blue knitted jumper with a hood and angelic shoulder-length hair.

Perhaps because of the overwhelming choice they offered, convenience stores magnified the haze in his head out of all proportion and created a tension inside him. Often he would decide in advance precisely what he was going to buy and the order in which he was going to select his items, but this time his mind had been elsewhere and he was unprepared. And besides, he felt he was being watched and wondered how many people there had read the suicide article, how many knew who he was and transferred all their antipathy towards modern society onto him. Who had scrutinized the picture of him in the paper, thought they saw something unwholesome in his features and squirmed in their seats with a horror shot through with pleasure at the thought that the source of this exciting news was *right here, right next door*?

Instead of looking around hopelessly with the child's innocent gaze resting on him, he decided to go straight over to the shelf of light bulbs and take his time lining them up in his basket while he got himself organized. He needed at least two small forty-watt bulbs of the narrow screw-in type and several of the standard size – sixty watts with the wider screw-in fitting.

'Well, hello, Sveinn,' said a voice from behind him – a gruff but oddly shrill voice which he thought he recognized but couldn't remember where from. Turning round, he was none the wiser. The lad who had addressed him was familiar, but no more than that. He was short and fair, with an oval face, his voice not yet broken, although he was certainly old enough.

'Odd bumping into you just now,' said the lad, toying ostentatiously with a tiny and very expensive brand of phone. 'I was just hanging up from Kjartan when I spotted you. He rang to tell me about it. You've got yourself in a nasty fix there, man.' When he saw that Sveinn couldn't place him he quickly added, 'I'm Lárus. We met at Kjartan's a while back, when he decided to celebrate his birthday six months late. Or six months early.'

'Right,' said Sveinn disinterestedly. 'Hello,' he added, and made an attempt to give a friendly nod, but was not sure whether it was a smile or an awkward grimace which spread across his face. He tried to dodge past and say goodbye as he did so, but the lad blocked his path, an eager look on his face. He came right up to Sveinn and leant in towards his chest, almost as if he was going to hug him over the basket of light bulbs.

'The thing is, I think I remember her,' he said in an undertone.

Sveinn looked at him blankly. He didn't have a clue what the lad was talking about or whether he was meant to say something in reply. His whole sense that there was a coherence in the world was dissipating, consigning him to a dizzy haze of random words and events.

A primitive desire to shove the lad out of his way welled up in him. But instead he leant back and eyed him suspiciously, trying to make it clear that he was not interested in taking this obscure conversation further.

'My shift finished at eight o'clock this morning,' whispered the lad, and his eyes shone with excitement. 'She was one of the last ones to drive through while I was on. It must have been her. There really isn't any traffic on Saturday mornings.'

Sveinn nodded, slowly at first and then more quickly as it dawned on him that young Lárus worked in the tollbooths at the entrance to Hvalfjörður Tunnel.

'I noticed her because I thought she was crying at first, but when she wound the window down I saw she just had this odd expression. She was clearly in an awful state. I don't remember if she paid by card or cash. If she paid by card we can easily get to her – she's a sitting duck. If she didn't we can still find her. There are cameras.'

The amusing thought crossed Sveinn's mind that the lad was willing to lay himself open to charges of misconduct for illegally obtaining information. But the lad's look of undisguised longing made it clear that he just wanted to be part of the adventure.

'Can you just hand out information like that, willy-nilly?' asked Sveinn, forcing himself to stand perfectly straight and still so as not to knock into the light bulbs behind him or the lad close in front of him, who came across like a fawning dog.

'My aunt is the shift supervisor up there,' said the lad. 'She taught me how to do it because she doesn't want to have to do the printouts herself every time. And if we need pictures I can definitely get her to help us.'

*You sad, sad boy*, thought Sveinn. *Do you need a world war or a natural disaster to feel proud of yourself? Clammy with longing to get one over on a neurotic woman just to make up for the privileged and secluded life you've led.*

Out loud he said, 'I'd just decided to ring the police and let them deal with it.'

This was far from the truth. He hadn't been thinking along those lines. At most he'd considered taking a trip to Reykjavík if there was a chance of reclaiming the doll, but he didn't want to make a circus out of it, with one fool after another taking centre stage. The more people who became involved, the more irritating he felt the whole situation would become.

'But thank you very much, anyway, mate,' he added. 'If you

should happen to come across her full name and where she lives, then do get in touch.'

The words were scarcely out of his mouth before the crest-fallen lad was back on his phone.

'P-I-N-O-C-C-H-I-O,' he spelled out loud.

'Why Pinocchio?' asked Sveinn.

The lad glanced up quickly and Sveinn saw that he was slightly taken aback.

*Good for you*, he thought when the lad managed to suppress his embarrassment and announce casually, 'Pinocchio's your nickname. Didn't you know?'

'No, I had no idea,' said Sveinn, and couldn't stop himself smiling. 'Why Pinocchio?'

The lad shrugged and said, 'You know. Pinocchio the wooden doll. It's not meant unkindly, you know. Most people round here get called something, unless they're so boring they're not worth gossiping about. Don't worry about it.'

'I don't suppose I'll lose much sleep over it,' said Sveinn, and gave a hearty laugh to end the conversation. As he walked away he called out his phone number over his shoulder to a drooping, blond head and two thumbs working the keys.

# 6

It was almost midnight and Ína was asleep, exhausted and spotlessly clean, having helped clear up in the kitchen and then
been allowed to play for over an hour in the bath. The two
women sat at the dining room table: Björg halfway through her
third or fourth cup of coffee and Lóa well on her way to emp-
tying the bottle of red wine.

'Well then,' said Björg, standing up and gazing dreamily at
the fading orange-red glow of the night sun which gilded the
Sound and Mount Esja, its gullies still striped with snow. She
opened the window; a chill crept in, bringing with it a gentle
hint of earth and seaweed.

Above all Lóa didn't want Björg to go straight to bed. The
contents of the bottle were safely filling her stomach like
precious treasure, feeding her desire for more than just superficial
conversation.

Björg, who had left her partner some weeks previously, had
been talking about her experiences on the housing market: the
greed of landlords, the desperation of people looking for a flat
and the high demand for accommodation which then forced
prices up. At the moment she could stay at her mother's and
Lóa's alternately, and she was forever saying how thankful she
was before admitting how sick and tired of it she'd become.
'I'm out on the street yet again, up to my eyes in debt, and
everyone apart from you has given up on me. People just aren't
interested in listening to my endless tales of misery.'

'I'll need nothing less than a miracle if you and Mum need to get rid of me at some point,' she said and laughed wearily. She stood by the open window and lit a cigarette, gazing silently.

'Wait a moment. I'll be back in a second,' said Lóa, realizing as she stood up how heavy her limbs felt. Surprisingly steady on her feet, she walked along the dimly lit hallway, which reminded her of another hallway. It seemed a hundred years ago that she'd been standing there, or perhaps it had only been in her imagination that she had fumbled her way along it in search of a bathroom. Instead she had found something quite different: a man's unfamiliar backside resting against a hard bed rail, a doll workshop and a dangerous, dark-haired female, who had led her onto a path of crime without uttering a word. Without so much as raising an eyebrow.

She knocked gently with one finger and opened the door without waiting for an answer.

Margrét had drawn the blackout blinds and lay on her back on the far side of the bed, right up against the wall. Her eyes, surprisingly bright in her feeble and withered body, followed Lóa's every movement. The only light came from a large alarm clock with luminous numbers which showed the whites of Margrét's eyes – the whitest white Lóa had ever seen, except perhaps in very young children.

When Margrét was admitted to hospital the whites had been oddly yellow, which, according to the doctor, was a sign her liver function was low. But now they were snowy white. That must be a good sign.

The doll sat undisturbed in the armchair next to the bed, except that Ína's multi-coloured flowery hat had been set jauntily on her head. Clearly Ína had slipped into Margrét's room earlier in the evening without Lóa noticing. The poor child was naturally very interested in the doll, although she had surprised her mother by not mentioning it at the dinner table.

Margrét took up virtually no space in the bed. All that empty space around her was no less heartbreaking than she was herself, with her jutting cheekbones and prominent eyes, and Lóa wanted to lie down next to her to share her body warmth, stroke the hair from her forehead and fill up the emptiness beside her, but she knew Margrét would never let her.

'Are you having difficulty getting to sleep, my love?' asked Lóa.

Margrét shrugged her shoulders impassively.

Lóa didn't ask whether she felt better having the doll next to her because she knew that no matter whether Margrét thought it was a good idea or not, she would say it wasn't. And besides, it was not intended to make her happy – it was more a kind of medicine.

She grasped the doll's hands – it wasn't like holding the hands of a sleeping person, it was more as though the doll gripped her back – and heaved her up out of the chair, eased her down gently onto the bed and settled her by Margrét's side, half on top of the duvet.

Margrét didn't look at the doll but continued to watch her mother. She didn't say, '*I can smell wine on you, Mum,*' or '*You're crazy.*' But perhaps she thought both.

Lóa picked up the folded woollen blanket from the arm of the chair and laid it over the doll. Even though she was in pyjamas buttoned up to the neck, the air was too chilly to have her lying there uncovered.

Margrét turned away and closed her eyes, and Lóa took the opportunity to behave as though this was all perfectly normal:

Margrét was drifting off to sleep and she was one of those stone-cold-sober women who spend their evenings watching TV. 'Good night,' she whispered, and closed the door quietly.

When she came back into the dining room Björg was sitting cross-legged and thumbing through an old copy of *Living Science*. Tiredness exaggerated Björg's short-sightedness and from the way she was peering at the magazine she was obviously sleepy. But she seemed to sense that Lóa needed a little more company this evening.

Björg put the magazine down and said, 'I've never heard you moan or complain – not even in circumstances which would overwhelm anybody else, one way or another.'

Lóa shook her head vigorously. 'What rubbish,' she said. And yet she couldn't help letting the praise touch some maudlin part of her brain which the wine had already loosened up. She winced whenever conversations turned to moaning women, and the last thing she wanted was to be one of them.

'So, how are you really?' asked Björg. 'Is what you were up to last night top secret?'

Lóa shook her head again. 'I didn't plan on being out all night.'

'What were you doing?'

'I just went for a drive. Up to Akranes,' said Lóa.

Björg laughed. 'To Akranes? Who do you know up there?'

Lóa looked down at her nails, bit one of them, then thought better of it and dropped her hands in her lap. She had almost forgotten the original reason for going, and now that she was about to explain it seemed ridiculous. She concentrated on keeping the worst bits to herself. She didn't have the courage, for example, to tell Björg that the reason for abandoning the girls, for what should only have been two hours, was to help her resist the bottle, along with the sudden compelling need to get as far away as possible from this house, which kept pressing in on her until she felt she was being buried alive.

'Do you remember Marta? The old woman who looked after the girls last winter?' asked Lóa, and her mouth went dry as she thought about the sequence of events she was revisiting.

Björg flicked away an imperceptible speck and said, 'Vaguely. I was so taken up with that red-haired stockbroker I was seeing that I wasn't exactly a regular visitor then.'

'No, we really missed you,' said Lóa pausing to think for a moment before she continued. 'Marta was a little eccentric, but she was good with the girls and kept the place clean, even though I hadn't made a particular point of that. I felt I'd struck lucky and thought she'd continue to be part of our lives, even when Ína became too old to need a childminder. She had no family or friends and I thought we would become like a family to her.'

Björg nodded and the sleepiness in her eyes gave way to interest.

'And then Ína started talking about finding a sliver of glass in her sandwich, in the packed lunch Marta had made for her to take to school. She kept on about it, so I asked her about it and whether it had happened more than once. Ína said it had really happened, but only once and I had to believe her, especially because she was so taken by Marta and had no reason to lie about her. There was nothing I could do other than ask Marta to leave, even though we, and especially Margrét, would all miss her. Marta had much more faith in Margrét than I did. Sometimes I was a little jealous, but mostly I was just relieved that Margrét had someone she could turn to.'

Lóa's eyes filled with tears, but her voice remained steady.

'Margrét has always kept herself to herself,' she said. 'She bottles everything up. Ever since she was little, even before she learnt to talk. Children are free-spirited. They just burst out with things all the time. But not Margrét. It was as if she'd been born with a tight rein on herself.'

Standing up, Björg walked over to the window again. She fiddled with the hanging mobile Ína had given Margrét for Christmas: white clay angels with golden trumpets. She prodded their bellies, watched them swing about and said, 'I know. Margrét has always been different. The quietest child I've ever known. I remember you made a point about it the first time you asked me to babysit her. You said I mustn't raise my voice – it was enough to tell her off gently. And you were right – she paid attention to everything I told her. I could hardly bring myself to leave her.'

'Feel free to smoke at the table,' said Lóa. 'We'll just air the room afterwards.'

Sitting back down, Björg stuffed her hands deep into her pockets. The sensitive lines around her mouth revealed how much she took Margrét's illness to heart.

Lóa looked away. Strange how she should crave empathy but couldn't handle it when it was offered to her. Feeling increasingly ill at ease, she continued her story.

'Marta smiled and made out it was nothing when I sacked her. It was weird, as though she wasn't human. It's difficult to explain to someone who wasn't there, but I felt as if I was standing in front of some creature who had no idea what a normal emotional response to the situation would be. I was filled with an indescribable aversion to her. I realized that I had disliked her all along without acknowledging it, and I felt very relieved when she left. I didn't doubt that I'd made the right decision.' Lóa looked at Björg. Her brows were drawn in deep furrows and her mouth was half open in confusion.

'I don't understand,' she said. 'Why did you even want her to feel bad when you fired her? She might have had her own reasons for reacting as she did.'

Lóa had begun shaking her head even before Björg finished her sentence. 'No,' she said. 'For one thing, she adored the girls and always talked as though there was no doubt she would be there for them until she passed away. She talked about the future as if it were a fait accompli: what she was going to give Margrét as a wedding present if she should be lucky enough to see the happy day and so on. And secondly, she was naive enough to confide in me that no-one else had been willing to employ her. No, no-one in her position would have gone without complaint. But it was as if she didn't know that she had every right to be aggrieved and to demand an explanation. It was as if she had no idea that it was normal to feel saddened, or angry even, and to start crying.

'I had prepared myself for all of that and had intended to tell her that of course she was welcome to visit as often as she liked. But I didn't get to that because she threw me so. I was so filled with disgust that I had to stop myself from pushing her out of the door and slamming the bolt home.'

Lóa was silent as she finished her wine. She was amazed that she didn't feel more tipsy. She felt a strange pulse beating at the bottom of her neck and kept having to swallow. She put her hand to her neck and continued, 'Then the au pair came from the Faroes and was with us for a year. When she left I took leave from work because of Margrét, as you know, so I haven't had to find a replacement. But the last I heard of Marta was that she had got a place in a care home in Akranes.'

'Oh, I see,' said Björg. 'You decided to go to Marta and ask her to speak to Margrét.'

'No,' said Lóa. 'I wasn't going to go that far. I just wanted to find out whether she's actually living in Akranes and then pop in to say hello. But before I made it to the town I got this puncture. So I don't even know what the care home looks like.'

'Why didn't you just change the tyre?' asked Björg. 'Did you sleep in the car?'

She looked briefly at Lóa and when she got no answer she reached over for a packet of incense which had lain forgotten on the windowsill for the last six months. The colours had faded in the sunlight and the paper was crinkled and warped as if the packet had got wet a few times. She opened it and as she carefully pulled out a stick flakes sprinkled out over the table top. They had not noticed the light fading in the room or thought to light any lamps or candles, so the flare of the lighter burned bright yellow in the gloom.

Lóa was thinking that the nights were still not completely light, when in the next breath she had a pang of conscience about her work. She imagined she was back at her office desk, a humming computer in front of her and a bronze lamp with a white glass shade, a Madagascan dragon tree filled the corner and a glass wall separated her from the owners of the business.

Björg poked the smoking stick of incense into the soil of a metre-high ficus plant, which Lóa had forgotten to water for weeks. The dark green leaves were beginning to droop, burned at the edges by the powerful spring sunlight. A waft of smoke hung round the plant and Lóa grimaced at the punishment it now had to endure on top of her neglect. It was the only pot plant still surviving. The others had all withered to their roots and made the living room into a sort of wasteland; there was even a spider's web on one of them.

When she was little, maybe five or six, she had amused herself for a whole afternoon pulling long blades of grass away from the walls around her garden, grasping the legs of the slender male spiders and throwing them into the web of a fat female. Someone had told her that the females ate males. The next morning she was buzzing with curiosity and excitement because her conscience was pricking her and because of the total power she had assumed over life and death. But when she ran out to see whether the female was pleased with her gifts her heart sank, because the web was nothing more than threads swaying eerily in the wind, the male bodies huddled together, neatly wrapped in finely spun silk.

Sitting at her dining room table in Framnesvegur, the adult Lóa said, 'The road to hell is paved with good intentions.'

Snorting with laughter, Björg allowed the lighter flame to glow for a while, before testing the heat of the metal with a rapid movement of her fingers. Under the table, her leg swayed in time to some rapid inner beat, which Lóa imagined sounded like the drum of a brass band on a fast march. The wall behind Björg was papered in muted golden tones with a glossy leaf pattern, and when she leant up against the wall two long, inter-twined leaf stems appeared to protrude from her head like gleaming antlers.

'No matter how hard I tried with the wheel brace, I couldn't undo the nuts,' said Lóa. 'I'd just picked up my phone and was trying to decide who to call, when a man came out of the house I'd driven up to when I turned off the A-road. I had no idea anyone lived there. I thought it was a garage. Anyway, there are lots of similar looking places out in the country. He offered to help me, but said he needed to finish his meal first. I was going to say no, because he was so surly, and then his expression changed, and it was as if the world would come to an end if I didn't let him change my tyre. I thought it was probably a question of honour – that as a true country man he wouldn't be able to look himself in the eye if he didn't show me the proper hospitality, even though I was uninvited and stranded there on his driveway.'

Björg's leg stopped swinging and instead she nodded, as if the drumbeat had moved up to her head. A black curl, which had been carefully tucked behind her ear, slipped onto her forehead, between equally black eyebrows, to form an upside-down cross on a pale background. Björg's skin paled to a milky white over winter and if her lips had been redder then the fairytale description would have fitted her perfectly: *hair like ebony, skin as white as snow, lips as red as the rose.*

Lóa hesitated, unsure how to continue the story. If she omitted to mention how she had downed the tranquillizing contents of two bottles of wine Björg would think she had jumped into bed with some trailer trash.

She took two deep, tense breaths and continued, 'He offered me red wine and I accepted half a glass. I was just going to sip it to keep him company or to calm my nerves or just to compensate for the bad luck – I don't remember exactly what I was thinking. But I got blind drunk and crashed out in his armchair in the living room. I woke around six and was hoping to get home before the girls woke and before Ína was up and about.' Lóa half smiled wearily, and was amazed again that Ína had not mentioned the doll. Ína, who had an uncontrollable desire to talk about everything that happened to her. Maybe she had sensed that her mother wanted to keep it a secret – Ína had become expert at sensing the unspoken.

'Did you drive home three or four hours after your binge?' said Björg.

Lóa sensed her muscles tense and her defences shoot up before she could even get a word out. 'What was I supposed to do?' she said, her voice almost an octave higher than usual. 'Pull over and wait for a bus? How do you think I felt waking massively hung over in that armchair and with the girls alone at home? I feel dreadful about this without you pointing the finger.'

Björg observed the restlessness with which the angels holding their horns circled round each other.

'I wasn't pointing the finger,' she said at last, and slid her hands into her sleeves. She clasped the ribbing of the cuffs in her fists and held them up. 'See, the cat has pulled back her claws,' she said. 'Now the mouse can come out of her hole.'

# 7

Sveinn was standing on a chair in the kitchen, unscrewing a broken bulb from its fitting. It was so badly worn that he had to hold onto it to prevent the fitting from coming loose from the socket. Old paint and rusty, brown debris rained down onto his hair and into his eyes. Supporting himself against the ceiling with his left hand, he slipped the bulb into one back pocket and fished the new bulb out of the other.

The socket squeaked as he pushed the bulb back in, and when it lit up between his fingers he gave such a start that he nearly jumped off the chair rather than fall off.

The bulb had gone the evening before, towards the end of the rather silent dinner. He had looked up from his empty plate and noticed that his guest had become an indistinct silhouette at the other side of the table. Lóa appeared indifferent to the fact that she could barely make out her own hands, so long as the glass still found its way to her lips, but nevertheless, he had felt he should step over to the light switch and flick it on. Except that the light hadn't flicked on but given a buzzing sound and then a bang.

That was the reason they'd moved into the living room, which in turn was the reason he had totally forgotten about the tyre. He hadn't even wondered why he hadn't gone to bed long before and why Lóa was still sitting opposite him, weighed down with all that pain, which was none of his business whatsoever.

But when he had finally had the sense to go out and see to

her car it was too late: she had been in no fit state to drive, and he hadn't minded if she stayed a little longer.

He had been too tired to work out whether he wanted to sleep with her. But he was never too tired to feel his loneliness, like barbed wire wrapped around his diaphragm.

Sveinn wiped the debris off his face and out of his hair and, taking a dustpan and brush from the broom cupboard, he brushed the table and the chair he'd been standing on and got the worst up off the floor.

And now what? He'd already put his shopping away, eaten a few slices of bread and read the papers for the second time that day, and he didn't feel like going back to bed.

His feet led him back towards the workshop, but he stopped halfway down the hall; it was too depressing to look at the disturbance from earlier that morning, and besides, he had no reason to go in there.

He considered driving over to the nearest DIY store, getting some paint and doing up the outside of the extension, making the walls as pristine as the window frames he had gone over the month before. But no, he simply didn't have the energy. Perhaps tomorrow. He really should change the cladding on the Nissen hut as well – the corrugated iron had begun to rust through the paint.

When he was not working he found himself at a loose end. As though he were an unwelcome intrusion into his own empty existence.

It hadn't always been like that. When he was a student, for example, he had enjoyed having free time. Meeting his mates and his fellow students for coffee and moving on to a few beers as the evening wore on. Reading books about art and engineering, even philosophy and novels.

That was a strange thought. He couldn't remotely identify with the young man he had once been. Had he really enjoyed reading? Had he been more noble-minded in those days? Had the palace of his mind been a grander and more glorious place? Or had he just been full of ambition and pretence? Perhaps the underlying reasoning had been along the lines of: I don't intend to look a fool in front of girls by not being able to follow them when they refer to Nietzsche or Susan Sontag. And I don't want to become one of those nitwits who don't know anything about anything and only think about making money.

If that was the case he had kept to his intentions to some extent: he had been a good conversationalist as a young man, and even today he barely gave money a second thought. But he had forgotten more or less everything he had ever read and felt uncomfortable around extremely intellectual people, particularly if they were women. He had the feeling that in their eyes he didn't have much to offer and was more what they would call a curiosity – someone they would enjoy having as a conversation piece, like in a Woody Allen film. Having bantered with him for three quarters of an hour, they would feel they had a better understanding of his psyche than he did, and any respect they felt for him would be akin to their respect for Aboriginal Australians or their less fortunate sisters who fought their way out of poverty through prostitution and lap dancing. They would think up all sorts of reasons for his choice of career, sub-conscious reasons which could be traced back to his childhood and the zeitgeist, which would have influenced him because he had neither the education nor the insight to see how sick the prevailing mood was.

His phone broke into his thoughts. On the backlit screen appeared the word *Unknown*. He answered, 'Hello? Hello?'

There was no response, not even breathing.

'Who is this?' he asked into the silence. The silence gave no response, but it crept up on him from behind, seeped into his heart and his head, until he began to feel as if he were not really alive, as if he were nothing more than a shell around his own malaise and his petty sorrows.

He tried to imagine the listener at the other end of the line, and pictured Lóa at home, reclining on a leather Chesterfield sofa, in her petticoat and with her hair uncombed. She was drumming her fingers on the back of the sofa and listening to him repeating himself – '*Hello? Hello?*' – like a well-trained monkey in a zoo.

'What do you want from me?' he said, and was about to say her name, tell her that everything was all right. '*Tell me where you live,*' he was going to say. '*Just give me your address and I'll come and fetch the doll and we can forget about it.*' But he had the feeling that no-one was listening, and taking the phone from his ear he saw that she'd rung off.

It wasn't that he was frightened exactly, but he was obliged to face up to the fact that he had got his own stalker, just like a celebrity. A female stalker, who sent him anonymous threats and called to listen to his voice, to make him edgy. It was amazing that he had shot so far up the ladder of fame. Stalkers were a status symbol, weren't they? And female stalkers were much rarer, and therefore more remarkable, than their male counterparts.

He returned to his mental picture of Lóa on the Chesterfield and chuckled at the petticoat he had dressed her up in. Women don't go around in petticoats, except perhaps in old films. *I'll be adding a cigarette in a holder and eyeshadow out to her temples next,* he thought.

His scalp itched from the debris from the bulb fitting and he considered having another shower. Wasn't there some other dirty job he could do, since he'd got so grubby already? Yes, he needed to clean the bathroom, particularly the basin and the toilet. But first it would be a good idea to change the bulb in the bedroom, although he couldn't remember ever having switched the light on since moving into the house.

There was no chair he could stand on in the bedroom, just the wicker laundry basket, which came halfway up his thigh. The pliable wicker meant it wasn't very stable, but if he was careful he should be able to keep his balance.

He flicked the switch a couple of times without the slightest idea whether he was turning it on or off. 'Eeny, meeny, miny, mo,' he murmured, flicking the switch up and down with every word. 'Catch a monkey by the toe; if he hollers let him go, eeny, meeny, miny, mo.'

Then he placed the basket in the middle of the floor and scrambled onto it with legs trembling like a new-born foal. He intended to repeat the same procedure: holding firmly onto the decrepit fitting while carefully unscrewing the bulb.

The thread on the bulb was half visible when a bright-blue light flashed across his fingers and a crippling jolt shot down his arm. He didn't know whether he was thrown sideways or had fallen straight down, but the dirt-cheap laminate came rushing up to meet his head. Whoever had chosen this flooring clearly hadn't given a damn about the house and equally probably wouldn't have given a damn about some idiot who was about to break his nose headbutting the floor in dramatic style.

He didn't even have the sense to put his arms out in defence, because none of this was happening in reality, not until he heard his knee crack and felt a resounding blow as the rest of his body crashed onto the ground. His forehead bounced once on the varnished surface and then everything fell silent. Only the gulls continued to cry outside the window and his trouser leg rustled as he tried to move.

Bit by bit, shock gave way to pain; his shoulder and knee hammering Morse-code messages to his head, which felt like it was clamped in a heavy vice. His right arm was unhurt and he fumbled above his head to see whether the wardrobe had fallen onto him, or even the wall, the roof or the sky.

His left shoulder had doubled in size, or was he lying on something? With difficulty, he managed to turn his head so that his nose, unbroken despite everything, was facing the spine of a thick book, and his eyes battled a haze of double vision to bring the letters into focus: *r . . . man,* he read. *Sherman.*

It was a hefty tome with a selection of photographs by the artist Cindy Sherman. A book he had bought many years ago when travelling then lugged home and barely looked at since. What was it doing on the floor?

*If they don't break your heart they'll settle for breaking your collarbone, whether you know them personally or not,* he thought, totally at random.

He didn't know how long he'd been lying there before he managed to wriggle to his feet, but he had the feeling that in that time he had dreamt a number of obscure dreams as he flitted in and out of consciousness, then promptly forgot them. Again and again he tried to put some weight on his right foot, but the pain shot up into his groin and filled his head with scalding steam, paralysing his mind and making him even more helpless. He stood on one leg and hopped the length of half a stride towards the door, nearly blacking out with pain, which this time struck his shoulder blade like a gong.

He quickly lay back down in case he lost his balance again. Lying there on the floor, utterly weak and beside himself with pain, he tried to use his head. Think. Where was the phone?

The phone was on the kitchen table. He had taken it out of his back pocket to make room for the light bulbs – the new bulb in one pocket, the broken bulb in the other – wasn't that just sheer genius on his part? Now he was here – rolling on the dusty floor among the dirty laundry, which had spilled out of the basket when he knocked it over as he fell – but the phone was there, a million miles away.

He tried to empty his mind, in the hope that this would help him concentrate better, but the blackness rose before his eyes.

In his dream he was dragging himself along a wall in a strange house, one leg severed at the knee, black blood dripping from the stump and his arm was like sausage meat in his soaking-wet shirt-sleeve, which he didn't dare roll up. He didn't even dare to look at this limp limb flapping at his side like some alien obscenity. He wanted to cut it off. Perhaps that was how he'd lost his leg. He had felt revolted by it and got rid of it. Where was he going? That's right, he was looking for his phone, which was ringing non-stop in the other room. Or was he trying to find the bathroom? God, he was desperate for a pee. He put his hand on his stomach and realized it was sliced open – he could feel his guts under his shirt and under his skin. He tried to hold them in as best he could. Then the fear took hold of him, wiping out every thought except that he didn't want to be alone. On no account. Death didn't matter, just as long as he didn't have to die alone. Why was there no-one here to help him?

'... I've rung the ambulance,' someone said, with a note of

eagerness in their voice. Touching his forehead, they laid two shaking fingers on the artery in his neck, clearly to check his pulse.

Sveinn pushed the groping hand away. 'I'm not dead yet, you idiot,' he heard himself saying. 'Don't touch me. You're disgusting. Who are you?'

'L . . . Lárus.' It was the lad who had stopped to talk to him in the shop earlier that day. 'The ambulance is on its way. Don't move or try to talk. She said you mustn't move – the woman on the phone,' he added, dithering. There was something Sveinn couldn't put his finger on, but which infuriated him. Yes, it was excitement. The lad found this exciting. Now he got to play the hero. Save the day. Of course, he would much rather they were out in the middle of nowhere and he had to dress the wounds himself. Find a slender branch to use as a splint, rip his shirt into bandages.

It was a relief that they were not in the middle of nowhere, but here in civilization, and the lad didn't get to play the knight in shining armour on his account. The only act of heroism he'd had to perform had been to ring for the ambulance and let some telephonist tell him what to do.

Pain and cold competed for Sveinn's attention. The lower half of his body felt especially cold, as if he were half lying in a snowdrift. He lifted his throbbing head, and when he saw that he'd wet himself he just wanted to give up and die. Alone or not alone. This lad, who was so unbelievably irritating, didn't truly count as company.

'Go and get the scissors,' sighed Sveinn. 'From the kitchen. And be quick about it.'

The lad obeyed without thinking and clearly knew where the kitchen was. He was playing his part so well that if he had been told to go and boil some water he would just have done it, without asking why.

Sveinn lay on his back, with Cindy Sherman for a pillow and the new bulb smashed to pieces in his back pocket, thinking he would rather be alone in his gory nightmares than here, soaked in urine and at the mercy of this oddball who seemed intent on waylaying him with his charity.

Here he was, running in with the scissors.

'Didn't your mother ever tell you not to run with scissors?' said Sveinn, trying to give a friendly smile.

'What did you say?' asked the lad, clearly deaf with excitement, glancing fearfully around the room. Perhaps he was trying to picture how the accident had happened. It was not surprising that he should wonder about it.

If the papers were anything to go by, most serious accidents occurred in the home, but this one must take the biscuit. When Sveinn read about all those domestic accidents, he imagined a forgetful old person suffering from dizziness, or a child too young to know any better – not men in their prime injuring themselves on books.

'How old are you, mate?' he asked.

'Nineteen.'

'Cut the trousers away. You know, like they do on TV, on *Casualty* or whatever it's called. Can you do that?'

'No,' said Lárus. 'I mean, the ambulance is coming in ten minutes and the woman said—'

'The woman doesn't need to know about it,' Sveinn interrupted. 'She thinks my back's broken. I don't know exactly what you told her, but look ...' He shifted slightly, despite the stabbing pain in his shoulder. 'You see, my spinal cord is fine.'

He pulled down the collar of his shirt to show where the

bone was protruding under the skin. 'I've broken my collarbone and there's something wrong with my knee. That's all. I swear it. Hurry up, mate. Just do as I tell you and it'll be OK.'

The lad got down on his knees and began to cut. He was quick and confident, Sveinn had to give him that, even though he was only nineteen and for some tragic reason his voice had not yet broken. He cut and tore in turn from the ankle to the groin and then the scissors hacked through the pocket, the double-stitching and everything that lay in their path.

He hadn't quite cut through the second trouser leg when Sveinn grabbed the scissors from him. He groaned with pain as he pulled the opened denim material from underneath him and began to cut open his soaking-wet underpants. Lárus made as if to help him, but one look from Sveinn stopped him.

'There are pyjamas in the cupboard over there,' said Sveinn. 'Quickly, go and get them for me. White with brown-and-burgundy stripes.'

Lying on his back like a stranded ewe, cutting with the wrong hand without being able to see properly was trickier than he expected. Twice he cut himself and inadvertently nicked his belly where it bulged over the elastic.

He flung the trousers into a corner followed by the ragged underpants. He grabbed a dirty short-sleeved T-shirt from the floor and dried himself all around before chucking the T-shirt in the same direction.

'Do you mean these?' asked Lárus, holding something up in the air which Sveinn, exhausted from his efforts, could only just make out.

'Bring them here,' he answered. 'Help me.'

They heard a vehicle pulling into the driveway, and with

shaking hands Lárus pulled the pyjama bottoms up over Sveinn's legs. Now they could hear voices, a man and a woman talking quickly in hushed tones, and the sound of gravel crunching underfoot. They rushed straight into the porch without knocking and had got as far as the kitchen when Sveinn snatched the waistband out of Lárus's hands and eased it under his buttocks and up over his goddamn prick.

'We made it, mate,' he said, to calm Lárus, who was standing sheepishly in the middle of the floor, peering into one corner after another as if he feared seeing something which could give them away. But Lárus didn't seem to hear. When the ambulance crew appeared in the doorway, having called *Hello* a number of times on their way down the hall, Lárus was standing there, as white as a sheet, as though he was responsible for everything.

'Well, hello,' said Sveinn, smiling to himself. The pyjamas were sticking to him slightly, but at least they were clean and dry. The butch dyke and the six-pack wouldn't have to look at his soaking crotch as if he were a drunk in the gutter, and nor would they have to put up with his foul temper because he felt so humiliated. He would be able to maintain a certain level of dignity and, in gratitude to the Almighty, he would make the trip for these guys in their red-and-blue overalls as pleasant as possible.

The woman crouched down by his side and looked him over. The overalls were straining round her sturdy thighs and clearly weren't designed for the female body. The straight-leg cut suited her colleague much better.

'Can you stand up?' she asked.

'I could earlier at least,' he replied.

'Can you walk?'

'No.'

She gently felt the collarbone, which was pressing up under Sveinn's shirt collar and he had to clench his jaw so as not to cry out.

'That's a nasty break,' she said.

Her colleague leant on the folded stretcher and whistled. It was a long undulating note which implied amazement and admiration. 'How did you do this, guv'nor?' he asked.

'I was changing a light bulb,' said Sveinn, with a guffaw, despite the agony which erupted at his shoulder blade and spread through him like poison.

'Were you standing on that basket, holding the bulb and waiting for ninety-nine more geniuses to come and rotate the house for you?' joked the ambulance man.

Sveinn lowered his eyelids. That was precisely the response he'd expected. Ambulance men are the most hard-bitten crew in the world. More merciless than white-collar criminals, rougher than waves on the open sea.

'Behave yourself, Jónsi,' said the woman. 'Bring the stretcher.'

Drunks brought out their toughest side. Drunks were made to walk out to the ambulance themselves, unless they were pouring blood or their hearts had stopped – then they were tossed, in the most compassionate manner, onto stretchers. When he was small, before his mother found God and AA, he'd had to call an ambulance three times in the same week, when the old dear had complained of pain that spread down her arm and her lips had turned blue. And he had been able to do nothing but look up at the men as they patted his blond head – he had been blond in those days, like Lárus – before they set about using the most brutal methods to wake his mother. They'd stuck the tips of pens under her nails, forcibly opened her eyes and shone a little torch into them, until she either lifted her hand or began to blink. Then she had been dragged to her feet with the ambulance men supporting her on either side. Except on the third and final occasion: then they had run out with her on a stretcher, leaving the front door open.

Perhaps it was more weariness than contempt which gave them their hardened expressions, but Sveinn had been ashamed that his mother wasn't really ill, and he had been ashamed that he wasn't as cool and tough as they were, just a little kid with his heart in his mouth.

The old dear? What a misnomer. She had only been about thirty when this happened. She'd been little more than a girl, constantly running away from hospitals and other institutions. Her memory had been shot to pieces so it was hard to say how old she seemed. She was sixty now and helped out at the treatment centre serving coffee and kindness.

'One, two and up-we-go,' said the woman, and they lifted him in unison and wheeled him towards the door. The woman had covered him with a thin, warm blanket and strangely he felt a deep gratitude towards her. *This is how suffering makes one tender-hearted,* he thought, and suddenly remembered the fire risk from the bulb, which was only partially fixed in the faulty light fitting, with an electric current running through it.

'Do me a favour, Lárus,' he said, and pointed to the light switch. 'Turn it off for me, will you?'

Lárus sat in the back of the ambulance without so much as a by-your-leave, and avoided looking Sveinn in the eye, as if he feared he would be sent packing if he drew attention to himself.

'Are you feeling fairly OK?' the woman asked.

'Yes, love,' replied Sveinn.

'You were lucky your friend here found you,' said the woman.

Lárus's pink ears turned pinker still.

'Good point,' said Sveinn, turning his head with difficulty towards Lárus. 'What were you doing at my place?'

Smiling indulgently, the woman moved towards the front of the vehicle and leant over the front seat so as not to interrupt their private conversation. Perhaps there was more to her than met the eye. Perhaps she was neither stupid nor vulgar, but one of those women who sense an atmosphere with their invisible antennae and know precisely how everyone is really feeling.

'I'd tried to call you a few times,' said Lárus quickly. 'You know, because of what we'd spoken about earlier. But you didn't pick up and I was beginning to think that you'd lost your phone or something. I drove by your place and saw your truck and decided there was no harm in knocking on the door, but as I was walking past the window you were just lying there and I saw that something was wrong, so I went straight in.'

Sveinn inhaled as deeply as he could without moving his collarbone and was surprised how indignant he felt. He should be relieved and grateful, not seized with the desire to get his hands on this Good Samaritan of his.

'What did you want to tell me that was so important?' said Sveinn, although he knew that by talking so casually in the presence of the ambulance crew he was totally destroying Lárus's fantasy that the two of them were conspirators in some kind of secret plot.

When Lárus didn't respond he added, 'Don't be so mysterious. We haven't got the Mafia or the police on our tail.'

The hurt was evident in Lárus's voice when he said, 'No.' But he was resolute and added, 'I've just found out what you needed to know. You can drive over to her place as soon as your shoulder's up to it and get back what she stole.'

'That didn't take you long,' said Sveinn. 'I was sort of wondering whether we shouldn't just let her have the wretched doll, since she wants it so much. What do you think?'

Lárus shrugged, utterly dejected. He seemed to long for Sveinn to take notice of him. He wanted to make himself invaluable. The poor lad didn't realize that all he needed to do to earn Sveinn's approval was to disappear off the face of the earth.

# 8

*Sunday Morning*

Lóa stood at the kitchen sink, looking out of the window at the yellow-and-red sloping corrugated roofs and at the newly sprouting grass which was beginning to peep up from beneath the yellow-brown tangle left from the year before. The colours were intensified in the bright morning light. She had a strange buzzing in her head which ran through her whole body, as if someone was playing bass notes too low to hear. It wasn't nearly bad enough to be termed a hangover – it was more what you'd call a good, cosy feeling; her nerves were humming like a milk-cooling system in a cowshed after milking time.

She slowly washed up the liquidizer jug and its base. The food supplement drink was sitting next to the fruit bowl in a tall tumbler made of opaque, pink glass, waiting to be taken in to Margrét. It reminded Lóa of an advert she'd once made for a new yoghurt drink which had just come onto the market.

The idea of work was like an indistinct memory and the image of the office at Borgartún was two-dimensional in her mind, as though on a TV screen.

The taxi journeys with her father, when she had been too small for her feet to reach the footwell, were much clearer in her memory: his large, meaty hands firmly fixed to the steering wheel, except when he'd steered with the tips of his thumb and forefinger to make her curl up with laughter. She had been so small and placid that some customers hadn't even noticed her until they leant forward to pay. She had been so silent when she got absorbed in looking out of the taxi window at all the houses, the streets, the cars, the people, the dogs and the ducks on the lake in the town centre. The other drivers had seemed wavering and uncertain of themselves, sometimes utterly lost in comparison with her father who had known the street names in the new districts when they were still just muddy plots whose borders had only been roughly paced out.

When they'd handed him the notes the money had looked small and valueless in his big, paw-like hand, the paper creased and wafer-thin. She had sat there with the money-bag in her lap, and he would pass the notes over, so that soon she had become more adept than him at giving the right change. He had always been so slow in finding the coins; you got the feeling that his barrel-chest blocked his view and the messages sent along his nerves down to his fingers got lost in the large expanse of his shoulders, which were broader than the car seat. The customers had often told her how good she was at mental arithmetic, that she should become a bank cashier when she grew up.

'Or a bank manager,' as her father had once said, one beautiful, bright frosty day.

The customer, a man with a stoop, wearing a brown tweed overcoat, had heartily agreed. 'Precisely, what was I thinking? We couldn't find a better bank manager than this young lady.'

And so the two of them had got talking about the state of the economy and the Central Bank and they hadn't noticed her blanking out their conversation, or seen her mind flitting high up above the rooftops. Up to the skies, clearer and bluer than in any advert.

Only a few months earlier, work had formed a large part of her life. Now she had to think hard to remember the projects she had left half-finished when she went on leave. There had been times when work was the only place she'd felt truly awake. When she wasn't in the office her mind had been half on ideas that tossed and turned around her subconscious; embarrassingly feeble ideas which were unremarkable until the waves of her conscious mind had smoothed and polished them. And then they emerged, brilliantly flawless, and awoke desire in the hearts of ordinary, weary people desperate for a share in their beauty. But that sort of beauty was nothing more than a crack in the door with the promise of a different kind of happiness just beyond. A different kind of happiness? In what way different? Her role was to half answer that question, to give a veiled notion of how.

It had been her role, but no longer.

She picked up the tumbler of drink supplement; it had become tepid. Margrét detested tepid drinks. In the freezer was a pink, heart-shaped-ice-cube mould. It was almost empty, just two hearts left, but that would have to do. The icy coldness numbed her palm on the way over to the glass. Lóa dried her wet hand on her skirt and, stirring the brimming glass with a dinner knife, carried it carefully in to Margrét.

Sensing an odd tiredness and grittiness at the back of her eyes, Lóa screwed up her face and rolled her eyes to release the tension. Suddenly she saw herself as the waitress on the cover of Supertramp's album *Breakfast in America*: the nylon uniform straining over her bosom, her suntanned complexion exaggerated by the white teeth of her endearing smile. All that was missing was the apron and the tray.

Björg was awake but still snuggled under her duvet on the sofa bed. Her things were all piled up on one corner of the dining room table: an open book, a glass of water, the silver rings which adorned her hands during the day, a packet of cigarettes and a lighter.

Rushing through the living room, Lóa made do with a wink as a good morning, then stood at Margrét's door. She knocked softly and waited a few seconds before opening the door and going in. Margrét lay curled up with her back right up against the doll's side. The doll was lying there with her eyes wide open, staring up at the ceiling as though someone had promised her a shadow-puppet performance on the white-painted surface. Margrét's face was not clearly visible in the cool half-light as she lay facing the wall, so it took Lóa a moment to realize that she was asleep. Her fragile ribcage rose and fell gently under the duvet, her eyes were closed and relaxed, her tousled hair looked like an abandoned nest. Lóa hadn't seen her sleeping for months – the doctor had said that she wouldn't sleep for more than three or four hours a night while her body was so thin. 'It's natural for her to be tearful,' the doctor had said. 'Wouldn't anyone be in this pitiful state, starved of food and sleep?'

Lóa put the tumbler on the bedside table and opened the curtains. The light made Margrét jerk her hand and shift her tousled head. She stretched out one leg and tried to roll onto her back, but was blocked by the doll. She sat up sharply, squinting as if a torch was being shone in her eyes. She looked like a little child who had been woken in the middle of the night. For a second Lóa was able to look into Margrét's soul, and she flinched at the torment she saw there.

'Bloody hell,' muttered Margrét and the childlike look melted from her face in a flash.

Lóa felt obliged to make up for Margrét's negativity with forced cheerfulness, even though she knew it would grate on Margrét's nerves.

'A very good morning to you. And what a gloriously beautiful spring morning it is too,' she said.

Margrét winced as though she was possessed by an evil spirit and her mother was holy water.

'It should definitely be warm enough after lunch to sit in the garden for a little while,' said Lóa. 'You can sit outside with your history books. It's the last exam tomorrow, isn't it? Then you're free, my love.'

'Yeah, then I get to go back into the nuthouse,' said Margrét, and her lips curled into a sarcastic smile and paper-fine creases appeared under her deadened eyes.

Lóa was at a loss. She couldn't go on pretending she was in a good mood. Margrét's misery was too heavy a burden for one person to carry alone.

'I expect you'll only need to be in hospital a few days, you've been doing so well,' she said.

Margrét snorted. 'Isn't it really you who's been doing so well?' she said. 'They'll definitely be pleased with you.'

Björg appeared in the doorway in matching dragonfly-patterned knickers and vest-top. 'Is this a pyjama party?' she asked. 'Is ...' she was about to add something, but was transfixed by the sight of the doll. A look of sheer amazement swept over her face so that she looked more like a painting of herself, a painting which could be called *Face to Face with the Unexpected*.

Lóa would have laughed, had there been an ounce of laughter left in her soul. Instead she just stood there awkwardly and had never felt so alone. Björg was smart and quick on the uptake, but now she seemed utterly gormless.

Then Björg's mouth closed and her eyes glazed over briefly, as though she was working something out in her head. She looked quickly at Lóa and then at Margrét, who was sitting hunched up in bed, biting her nails.

She was totally absorbed in this humdrum activity until she exclaimed in surprise, 'Shit!' and looked up, a drop of blood hanging on her lower lip and another running down her thumb, down to her emaciated wrist.

Lóa stared at the precious fluid as if she had never seen blood before, as if it wasn't just a drop of blood but Margrét's very life which was running out of her, right before her eyes. Lóa began to black out. Everything went dark except for the drop of blood, bright red like a redcurrant from hell. 'God *damn* it,' she heard herself say in a pinched voice and she put her hand over her mouth. Her palm still smelled slightly of the ice cubes she'd held.

She jumped when Björg came to her, smelling of sleep and Dior perfume from the previous day, and put her arm round her neck and kissed her on the cheek. Her lips felt cool against Lóa's burning skin.

'I'll do it,' said Björg, and nodded her head towards the glass on the bedside table. 'You go through and talk to Ína. She's awake; I heard her singing in her room.'

Lóa nodded, her hand still over her mouth, and stumbled towards the hallway. It was like peering through a window pane patterned with hoar frost as tears blocked her view, and the lump in her throat was the size of Margrét's bony fist.

The thought came to her of the tobacco on the living room table. In the old days, when she used to smoke, she'd sometimes been amazed at the effect of tobacco – stopping tears which were determined to fall. They even disappeared back into your eyes once you'd got halfway down a cigarette.

Maybe not. Ína would be shocked if she saw her smoking,

and anyway, the smoke would probably make her feel queasy. She rubbed her temples gently and swallowed again and again. She considered going to the bathroom and splashing her face with water, but feared that once she'd locked the door she might begin to weep uncontrollably.

She strode resolutely towards Ína's bedroom and pushed open the door. Ína sat on the floor with her legs outstretched, holding a naked Barbie doll whose hand was permanently clasped round a tiny microphone. Lóa noticed that the rounded plastic bust had no nipples.

When Ína looked up her eyes became wide with fear. 'What's the matter, Mum?' she asked.

'Nothing,' replied Lóa.

Ína looked bewildered, as she always did when she was lied to, and, holding the doll by the hair, swung her round a few times before she jumped to her feet and said, 'Shall we go and get the bike now?'

'What bike?' said Lóa.

'The bike you said I could have for a present this summer. You said so yesterday. You said we'd go tomorrow to buy me a bike as a present, and now it is tomorrow.'

While she was talking, she followed Lóa through into the kitchen, waiting for an answer, her eyes eager with anticipation.

Lóa unscrewed the lid of the coffee jar and said, 'Oh, darling, is that what I said? I meant on Monday. It's Sunday today and the shops are closed on Sundays.'

Ína rolled her eyes. 'The shops aren't closed on Sundays. We've often gone shopping on a Sunday,' she said, and holding her right hand like a revolver, she aimed it at her head, clicked her tongue to release the safety catch and fired, making the appropriate noises.

Lóa rolled her eyes back. She detested this gesture which Ína had adopted from her father. He mimicked this action when he'd said something which was supposed to be funny but which had somehow missed the mark. Ína, however, did it all the time, when someone, herself included, said something she thought was stupid, strange, ridiculous or just wrong.

'Can't we go straight away?' Ína pestered. 'I'm going to a birthday party tomorrow, remember? And we've still got the costume to make. I'm going to be an elfin queen with a magic wand.'

'The birthday party isn't until later in the afternoon, darling. That gives us enough time to do both.'

'But I need to practise riding my bike for when I go to Dad's.'

'What do you mean, practise? You already know how to ride a bike,' said Lóa wearily, switching on the coffee machine.

'Practise weaving in and out and riding with no hands and stuff,' said Ína anxiously, adrift in her own powerlessness like a mine on the open sea. The poor girl always suffered from a sort of stage fright before she went to her father's. He adored her, but she always had to compete with her two little half-brothers for his attention. Lóa saw how these competitions were conducted in deadly earnest, and she felt for Ína, who was trounced on all sides: on a daily basis by Margrét, the prisoner from Belsen who at that moment was being tortured and probably interrogated in her bedroom, and every other weekend by two hyperactive little rascals who were just at that manic age.

'We'll go and buy you a bike tomorrow, while Margrét is doing her history exam,' said Lóa. 'I promise you. On my honour. You'll have the whole week to practise on it. You're not going to your dad's until Friday. And now, not another word about it.'

Ína stuck out her tongue and blew a long raspberry, before getting the Coco Pops from the cupboard and struggling with a two-litre carton of full-cream milk from the fridge.

Lóa left her to it and, wandering into the living room, ran her finger along the bookshelf and looked at the straight line left in the dust. She tried unsuccessfully to blow the dust away and wiped her hand across her stomach, pretending not to notice the pale streak left on her navy-blue angora jumper.

She slipped back along the hallway towards Margrét's room and leant up against the dark wood. She heard Margrét mumbling but couldn't make out the words.

'How come?' she heard Björg saying, and felt sick because Björg's voice sounded so much stronger and more youthful than Margrét's.

Later that day, Lóa and Björg were sitting at the dining room table over dregs of cold coffee, curled slices of ham, yellowing cheese and a white jug of milk which had been boiled, but whose heat had long since ebbed away. Margrét was in her room studying and Ína had gone out into the garden to play with a friend from over the road.

Lóa had hurriedly explained the situation with the doll, hoping that Björg would look up and say, *'I understand. Of course there's no question about it. Margrét needs the doll more than anyone and that totally justifies what you did.'*

But Björg hadn't said anything of the kind and there was no understanding in her eyes; Lóa wasn't sure whether it was patience or despair she saw there. And when, through the rushing in her ears, Lóa heard that she was repeating herself, like someone championing a lost cause, she shut her mouth tightly and sat in an uneasy silence.

Björg had slid her bare feet to the front of the chair cushion and was resting her head on her knees which were pulled up under her chin; the dragonflies still flew round her midriff. She seemed to know that Lóa couldn't cope with straight talking, or at least that it was important to be careful how she put things to her.

Then Lóa asked, 'What did Margrét say?'

Björg sighed and slid her feet back onto the floor before answering, 'She was full of remorse and said she hadn't intended to draw blood. She's just got this nasty habit of nibbling the skin around her nails, but then there was no dry skin left and that's why she inadvertently bit herself. She seemed to understand how upsetting it was for you, or perhaps she was just afraid that her rations would be increased to make up for the calories in that one drop of blood.' Björg attempted a smile.

The wretchedness of the situation made Lóa give a grim laugh.

'She cried a little and said she knows she's a hideous wretch, but she just can't help it,' said Björg. 'I asked her to tell me how she's feeling and why she's doing this to herself. I just asked it almost as a rhetorical question, for the sake of something to say, and wasn't expecting an answer as such. But she tried, the poor little love. She tried to give me some kind of reason.'

Lóa sat staring into her coffee cup, at the light-brown film across the bottom which seemed to be edging its way up the porcelain.

Björg brought her palms down firmly on the table and said, 'Don't look like that. She's in good hands. We're looking after her and all the staff down at the hospital are looking after her.'

Lóa gave a false smile which made her feel that her face was soft and sticky like a clown's.

'That's right,' laughed Björg. 'Good for you. I can't tell you precisely what she said because it was rather confusing. But essentially she said that she longed for something crystal clear and utterly perfect, that the hunger opened an empty space within her which let in light and dust where light and dust don't normally reach. She said she could picture a ballet hall with parquet flooring on the tenth floor somewhere in New York. The late-afternoon sun is shining in at an angle through the window. It falls on the floor in a cone of swirling dust and the peace there is endless. And although there is a gloomy sadness hanging over the room, there is just so much space.'

'I can't understand this,' said Lóa. 'I don't understand a word of this.'

'That's just what she said,' said Björg, looking apologetically at Lóa from under her straight, dark eyebrows. 'She said that you didn't understand her. The one thing she wants in life is an expanse of tranquillity, fresh as crystal, and that you do nothing but crowd that space with stuff and more stuff, until there is no space left. She said she hates all those tasteless things, all those unnecessary words and colours, smells which blend together, and the never-ending noise surrounding everything. Her idea of perfection is so stark that when she's finished picking at all the knots, there is nothing left in her world. I pointed out this little flaw in her design and she just said again that she needed space. She went on about this word, *space,* as though she needed a hundred square metres of floor-space and four-metre-high ceilings just to be able to breathe.'

The tears began to well up again, and Lóa had to swallow hard before she answered. 'If she wants me to give her the space to kill herself so she can have a minimalist funeral in a huge dome of a church with hardly any mourners, she can think again. She's not getting any goddamned minimalist burial with white flowers,' she exclaimed, not realizing how much she had raised her voice.

'Shh now,' said Björg. 'Not so loud. She made me promise not to tell you about all this, realizing at the same time that I would, of course. And she said something else that I couldn't fathom. I'm not even sure if I should bother to repeat it.'

Lóa shrugged her shoulders.

'Well, OK then,' said Björg, leaning forward across the table so that her fingers were touching the cup in front of Lóa. 'All right. I'll try so you don't think it's anything serious. It's just that when Margrét had finished her drink she suddenly began sobbing. I asked her why she was crying and in between sobs she told me that when she saw the blood earlier it reminded her so much of something that happened a couple of years ago, when Ína was five. Margrét had been twisting a sharp knife in her fingers and cut herself on purpose and showed Ína the cut, just to frighten her a little. But Ína's expression glazed over and she grabbed Margrét's hand and tried to pull it towards her mouth, as if she was in a trance. When Margrét realized that Ína was going to lick the cut she whipped her hand away and pushed Ína off her chair, and her head hit the wall and she began to scream.'

'I don't remember this,' said Lóa.

'Perhaps you were in the next room, and they may not have explained it very clearly to you – both were in shock and children don't know how to put things like that into words. They just say, *"She pushed me"* or *"He kicked me"*. And that's settled. Isn't that right?'

'I suppose so,' replied Lóa.

'I didn't understand why she was bringing it up again now,

let alone why she was crying about it, as though it was somehow important, as though fighting between siblings isn't a daily occurrence in most families. So I stroked her hair – I had to lean over that weird and wonderful object you dragged back from Akranes – and I asked if she had a guilty conscience about what she'd done, but she shook her head and screwed her eyes tight shut, as though I smelled bad, as though my hand was pressing down on her unbearably, even though I had only gently touched her forehead. And I asked her why she was crying so and she sobbed into the pillow, *"I don't know"* and then I was about to say something, I can't remember what it was, and she said again, *"I don't know"* and then she asked me to leave,' said Björg, and she glanced towards the door leading to the hallway.

# PART TWO

# 9

*Sunday Morning to Monday Afternoon*

Sunday was as dreary and discordant as a church choir in a sparsely populated country parish, and Sveinn was sitting at his computer in the corner of his workshop. He had been sent home the previous evening in the only taxi the town boasted, with his arm in a sling, his knee in a tight support bandage and painkillers in the pocket of his Barbour. The painkillers were called Tramadol, and among the possible side effects listed were: nausea, vomiting, constipation, drowsiness, dizziness, anxiety, headaches, mood swings and dry mouth. Lárus had picked up the prescription for him at the chemist and been sent to fetch his shoes and anorak.

Sveinn was still in his striped pyjama bottoms and shoes without socks, and although he was shivering he wore nothing on top. The phone and the Tramadol were within arm's reach so he wouldn't have to get up unnecessarily. He had already taken more than the recommended daily dosage, even though the day was nowhere near over – it was only around two o'clock – and he could feel the effects: he was sluggish with sleepiness and his head felt like it was filled with wool.

The very thought of not being able to get into the shower for a week made him feel claustrophobic. When he got up he'd washed himself with a wet flannel, like an old-age pensioner, but it wasn't enough; he needed a torrent of steaming hot water to cascade over him, pouring onto the concrete floor with a purifying crash.

The screen on his phone lit up and the ringtone, mimicking the sound of an old-fashioned telephone, resounded more harshly in his ear than usual. It was accompanied by a harsh grating sound, which pierced the glass roof of his senses like hobnail boots on ice.

'Yes,' Sveinn answered.

It was Kjartan.

'Ha, ha, ha, hello, old pal,' said Kjartan.

'Hi.'

'So you managed to flatten yourself with a Russian legsweep, did you? Any broken bones?'

'I guess I did. But I only broke one bone.'

'I didn't know you were a wrestling man,' said Kjartan. 'I prefer the Icelandic form of wrestling myself. You have to admit, it's a classier sport. The type you and your kind practise is just for hoodlums. Ha, ha. But I'm just a naive country boy, not university-educated like you.'

'Well, I'm glad you can laugh at my misfortune,' retorted Sveinn. 'Then it wasn't all for nothing.'

'No, it wasn't,' replied Kjartan. 'How are you anyway, old pal? Are you starving to death? Can I get you anything?'

'No thanks. I don't need anything.'

'Are you sure?'

'Yes.'

'OK, then I won't bother you any longer. It sounds like you could do with some rest, get some shut-eye, as they say, eh? But ring me if you need anything. Don't go driving while high on that dope from the doctor, do you hear?'

'No, no.'

'OK then, mate. Bye for now,' said Kjartan, and hung up before Sveinn could thank him or say goodbye.

He became aware of a nasty nagging pain in his shoulder and, without thinking, leant across for the tablets. *Just one more,* he thought. *And then no more until after supper.*

He opened up his inbox, expecting to trawl through pages of unread emails. He ran his eyes down the orders without paying them too much attention. *Later,* he thought. *I'll reply to them when I'm feeling more up to it.*

Outstanding order forms lay in a pile next to the printer, and for the first time since he'd started the business he wondered whether he should get himself an assistant or a secretary.

The fifth email he opened wasn't an order or an enquiry. The sender was athena@gmail.com.

*How many lives do you reckon you have ruined, roughly speaking?* Athena wrote.

> *The world is a crock of shit and the present is a caricature of what it should be, not least because of men like you who go out of your way to degrade everything that's good and beautiful in life.*

Men like you? What was so familiar about that phrase? That's right, hadn't Kjartan just said something similar when he accused him of being into wrestling? This time he was accused of being evil incarnate. No small honour, albeit a dubious one. He was a powerful man indeed if Mrs Athena/Lóa Hansdóttir – Lóa Hans' daughter – was to be believed. And what did she mean when she said he was degrading everything that's good and beautiful? Were women synonymous with everything good and beautiful in her mind? Did this mean he was degrading them? He wasn't degrading women. His job was to create beautiful likenesses of women. Images. Nothing else.

Why was it considered acceptable to paint a picture of a woman, but not to make a likeness of one?

Perhaps a more pressing question was this: why was he mentally arguing with a head case when it would be better to spend his time and energy on something else? Like reading the orders which had come in over the weekend. Or thinking about the idea of getting a secretary. Perhaps his friend Lóa could be persuaded to take the job? If she wasn't too busy writing derogatory emails and obituaries for the living.

Further down the screen was another email from her:

*Maybe you believe that everyone is as decadent as you, but that is not the case. Some of us just want to live in peace, free from the sick pleasures of degenerates like you . . .*

(There it was again – *men like you, you and your kind.*)

*. . . and live a normal family life.*

(Nah!)

*You may think you're this amazing artist and therefore beyond good and evil, but you're nothing more than a scumbag and a pervert.*

A pervert? That was one step too far, and something snapped inside him. If she'd been standing in front of him he would have yelled at her to sort her own issues out and shut up once and for all. Amen! The woman was clearly a sandwich short of a picnic and needed proper help. He resolved not to read any more of her messages, but then immediately broke his resolution. She might warn him she was going to turn up with the heavy mob. If so, wouldn't it be better for him to know about it and make contingency plans, whatever they might be? Get himself a large dog? Ring the bloody cops?

He leant back in his chair, closed his eyes, sensed his breathing deepen and felt as if his consciousness was collecting together into a single point on his forehead.

Then *Raven-Black Lola* sat on a chair in front of him, her hand resting on the seat just in front of her groin.

*'I don't know,'* she said, without moving her lips. *'I don't know. It doesn't matter. It's all the same to me.'*

She wasn't as he remembered her. Her face should have been oval, the expression on her mouth one of surprise and the set of her eyes should have conveyed tenderness. But there she was, looking as if she wished him harm. It wasn't meant to be like that, and the only way to resolve it was to make a new impression of her head.

*'I don't know,'* she said, without a flicker of movement in her face.

'You don't know what?' he asked.

*'I don't know,'* she said.

'I wasn't asking you,' he replied.

*'It doesn't matter,'* she said.

He began to feel frightened, without knowing why, and was filled with such antipathy and disgust that he couldn't breathe. He woke up with a loud snoring noise to find his head lolling on his chest and a dagger piercing his shoulder.

'Jesus Christ,' he said, and rubbed his aching neck.

He moved across into the bedroom, but sleep eluded him. He lay there for a long time, his eyes tightly shut and his arms clutching the duvet. The sun shone obliquely through the window; it had already disappeared beyond the far corner. His collarbone was extremely painful and his knee throbbed uncomfortably. A petrol mower sputtered into life nearby. The neighbours had clearly decided to cut the grass before it grew – mowing it as a precaution. Interesting notion.

The noise from the mower sent a tingle down his spine and vibrated warmly against his innards. And what was that? A tingling in his groin? An involuntary erection. He hadn't been thinking of anything other than how sorry for himself he felt at being taken out of action in such a comical way and having all this pain to contend with. All because of one light bulb, which he didn't even need to use.

He sighed and massaged himself with the duvet. That only intensified the desire. He didn't want to masturbate. That would be too sad. To lie there unable to work, chock full of deadening medication, having degraded everything that was good and beautiful in the world, with no-one but his mother to mourn him should he suddenly kick the bucket. And then to wank in this pain-filled loneliness? No way.

Easing himself up onto his feet, he stumbled back into the workshop with the duvet under his arm. He spread it out on the floor and fetching the stool from the storeroom, he climbed up and took down one of the four dolls he had hung up to dry the Friday before. The ruler which was holding her feet apart fell to the floor and slid across towards the wall.

He laid her on her back on the duvet, pulled his pyjama bottoms down his thighs and, closing his eyes, he prepared to enter her. But he only got halfway – she was too tacky. It was almost painful. He clambered off her with his pyjama bottoms round his ankles and concentrated on not seeing himself objectively, tried not to be aware that this was one of those events which, put together, determined how his life would unfold. His life story.

He rummaged in the box where *Raven-Black Lola* had been until he found the tube of lubricating gel and put some on, the white foam balls sticking to the cotton of his pyjama bottoms. Back on the floor, he let the weight of his body rest against those pert breasts and flat stomach. It worked this time, and for a second he felt pleased at what a good design she was. He'd forgotten that when they were in use they weren't just inanimate objects. The vagina was receptive, as though it really didn't want to let go of him, and the weight of the dolls, the resistance offered by their bodies and the suspension meant they virtually moved under you.

He reached out for her hair to pull himself up a little, but grasped at nothingness. What was he thinking? It was rather unpleasant to say the least to mount them before they had their heads fixed on. He'd never done that before. But then he'd never used them for his own pleasure, only to test them when he was developing the vagina.

He pulled himself together and tried to finish the job, but his member had started to go limp inside her.

The heads were ready, carefully wrapped in plastic in the storeroom, so he went and got one and fixed it in place. More lubricating gel. How come he felt so pathetically unsure of himself? He wasn't too bloody posh for his own products. He tried to see the doll as *they* saw them – the customers who adored them and wrote him long, inspired letters thanking him for having created the dolls. He tried to convince himself that the object underneath him was sexy, to get rid of the distance he had allowed to come between them. They weren't just beauti-fully crafted works, they were replicas of beauty, oozing sex appeal. Lifeless, but beautiful. And there was nothing wrong with indulging himself as he was now doing, for the first time. Smooth, flowing, blonde hair, an inviting mouth and patient eyes made of glass, without a trace of dissatisfaction or judgement in them. A firm body, slender arms. It was completely natural to be enchanted by them. It was normal to want to take them, even though they were inanimate.

Then something happened which he would have done anything to have avoided: he saw himself through the eyes of an imagined observer. With his bum up in the air like a full moon, his arm in a sling, groaning with every thrust because his shoulder couldn't tolerate any sharp movement. He saw the workshop and himself in the middle of the floor, in this scintillating company. All the pictures on the walls which were meant to give him inspiration and remind him of the nobility of his craft, the unfinished floor with its old oil stains, the merciless artist's light which fell on him from above. Contempt unexpectedly poured over him from a huge dish of poison he had kept hidden in his mind without even realizing it.

Sveinn's arrogance towards his customers had been dripping its poison into this dish for years. He had always looked down on them as inferior and deserving his pity, as though he was helping them, making their lives more bearable. He was filled with disgust at himself for having sunk to their level.

When had he managed to convince himself that he was a cut above the rest? Perhaps he'd always thought it; maybe he'd gradually made a habit of hardening himself against other people's prejudices.

Giving up was almost as peaceful as it was inevitable, and he lay on top of her for a while, his semi-erect member against her soft thigh. Then he went into the storeroom and fetching the funnel, he filled it with hot water and mild detergent and washed the lubricating gel from inside the doll, before hanging her up again. He tried to shake the worst of the gel off the duvet, but the muck wouldn't budge and again he had to give up. He held the edge of the duvet with his teeth and used his good arm to pull the cover off. Still out of breath from the effort, he plodded slowly back to the bedroom, dropped the duvet cover into the rickety laundry basket and lay down with the coverless duvet pulled up over his head, leaving his bare feet poking out.

Drowsiness caressed him for a long while before he finally succumbed to sleep. He got up twice, once to pee and once to get his painkillers and a glass of water and to turn off his phone. Through the silence of the evening and the short half-lit night he slept peacefully.

Sveinn awoke with a stabbing white pain in his head and shoulders, but before he had even managed to open his eyes, he was already feeling unbearably bored. He couldn't live like this. He had to go out and do something. His mouth tasted of medicine and he had heartburn – his stomach felt as if it had been scoured with sandpaper.

The coffee machine was spluttering and gurgling more vociferously than usual, Sveinn thought, and he took a slurp of milk from the carton before going into the bathroom. He wiped the sleep off with a burning-hot flannel, washed his armpits and balls thoroughly before putting on a shirt and the most loose-fitting trousers he could find, to make getting dressed one-handed more manageable. He munched on four rounds of toast while flicking through the papers.

Tramadol and more coffee. He waited for a revelation, or at

least some hint from within, about how to spend the day when you're in no fit state to do anything. He skimmed the papers again but found nothing of interest.

He looked at his car keys, turned his phone on and put them both in his pocket, slipping on his shoes on the way out to the car. He forgot the slip of paper Lárus had given him with the address on. It didn't matter – he knew it off by heart: Framnesvegur 19.

The wind blew the sunshine and buffeted the car. Last season's long, yellowy grass along the kerb offered little resistance, as though shrinking from the brilliant light, just like Sveinn's sensitive eyes. He fumbled in the glove compartment for his sunglasses. What had he done with them?

He experienced a sudden pain in his knee each time he moved his foot onto the accelerator.

Just as he was coming down to the A-road, a sporty, silver-grey Hyundai pulled up in front of him and Lárus jumped out of the car. He banged on the window eagerly and had begun to speak before Sveinn managed to wind the window down.

'. . . but you didn't answer the phone so I decided to drive round and check on you.'

'Uh-ha,' replied Sveinn.

'Where are you going anyway? Aren't you still on medication? Would you like me to give you a lift? I've got nothing on until the morning.'

'I'm not going far,' said Sveinn.

'Aren't you going to Reykjavík then? I thought perhaps . . .' Lárus's eyes were darting to and fro, like a child afraid of missing out on something. He was bursting with so much longing that Sveinn almost felt for him. If it had been anyone else he would probably have been full of empathy, told him what he was doing or even let him tag along for the ride. But there was something in Lárus's manner which was unforgiveable – something opposite to original sin which you couldn't get angry at.

'Don't worry about it,' said Sveinn. 'Just stop thinking about it.'

Lárus suddenly appeared wary. A cloud passed over his innocent expression. Maybe the gods – out of cruelty or some harsh mercy – had revealed to him how he must come across to Sveinn in all his eagerness. 'Yes, no, no,' he said. 'I wasn't thinking about it particularly . . .'

'Thanks for your help,' said Sveinn. 'Obviously I owe you one. Let me know if I can do anything for you.' And he nodded impatiently towards the silver-grey car blocking his path.

'It was nothing,' said Lárus, swallowing with difficulty. Then he walked downcast back to his car and moved it so that Sveinn could be on his way.

Lárus and his car dwindled in the rear-view mirror until they disappeared altogether, and then Sveinn began to feel sorry for him. The empathy which had been entirely lacking a few seconds earlier now flooded over him like a tidal wave, which propelled the car along and washed it up on a totally different road which looked just like the first but was somewhere else altogether. There are innumerable holes in time and space – he'd always known that. And a person's character was like water flowing in and out of these holes. One minute you could be as solid as a rock, untouchable, and the next minute have difficulty defining where self ends and others begin. Right now, he felt he'd no right to keep rejecting this well-meaning boy who obviously needed a role model – or something from Sveinn that he was denying him.

What nonsense. It wasn't as if he owed Lárus anything. It wasn't as if Lárus was his son. He was just a lad at a loose end who needed to learn the hard way.

The fierce winds whipped and tore at the white-crested waves as far as the eye could see. Cirrus clouds ruffled the sky. The wilting grass, the feeling in his body, in his thoughts – yes, everything was somehow skittish, tousled and unruly. That was why the world longed for death, the man with the scythe, the Angel of Death, who sliced off the jagged edges, lightened the load.

His thoughts turned to Lóa, who had driven this route only two days earlier – not in such gales, but the storm in her head must have made up for that – with an innocent doll on the backseat. Or in the boot? Would she have put *Raven-Black Lola* in the boot or on the back seat? That would obviously depend on whether she thought she was rescuing her from the jaws of evil or arresting her for indecency. And why wasn't that enough? Why couldn't she just leave him alone having made off with his most precious piece of craftsmanship? Maybe deep down she was infatuated with him.

What was it Freud said? *Behind every fear lies desire and behind every desire lies fear.* If something touches you your eyes and your heart are drawn towards it. He had clearly touched her in some way. Otherwise she wouldn't act like this towards him.

Reykjavík was a strangely out-of-the-way place. A half-built, unfinished expanse of land, with hideous giant shacks scattered over it. Once it had been a pretty fishing village. Now it resembled a weary industrial city, lacking in culture.

He found the volume of traffic stressful and it dawned on him that he hadn't been into town for weeks or months. He'd become a country bumpkin. Like Kjartan. Or Lárus. The thought sent a shiver down his spine. It was probably time he thought about getting one of those shacks there on the outskirts of town. It had simply been coincidence that led him to move to Akranes – someone had told him about a decent-sized place which was vacant and could doubtless be rented for a pittance – just as sheer coincidence had led him to specialize in doll-making. It had been like any other marriage of convenience, and as time went by he'd grown to love this role that fate had allotted him.

He'd just finished scraping his way through art college and was full of disappointment: he had hoped the course would deal more with methods and how to work with materials and less with nebulous ideas.

What some people called the history of twentieth-century ideas he called a popularity contest for the cleverest title. Anybody could come up with smart ideas, couldn't they? He'd never belonged on that course. How on earth had he managed to fool them into letting him on in the first place?

Never mind. He'd got hold of the materials through an acquaintance his then-girlfriend had among some theatrical types in Sweden and had been given a helping hand to make his first doll – a lass with pudgy cheeks and copper curls. He'd spent all the Easter holidays on it, bent double and slaving away in Stockholm, while his girlfriend worked her way through the bars and coffee shops with the theatre crowd. This prototype then became his graduation project, and on the opening day of the exhibition he had received four offers for it. He had been so desperate for the money and for recognition that he had accepted all four offers and, with the buyers' agreement that he could make a limited run, had shot off to make nine more, exactly the same. He'd marked their soles with a number, had a respectable-looking certificate printed on official bond paper, stating that each doll was one of only ten of its type in the world, and collected a pile of money which he had no idea what to do with. He had been the only one from his year to profit from his graduation project.

He had then slammed the door on his art with gratifying finality. He'd left that messy, slimy temple for good. He'd locked the door after himself, and every moment since he'd been trying to wipe any living traces of art from his hands. He had succeeded tolerably well. But now he felt as though something dirty was trying to envelop him. Maybe that was because he hadn't stepped in the shower since Saturday.

He drove slowly into Framnesvegur, looking out for number nineteen. He pulled up on the opposite side of the road and sat there, completely unsure what to do next. He began to get out of the car, but then stopped; the wind managed to tousle his hair before he slammed the door shut again. He tried to picture their meeting, but couldn't imagine how Lóa would react when she saw him on the doorstep, whether she would be scared or angry or make out she didn't know him.

The minutes ticked by and after about a quarter of an hour, he made to get out of the car again, but before his feet touched the pavement, the door of number nineteen opened and Lóa emerged, nodding her head in response to the chubby young girl at her heels, who was talking nineteen to the dozen. The occasional ringing vowel sound reached his ears through the strong wind and the windscreen which separated them. The girl's silent hopping and jumping was like a miraculous display of boundless energy and it looked as if she might take to the air at any moment.

Lóa put both their seatbelts on and drove off without noticing Sveinn, who sat there, forcing himself not to sink down and disappear below the windscreen. He didn't want this sudden insecurity to get the better of him entirely.

It was a relief to see her drive off. There was little point in knocking on her door when she wasn't there. Yet he couldn't allow himself to use this as an excuse to hurry back home – that would be too much like admitting defeat, almost running away with his tail between his legs.

So what should he do? Find himself some errand to run in the city? Buy something?

Whenever he bought something that wasn't a necessity he always regretted it. He ended up disliking the purchase, thinking it tasteless and vulgar – a foolish example of man's desire to make things – and he felt ashamed of falling, yet again, into the trap of believing that some superfluous object would bring him pleasure.

There was little else he could do then but settle himself down in a café, read the papers and drink coffee. He really wasn't at all comfortable with the idea though. He thought he would stick out as a country bumpkin who'd been out of touch with the ways of the world for too long.

Outside Hotel Borg, he observed himself climbing out of his car, a new, American pickup truck which had cost him an arm and a leg – numerous arms and legs, to be precise – wearing old, baggy trousers and a well-washed woollen sweater over his shirt, his face scratched and his hair dirty. And a ditty came to mind which someone had made up about one of his teachers at art college who had come into money and blown his inheritance on a brand new BMW.

> *He was a bit of a lout*
> *Till money came his way*
> *But now he's swanning about*
> *In a BMW coupé.*

And he laughed to himself as he fed the meter with a hundred króna coin.

He took his pile of newspapers and settled himself at a table with a view over the little square presided over by a statue of an unknown office worker. But he found it difficult to concentrate on reading and tried to conjure up an image of Lóa instead.

She had lovely hands and a sad but enchanting smile which went well with her innocent, blonde waves. Her body reminded him of type number seven, except she was considerably stouter round the middle. The steady, yet somehow uncertain, look in her eyes indicated she was hardworking but didn't always foresee what she was getting herself into.

Having mentally dissected and analysed each aspect of her, he couldn't find any reason for the indecision which had come over him earlier. She was just a person. A woman. A spare rib, as they used to say in the school playground in the old days. Besides, he was in the right, and the same couldn't be said for her. Theft was a criminal offence, as was harassment, especially when it involved direct or indirect threats.

The waiter who brought his coffee was so impersonal that it was almost as if he wasn't there. His social persona must have been more impenetrable than most, or else he had no soul – he seemed no more than an empty shell.

It was an unpleasant kind of courtesy, a form of violence in Sveinn's view. He set great store by the fact that what he manufactured at least appeared to have a soul – he did all he could to portray an inner life in his girls' faces.

How did he go about this? How was it ever possible to make a zombie alluring?

First of all, the eyes must be big, but not too big – not so that they looked terrified, like someone in a horror film. It was easy to get this wrong and create something sinister rather than appealing.

It was also important that they were sweet-looking, rather than absolutely beautiful. They needed a hint of cartoon appeal. Disney. A face made up purely of soft strokes. No angular actress's cheekbones.

But this was all unimportant compared to the most carefully guarded, top-secret ingredient, the thing everybody saw but nobody noticed, the cunning optical illusion which spoke directly to the beholder's subconscious . . .

The girls' faces appeared to be fully symmetrical, but they weren't. Before casting the faces in the plaster mould he went to some lengths to make their profiles very slightly different and yet similar enough that people would think they were looking at man-made perfection. And this was true to a certain extent. If you were talking about perfection then it could only ever be man-made, though not in the sense people imagined when they looked at the dolls.

It is impossible to find a true circle in nature, and human faces are never entirely symmetrical. A right-handed person's left arm is marginally thinner than her right arm, and her left hand is fractionally smaller than her right, because they are less often used. He copied nature in this respect, without it being obvious to the naked eye.

He was convinced that this was one of the reasons his dolls

were so successful. Some customers wrote to him to say that their doll was more than a tool for gratification, that it provided them with more companionship than they had believed an inanimate object could because they felt the doll had a real personality.

One customer had gone as far as outlining her tastes and personality traits: if his beloved were a physical woman she would be a dreamy university student, walking around with a colourful scarf around her neck and would always have a book under her arm, something like *The Bell Jar* by Sylvia Plath.

Whenever Sveinn thought about this particular letter he couldn't hold back a shadow of a smile. *The Bell Jar* was undeniably one of the iconic novels of twentieth-century feminism. There was something tragi-comic about buying a sex doll and pretending she was an avid reader and a feminist.

He was often relieved that he didn't have to socialize with his customers. He'd be at a loss to know what to say to the Sylvia Plath admirer.

But anyway, it wasn't his job to judge the people who bought from him. And nor did he see it as his job to please everyone all the time. He had no interest in calculated marketing; he paid no attention to what the average man might think was most desirable in a sex doll's character. He just wanted to create a good product. That was where the enjoyment lay. That's what gave him his real reward.

The unknown office worker stooped unwaveringly on his plinth, his head and shoulders a box-shaped boulder. His briefcase must be sinking down after all this time, like his beautifully sculpted stone suit. What was the real reward of his work?

Swallowing another Tramadol tablet with the dregs of his

coffee, Sveinn decided to go home. He couldn't hang around endlessly, without any idea how long he'd have to wait. He would stop by Framnesvegur again, and if there was no-one in he would just drive home and try to forget the whole thing. He could make another model of *Raven-Black Lola* when he was fit for work again.

He looked up and down the street in search of Lóa's green Renault, but couldn't see it anywhere. He pulled up directly outside her house and considered leaving the ignition on, but decided that was unnecessary – whether anyone was at home or not, he wasn't planning on storming the house and then making a quick getaway like a robber. His heart beat faster as he read the names under the bell. Was her second name Hansdóttir, or had he made a mistake?

He was none the wiser, because only the first names were written, in awkward capitals: *Lóa, Margrét and Ína*. They were decorated with pink-and-brown butterflies. Clearly the work of a child who'd recently learned the alphabet.

The intercom was pressed almost as soon as he rang the bell. An eager voice said, 'Hello?' and immediately a sharp buzzing told him the door was open.

A young woman came running down the stairs; her expression was deadly serious and she was clearly disappointed that he wasn't someone else. Who had she been expecting? Lóa?

Maybe Lóa had made off with her loot and was now driving round the national ring road looking for some suitable cliff to jump from with *Raven-Black Lola* in her arms. Lóa was clearly sorely missed by this sister of hers, or lover or friend – whoever she was.

'Good afternoon,' said Sveinn, wondering why he had to

sound like a none-too-hopeful salesman. 'May I have a word with the lady of the house?'

The woman looked at him frowning. Jet-black hair, probably dyed, fell onto her forehead, almost covering one eye. She was pretty but slightly haggard. Maybe she'd had a lot to cope with in her life.

Her hair and build reminded him of the short-haired doll with the Asian face and body type number 4, which he would finish off as soon as he was fit for work again, box up and send to Helsinki. Both were quite slim-hipped, with small breasts and smooth, dark hair cut in a boyish style with a heavy fringe.

'She's not at home,' said the woman, tucking her long fringe back behind her ear.

He wasn't sure whether to believe her. Why had she bounded towards him like a guard dog?

'You see,' he said, staring straight at her. 'I don't actually need to speak to her. I just need to pick up something she borrowed from me.'

The woman hesitated, but didn't look like she was going to let him in. 'Can't you come back later?' she asked. 'It's not exactly convenient right now.'

'No, I can't come back later,' he said. And when she hesitated instead of getting defensive he felt sure that she knew what he was referring to.

She turned round and trotted up the stairs, indicating that he should follow.

'There's no need to take off your shoes,' she said, without turning round in the doorway. Without looking at him.

He followed her in and stood there in the middle of the room, unsure what to do, while she leant against the dining room table with her arms folded.

The first thing he noticed was the withered pot plants eve-rywhere: on the windowsills, up on an old chest and on the bottom bookshelf. There was another one in a decorative pot with a circular lace mat underneath on top of the television. Who on earth would live among dead plants? Yellowing and covered in dust. Not a trace of green, except on the metre-high tree which dominated the window and showed signs of life even though it had shed half its leaves. A strange sign of neglect in an apartment which was otherwise rather fussy for his liking. There was furniture from expensive designer shops, a display cabinet full of hand-painted Danish and Chinese ceramics, glossy wallpaper, large Persian rugs, cushions and bolsters of damask silk. What message was all this bourgeouis prosperity meant to convey? Lóa didn't look like a high-flyer with a salary to match. Maybe she had a wealthy husband. Or a wealthy ex-husband?

Then he noticed what an unusual design the apartment was. It had a double-height room with open beams above the living room and kitchen, looking up into an empty shadowy space. It looked as if the intention had been to build an attic room or a den under the beams, but this plan had never been realized.

A door, which had once led into the attic from the old stair-case, was suspended above the display cabinet. There were no stairs to be seen, which implied that there was no way up into this marvellous loft which someone had gone to a lot of trouble to build.

He slowly turned full circle and looked over the half-finished maze of carpentry in this otherwise ordinary apartment, and then his gaze fell upon an older woman sitting on the sofa. Her hand was half raised as though she wasn't entirely sure whether to greet him or not, but when their eyes met she stood up and walked towards him with her hand outstretched. It was small, silky soft and bony.

'Hello,' she said, and she seemed hesitant, if not downright afraid. 'Are you a friend of Lóa's?'

He couldn't help staring at her.

Since he'd started producing his dolls, he had only made five 'older' dolls and had never succeeded in getting the wrinkles round the eyes right. No matter how hard he tried to create soft laughter lines, they always ended up looking more like cold lines of bitterness.

The woman whose hand he was holding had exactly the lines he'd tried unsuccessfully to achieve. Where did the difference lie? He'd made the wrinkles fan out like crows' feet. He'd made them as deep. Perhaps it was the slight difference in colouring. On the dolls' faces shadows made the lines appear darker, but real wrinkles were actually lighter than the face, because they had not been exposed to sunlight.

Withdrawing her hand, the woman glanced away and then back at the sling stretched diagonally across his chest. Why was she looking at him like that? Yes, of course, she was waiting for his response.

'I'm sorry, I . . .' he began, but he had no story ready, so he rolled his eyes wearily and began again. 'No, not exactly. She borrowed something from me temporarily and I've come to pick it up.'

He looked at the younger woman who had answered the door. She nodded her head in the direction of the hallway off the living room. He hobbled across the floor and down the hall, as she'd indicated, and opened the first door he came to. It was a store cupboard, its wide shelves stacked with tools, toys, electrical appliances, boxes and bags.

Suddenly the younger woman was standing behind him. He could smell her perfume, and her anxiety too, he thought. There was something odd going on here, something sinister.

'She's not here,' said the woman.

Did she mean Lóa or *Raven-Black Lola*?

He turned towards her and was going to ask if something was wrong, but she'd already turned her back and was standing in an open doorway further down the hall.

'Is she in there?' he asked, still unsure who they were talking about.

'Yes,' the woman replied, and from the hesitation in her voice he sensed she too was uncertain whether they were referring to the same thing. But she walked into the room and clearly intended for him to follow her.

It was a large, spartan living space, with parquet flooring, the same as throughout the apartment, a desk, a chest of drawers, a cupboard and a large bed. And there on the bed was *Raven-Black Lola*, dressed in night clothes, her hair in a tangle and a shiny, red, heart-shaped sticker on her forehead.

He was so taken aback that, without thinking, he stepped too firmly onto his right leg. The pain exploded in his knee and shot right up into his hip. Screwing his eyes tight shut, he groaned in agony. But when he met the questioning look of the woman standing at his side he gritted his teeth, held out his hand and said, 'I'm Sveinn. I designed this doll.'

Nodding, the woman shook his hand. Her long, slender fingers were ice-cold.

'I'm Björg,' she said. 'Lóa's friend. How do you intend to . . .?'

Good question. He hadn't thought about that. He was used to giving them a fireman's lift when he needed to move them. They only weighed about fifty kilos.

He sat down by the doll's knees and pulled her up into a sitting position, then leant in towards her with his good shoulder against her stomach. He tried to stand up, but the weight was too great. 'Would you lift her slightly?' he said.

Lóa's friend obliged. She supported the doll's back with one hand and fumbled for a grip with the other, until she realized that there was nothing for it but to take hold of the groin and lift with all her strength, while Sveinn struggled to his feet, with the doll slung like a bag of salt over his shoulder.

'The pyjamas . . .' said Lóa's friend staring blankly. Then a grin crept over her face. 'Me Tarzan, you Jane,' she said, and gave a hollow laugh.

'I'll post you the night clothes either tomorrow or the next day,' he said, staggering through into the living room, where he saw the older woman, wide-eyed with amazement. Maybe she hadn't been introduced to *Raven-Black Lola*.

'Goodbye,' he said, but didn't hear her response, if she even gave one.

On the stairs he met Lóa. She was in a great hurry, still with the little one in tow.

He expected her to show some reaction – to show remorse, apologize or shower him with confusing explanations. But that didn't happen. Certainly she was surprised to see him. Her eyes narrowed and she gave a sharp intake of breath, but then just as quickly she seemed oblivious to his presence, as though he was just something on the staircase, something large which blocked her way, and she rushed past him with the girl at her heels. Then for some reason the girl burst into tears. He watched the tears begin to run down her cheeks and her lower lip quiver to reveal her teeth. Her sobs reverberated off the walls then were drowned by the thick stair carpet.

Had the doll been for her? The sticker on the forehead suggested so, but the room *Raven-Black Lola* had been lying in wasn't a little girl's bedroom; it was more like a room in a smart guest house.

Suddenly he saw red. What right did this woman think she had to cut him dead like that? He had shown her nothing but neighbourliness and she had repaid him with deception, doll-napping and now outright hostility. It wasn't his problem she was in a hurry. She could at least greet him, state her case, even apologize. Blanking him because there was some female conspiracy, or God knows what, brewing upstairs just wasn't on.

He stumbled back into the apartment, carrying his burden, and this time it wasn't only Lóa but all of them who made as if they didn't see him. Apart from the little girl, who stared at him, sniffing and red-eyed, as he laid *Raven-Black Lola* carefully on the sofa.

He looked at the crying child and shuddered, thinking of all the orders he'd received and rejected – orders for dolls with a child's body.

Maybe he had a moral obligation to swallow his objections and produce such dolls. That was better than men assaulting vulnerable children. Could he do it? It was his job, after all, but why should he dirty his hands with something which disgusted him?

'Mum, what's the time? We're going to be late for the party,' cried the girl. 'And I don't have a costume. I can't go to the party without a costume.'

'Darling, we'll find you something in a minute,' said Lóa.

'Nooo, I need a proper costume. They'll all be in proper costumes and I don't want to be late!'

'Mum, will you take Ína to this party and let her stay with you overnight?' asked Lóa.

'Of course I will, dear,' replied her mother.

'What did the police say?' asked Lóa's friend.

'They told me to come back tomorrow,' said Lóa, choked with emotion, as if a strong hand was gripping her throat.

Sveinn became uneasy. Maybe he should leave, get away from this house filled with fear, take himself down to his car and drive home to his simple rural idyll.

But he needed help getting *Raven-Black Lola* back up onto his shoulder.

'Excuse me,' he said.

But the three women didn't hear him. Now they were laughing like idiots. What was going on here?

The little girl came running back in, her cheeks still wet, carrying a large, red hairbrush. She settled herself down next to the doll, but the hairbrush got stuck in the tangles.

Sveinn walked over to her and made an attempt at kneeling down beside her, even though his knee wasn't up to it.

'What's your name, little one?' he asked, as he began carefully to work at the tangle.

'Ína,' she replied.

'And how old are you, Ína?'

'Seven.'

He gathered the doll's silky, black hair together in one hand and offered it to Ína saying, 'If you begin at the bottom here, look, it's much easier.'

# 10

The sales assistant in the bicycle shop was a cheerful lad, not much more than twenty, with a number one haircut and a hoodie with a gigantic picture of a motorbike on it.

'I'll help you out to the car with this, as it's so windy,' he said, picking up Ína's new bicycle: silver, with a pink bell on the handlebars, red mudguards and a red stand.

Ína was going to run ahead of them, but Lóa caught hold of her arm. 'Hold my hand. I don't want you disappearing under a car.'

She unlocked the car with the remote and held firmly onto Ína while the lad put the bike in the boot. She let Ína in on the driver's side then gently coaxed her across into the passenger seat.

The lad waved and ran across the car park, his head down and his hood billowing out like a sail in the wind.

Ína was buzzing with excitement and couldn't keep quiet or sit still. She knelt on the front seat, held the headrest with both hands and bounced up and down, singing in a southern drawl, 'Looong Jooohn Silveerrrr.'

'Sit down properly and put on your belt,' said Lóa. 'Now. This instant. We're already late picking Margrét up.'

'Silverrrr!' said Ína, half deaf with ecstasy over their purchase.

Lóa gave up, secured the seatbelt across her daughter's back and thighs and reversed out of the parking space. The clock on

147

the dashboard read 14:50. The exam had finished twenty minutes before and it was a ten-minute drive to Hagaskóli, where Margrét would be sitting waiting for them. She was well accustomed to hanging around waiting for her mother, who always imagined she could fit everything on her to-do list into an impossibly short time.

'I'm gonna choke,' said Ína, who had wriggled round and was now sitting properly on the seat, with the belt stretched across her neck.

Lóa reached behind her for the booster seat, which she handed to Ína, who slid it under her bottom.

'Ooh, that was close, Mum. I could hardly breathe,' said Ína. Then added, 'Margrét will be madly jealous when she sees my bike.'

'Do you think so?' said Lóa. 'Do you think she'd like a bike like yours too?'

Ína made her hand into a gun, aimed at her own head, clicked her tongue twice — that was the safety catch — and fired with a hissing sound. Which meant that was a stupid question. Either because *obviously* Margrét wanted a bike like hers, or because *obviously* she didn't. Lóa wasn't sure how things worked in Ína's mind, which was sometimes so grown up and sometimes quite the opposite.

Parking the car in the nearest available space, Lóa left the engine running and told Ína to wait while she ran into the building. But Margrét was nowhere to be seen. Her outdoor clothes were hanging on a hook, along with her bag of wet swimming things. The corridor smelled like wet gloves and stale bread, with a hint of disinfectant.

Running her finger down the timetable pinned up on the wall, Lóa found the number of the room where Margrét had sat her exam and hurried along to it. The door wasn't locked and the room was empty. The windows were all closed, but one of them was loose and gusts of wind howled through the gaps. Outside, the weather was worsening; it pounded the lonely basketball net, and the straggly birches were almost bent double.

On the table nearest the door lay a rocket-shaped rubber. Margrét had a rubber like that and Lóa stuffed it into her pocket before hurrying out into the corridor, straight into a weary-looking man with grey hair. He looked at her questioningly.

'I've come to pick up my daughter. She had an exam earlier,' said Lóa.

The man looked around slowly and said, 'I think they've all gone.'

'That can't be right,' she said, and stared at the man as though he could conjure Margrét up out of nowhere, have her suddenly appear before their eyes.

He shrugged and walked on, leaving Lóa to watch him disappear into the staffroom. She fumbled in her coat pocket for her phone and rang Margrét's number. A muffled R & B ringtone sounded behind her. Spinning round, she walked towards the noise. The tinny, hip-gyrating beat was coming from the metallic-red mobile phone vibrating in Margrét's denim jacket. Lóa stuffed it into her pocket with the rubber, and pressed the red button on her own phone to silence the ringing. Grabbing the jacket from the hook, Lóa charged down the corridor towards the staffroom and marched in without knocking. She stood facing the grey-haired man, who was sitting with three women, one very young and two middle-aged. All were holding coffee mugs, except the young woman, who was sorting out knitting needles and brightly coloured wools. They all looked at her as if she had caught them doing something they shouldn't.

Lóa spoke directly to the grey-haired man, 'I found her jacket and her phone. She must be here somewhere.'

The man looked uncomfortable, but said nothing.

'Where could she be?' asked Lóa. 'Where's the library?'

'It's closed,' the man said.

'Where's she most likely to wait? You have to help me. She's seriously ill. I don't want her wandering around somewhere alone . . .'

'Maybe she's just walked or taken the bus home?' suggested the man.

'And left her phone behind? That's hardly likely.'

Looking at a loss, the man turned to one of his colleagues, a well-built woman in a knee-length skirt and a white blouse, with blonde highlights in her short hair.

'None of us were advised there would be a student attending the exam who was unwell,' said the woman. 'We could have kept an eye on her if we'd been informed.'

Margrét had this effect on people even when she wasn't present – they fell over backwards to deny any responsibility.

'What did you say her name was?' asked the woman.

'Margrét,' replied Lóa. 'Margrét Hjálmarsdóttir, in 10A.'

Lóa saw from their expressions that they knew who she was. She was probably one of the most exciting topics of conversation in the staffroom. The skeleton from 10A, who was such a diligent student.

'Perhaps she just slipped out to the toilet,' suggested the young woman with the knitting needles.

The third woman, who hadn't yet said anything, was putting on her coat and fastening her large, shabby leather briefcase. As she squeezed past Lóa, she put a delicate, pale hand on her shoulder and, with eyes full of sympathy, said softly, 'All the best, dear.'

Lóa thought her knees would buckle. Part of her longed to fall into the embrace of this woman, who was about the same age as her mother, to accept the sympathy, to cry for help.

But involuntarily she shrank back from the contact, as if to shake off this negative omen. How could a strange woman dare to look at her as though Margrét was as good as gone? As if her physical death was no more than a mere formality to be endured in due course.

The wild weather entered through the outside door as it opened, and banged in the wind instead of closing slowly as it should. The woman with the shabby leather case paid no attention. She was nearly blown around the corner and didn't look back. It felt as if the whole building was about to explode.

Deafened by the noise, Lóa was startled when the man hurried past her. He rushed over to the outside door, and pulled with all his strength – first the door handle, which slipped from his grasp like a slippery eel, then the door itself, right above the lock.

The wind eased for a moment, long enough for the door to bang shut. The man whipped his hands away, but was too late: the fingertips of his left hand got caught – Lóa saw it all clearly, as if in slow motion. The man staggered back from the door with a long howl. The colour drained from his cheeks, his lips went pale and he bent over the injured hand, nursing it against his stomach; he was trembling all over, his eyes wide like a frightened mare.

Lóa's stomach churned – with disgust or empathy, she wasn't

sure which – and she moved out of the way to let the two women reach him.

Then everything happened very quickly. The older woman put her arm round the man and led him gently towards the door. 'Ouch, that looks bad,' she said. 'They're broken for sure.'

Running back into the staffroom, the younger woman picked up their coats and bags. Then they all disappeared out of the door, leaving it wide open, and leaving Lóa behind. She could hardly hear for the noise of the wind.

There was a smashing sound from inside the staffroom, and Lóa went back in to see that an empty glass had fallen from the windowsill by an open window and lay shattered on the pavement below.

When she closed the window silence fell over the room like darkness, and Lóa heard her own thoughts and footsteps as she switched off the light and went out into the corridor. The wind still held the outside door in its grip, but no longer seemed like it was going to lift the building from its foundations.

Margrét's denim jacket hung, light as a feather, over her arm. It was surprising that she should have left this pathetically scanty, flimsy piece of clothing hanging there as it was one of her favourites.

Lóa checked all the classrooms that weren't locked. Then the toilets. The women's toilets had seven narrow cubicles and one which was considerably wider, a whole wall of closed dark-green doors. There were white tiles on the floor, walls and ceiling and white washbasins.

'Margrét?' she called. Her voice echoed cold and hollow off the hard surfaces, and reverberated against her own chest.

Then into the men's toilets. But she backed out again.

Margrét would never have dreamed of hiding herself in there.

There was nowhere left to look. Lóa knew that Margrét wasn't in the building. She'd run away. She didn't want to go back to the loony bin.

*Bloody fucking hell.*

Anguish crawled under her skin, like cold, clammy seaweed, twining itself round her body and up her neck. She felt the pulse in her throat beating rapidly; her mouth was dry. Ína was alone in the car and surely beside herself with impatience by now.

The irrational fear swept over her that maybe Ína had run off as well. Lóa knew it couldn't be true, and yet she couldn't stop herself running along seemingly endless corridors towards the weather-beaten door, which was about to bang shut as she pushed it open and ran out towards the car park.

Ína was still in the car, thank God, but her agitation showed in every expression and every movement. When she saw her mother she gave a jump and leapt out of the car, then ran back in and slammed the door. Her relief gave way to distress at being left for so long.

'Where were you? I'm freezing,' she said, chattering her teeth loudly, the minute Lóa was sitting in the car next to her.

'I'm so sorry, my love,' said Lóa. 'Are you really cold? Why didn't you put your anorak on?' She reached behind her for the hooded anorak on the back seat and wrapped Ína up in it. Lóa cuddled her on her lap for a moment, but when she picked up the warm scent from the nape of Ína's neck she was overcome with emotion and pushed the child away again.

'Where's Margrét?' Ína asked.

'I don't know,' said Lóa, putting the denim jacket on the back seat. 'Maybe she's just walked home.'

'But it's horrible weather!'

'Maybe,' replied Lóa. 'I don't know, darling. Please, put your seatbelt on.'

'OK,' said Ína, and suddenly remembering that she was the Little Match Girl, almost frozen to death, she fumbled for the seatbelt as if her fingers were numb and she kept losing her grip, chattering her teeth loudly all the while.

Lóa picked up the phone and stared at it, before deciding to call Björg.

'Hi,' Björg answered.

'Are you at home?' asked Lóa.

'At yours? No. Why?'

'Margrét's disappeared.'

A shocked silence at the other end of the line brought Lóa to her senses. 'She's not at the school,' she added. 'When I arrived to fetch her she'd gone, and left her phone and her jacket behind. And I don't know where she could have . . .'

'Go straight to the police and report her missing,' said Björg. 'And ring your mum. I'll be back in about half an hour.'

Lóa's hands were numb. She put the phone down on the dashboard and looked at Ína, who stared back, motionless as a statue.

'It's all right,' said Lóa, clasping both of Ína's hands tightly. 'I'll ring Grandma and ask her to come over so there's someone at home if Margrét gets there before us.'

The police station was a low building compared to those around it. The front had an off-putting brown facade. Ína trotted docilely by her mother's side, with her anorak zipped up to her chin. She hadn't said a word since the school car park.

The air was dry and musty in the waiting room. There were chairs and benches covered in fake leather, an oblong desk with ten different sorts of form and, in a glass cubicle, a woman rushed off her feet.

Ína plodded over to one of the benches and plonked herself down in the middle. It was as though she was no longer a child, bursting with energy, but merely a body which needed to be put somewhere. Her feet didn't quite reach the ground and, rather than swinging them, she just let them dangle there. A boot fell off one foot and landed on the floor with a thud, revealing a pink sock embroidered with red flowers.

Lóa walked uncertainly over to the glass cubicle, suddenly doubting her right to march in and expect the system to leap to her aid. Although she kept her calm and composure, for the first time in her life she feared being taken for a silly, hysterical woman, and that these officers of the law would smell wine on her, even though she hadn't been drinking.

'Excuse me,' she said to the woman, who then deigned to look up at her, still frowning with concentration. 'Excuse me,' Lóa repeated, as if the woman wouldn't hear her unless they made eye contact. 'My daughter has disappeared. She has run away. Have I come to the right department to report a missing person?'

The woman looked sideways at Ína and said, 'How old is she and how long is it since you last saw her?'

'She's fifteen, nearly sixteen. I drove her to school this morning and when I went to pick her up she had gone, leaving her phone and jacket behind,' said Lóa, holding up Margrét's phone as evidence.

The woman stared at her in disbelief. 'Sixteen years old?' she said, slowly and clearly, as if hoping something would click with Lóa and she would shake her head, burst out laughing and say, *'Oh, of course. She's nearly sixteen years old. What was I thinking? You just can't get used to them growing up so fast, can you?'*

'No,' said Lóa, her voice cracking. She realized she'd been gabbling. 'My daughter is a danger to herself and should be in hospital, in the mental health unit. She's ill and has no friends and she definitely hasn't just gone off with some schoolmates. She's run away because she didn't want to go back to hospital. But she must – it's a matter of life and death.'

'I see,' said the woman reluctantly. 'Do you have a photo of her?'

Lóa took her wallet out of her pocket and, with trembling fingers, rifled through the bits of paper and receipts until she found a passport photo of Margrét, which she handed to the woman through the gap between the glass and the counter.

'It was taken on her fourteenth birthday. But she doesn't look like that any more. She's lost just over three stone since then.'

The woman took the photo and attached it to a blank sheet of paper with a paperclip. 'Come back if she hasn't turned up by tomorrow morning. And try to find a more recent photograph of her,' she said. 'But she'll probably come home by tonight. They usually do.' Her eyes as she said this expressed both empathy and firmness. This was an expression which no-one could achieve without spending a long time behind a counter surrounded by glass, and Lóa realized that neither threats nor negotiation would have any effect. She knew that if she maintained her composure she might be taken seriously – but not otherwise.

Ína followed her mother back to the car without protest, but didn't make a move to get out when Lóa parked the car outside their house.

'Shouldn't we go and look for Margrét?' she asked, anguish written right across her face.

'We will, my love, but not just yet,' said Lóa. 'First we need to say hello to Grandma and Björg and decide where we're going to look. There's no point in just driving round without knowing where we're going. Reykjavík's a big place.'

'How big?' asked Ína quietly.

'Well, there are thousands of buildings and hundreds of streets,' said Lóa.

And they walked into the house without giving a thought to the bike in the boot.

On the stairway, they bumped into the doll-maker. He had one arm in a sling and Margrét's summer present slung over his shoulder. The doll's arms hung limply down his back and her lifeless hands were striking his thighs with each step he took. The checked flannelling stretched over her curvaceous backside, which rested up against his head. He was red in the face and grimacing with the strain, and probably also from pain: he seemed unable to put his weight down properly on one foot.

Lóa's heart sank with fear or shame – maybe both. She'd forgotten all about this man and his doll. But now he'd reclaimed it and that was fine. She couldn't care less.

But what if he was going to report it to the police? Or had even already done so? Perhaps they were on their way over right now.

It was a frightening thought. She couldn't deal with this. She would have to talk to him, offer to make it up to him, ask him to forgive her, explain that she hadn't been quite herself that morning. But not now. She didn't have it in her right now.

As she walked into the room, her mother jumped up from the sofa and Björg leapt to her feet from one of the dining room chairs. They came up close, as if drawn by some magnet inside her, or as if they were expecting to support her so she didn't fall over.

Björg stretched out her arms to embrace her, nearly wrapping herself around Lóa, her long fingers pressing against the back of Lóa's neck. 'Don't worry too much,' she whispered, even though there was no particular reason to whisper, except perhaps not to upset Ína.

Loosening her grasp, she looked over Lóa's shoulder. Lóa turned and followed her gaze: Sveinn had come back in and was struggling to shift his burden onto the sofa.

Lóa's mother hadn't taken her eyes off him. She was clearly trying to work out what he was doing there, but was too discreet to ask. Or maybe she feared what the answer might be.

Lóa didn't have the energy to give any explanation and she wasn't up to dealing with the doll-maker, so she leaned in to the two women and thanked them for coming.

Ína started sobbing loudly, repeating over and over that she didn't want to be late for the birthday party. 'Margrét's right,' she wailed. 'You're never on time. I'm always getting told off for being late when it's not my fault.'

Taking hold of her mother's hand, Lóa asked, 'Will you take Ína home with you and let her stay the night?'

'Of course, darling,' replied her mother.

'And could you maybe buy her a costume and take her to this party?'

'Where will I get one?'

'I don't know,' said Lóa, and called out to Ína, who had run out of the room, 'Grandma will take you to buy a birthday present and an elfin queen costume, my love, and the two of you will definitely get there on time!'

There was no response from Ína, who was clearly digesting this offer.

Lóa found herself glancing at Sveinn, who was busy looking around and seemed fascinated by the renovations, though they were only half finished. Maybe it would be a good idea to delay him. Perhaps she would be able to avoid further embarrassment if she befriended him and got him on her side. She couldn't shake off the thought that if he reported the theft to the police then she would be in a very difficult position. The police wouldn't take Margrét's disappearance seriously, or might in some way blame her for it. They would be bound to think she was dishonest about everything because she was a thief.

She looked away quickly when she felt Sveinn was about to turn towards her. She tried to marshal her thoughts, but when she had registered that Margrét wasn't waiting for her outside the classroom, as they had agreed, it was as if a smoke alarm had gone off in her head and she couldn't stop the awful noise when everything inside her was in turmoil.

Björg folded her arms and asked, 'What did the police say?'

'They told me to come back tomorrow,' replied Lóa.

'She'll turn up this evening, you'll see,' said Lóa's mother, patting her reassuringly on the arm.

'That's what the woman in the glass cubicle said,' responded Lóa, and the tension in her throat gave way to a burst of laughter.

'The woman in the glass cubicle?' Björg echoed.

'The one I talked to in reception at the police station.'

'Oh, her! The gatekeeper of patriarchy!' said Björg. 'Does she really exist? I thought she was only an urban myth.'

They all laughed, Lóa's mother loudest of all – like a tipsy choirmistress, her eyes wet with tears.

# 11

*Monday Evening*

Lóa was standing over him, her hand resting on his good shoulder, saying something. Sveinn heard the words but didn't understand them, and even though she was speaking in a clear and gentle voice, the consonants sounded like gunshots and the vowels sank somewhere cold, deep in his brain.

He was lying on the sofa, half on top of *Raven-Black Lola*. He felt chilled to the bone and utterly exhausted. Lóa had lit numerous candles and drawn the curtains. Outside, the evening light was trying to penetrate the cracks around the thick, red velvet. *People don't usually light candles at this time of year, when there's constant daylight*, he thought.

They were alone in the room. Sveinn couldn't stop his mind straying to the unfortunate writer in the Stephen King novel *Misery*. It was about a man who was held captive in his own home by a fanatic: a mentally ill woman who smashed his knee with a sledgehammer so he couldn't escape.

A shiver ran down his spine, but the fear didn't take hold. Part of him was amused that he should be lying here, only just awake, feeling rather undignified and scared. What was he thinking, falling asleep in the home of his would-be executioner? It was almost as if he was offering himself up, as if he wanted her to harm him.

He sat up and made his arm more comfortable in the sling. He now remembered his head feeling heavy and how he'd intended to rest it briefly on the back of the sofa with the doll next to him, looking elegant with her hair newly brushed. He'd intended to speak to Lóa privately, in order to clear things up before he drove home. If she reacted badly then he would give as good as he got. He'd retaliate if she started threatening him. But he'd clearly managed to fall asleep in this bizarre position, and now here was the lady of the house standing over him, telling him that they'd tried unsuccessfully to wake him. The red triangle on the bottle of pills obviously wasn't just for decoration.

He let her help him into the bedroom where he'd found *Raven-Black Lola* earlier that day.

'Where are the others?' Sveinn asked, when she'd pulled a duvet with a creamy-white cover up over him.

'Mum took Ína home with her and Björg is on her shift at the hospital. She's a healthcare assistant,' replied Lóa. Even though she was being helpful and kind she was so aloof that he felt uneasy. It was as if he had done something wrong, as contradictory as that seemed.

She turned off the light on her way out of the bedroom, and he heard her sit down at the dining room table, tap the keys on her laptop and scribble something on a piece of paper. Or at least, that was what he imagined from the faint noises which floated through from the living room.

Reaching in his pocket for his phone, he saw that Lárus had rung twice, but not a dicky bird from his stalker. But then why would she bother to ring him when he lay sleeping in her house? Everything pointed to the same conclusion, and suddenly it seemed ridiculous to waste more time pussyfooting around. It was the law of the jungle – such matters should be firmly dealt with, not be allowed to run on and get blown out of all proportion until they become insurmountable. If he was going to hell in a handcart, then at least he wanted to be steering.

He pictured Lóa in a candlelit room, wearing a floor-length, green dress, her long nails painted red, pouring poison from an emerald-studded pendant into a goblet filled with blood-red wine.

Sveinn rattled the bottle of pills and, hearing a fairly empty sound, was filled with dismay. He shook the pills out into his hand and counted: one, two, three. He would have to make do with just one this time, even though he longed to take them all at once. He broke the pill in two, but had difficulty swallowing it. His mouth felt like it was lined with paper and he was left with a powerful aftertaste – he had to get some water.

The warm, light duvet smelled slightly of fabric conditioner. He felt a pang of regret once he'd thrown it off and was sitting at the foot of the bed. His head was spinning and a fuzzy blackness affected his vision. Maybe it was just as well he only had two pills left if he wanted to drive home in the morning. Then he would have to go and get himself some more.

Lóa barely looked up when he appeared in the doorway; she was so absorbed in writing on a sheet of paper. There was a whitish-blue aura around her from the computer screen; her face and neck were lit up, everything else was bathed in soft candlelight. It would have been a beautiful, peaceful sight if it hadn't been for the tension in the air. All else simply gave way under its weight. Which made it difficult to say anything, let alone broach such a complicated and sensitive subject.

Limping silently past her, Sveinn made his way to the bathroom, where he let the water run cold, so cold that his fingers hurt under the icy jet. Then he took gulp after gulp straight from the tap, until his lips and gums were almost numb and his stomach felt bloated.

He made his way back to the living room with a refreshing coolness in his mouth and throat, his eyes moist with relief. Sitting down at the heavy oak table opposite Lóa, he watched her over the silver laptop. He looked at her glasses, which were clearly ridiculously expensive, probably designed by some homosexual prodigy in Paris or New York. He looked at her wavy, blonde hair, which, in this light, reminded him of the way tinsel used to shine in the Christmas lights in the old days.

'Lóa, is your surname Hansdóttir?'

'What do you mean?' she asked, so totally unperturbed by the question that he was thrown.

Frowning, she looked straight through him, opened her mouth, put her tongue behind her teeth as if she was about to say something and then turned back to the screen in silence.

This conversation wasn't going the way he'd planned. There was something going on which he didn't know about and didn't understand, but which he longed to put right. He wanted to redeem himself by putting it right, whatever it was. Everything he had witnessed in this home was a silent cry for help, and he'd fallen asleep in the middle of it. But now he was wide awake and his anger had largely dissipated. The poor woman must be a sandwich short of a picnic because she wasn't reacting: not to him turning up unexpectedly on her doorstep, or to the fact that he'd clearly indicated he knew who the hate-mail writer was. Things weren't what he'd thought they were. He would have to get a better grip on things.

He hadn't intended to get drawn into someone else's problems, but it was too late now. Lóa was sitting opposite him like a neon sign spelling out mysteriously coded messages he thought were meant for him. A code he was meant to break. Why? It didn't matter. Probably it was no more than a coincidence, that he was there when there was a problem to be resolved, but the task was no less pressing. The world was driven by coincidences. Some people claimed they didn't believe in coincidence. Sveinn didn't believe in fate, but he believed in coincidences which directed the course of people's lives with varying degrees of forcefulness, like a pawn on a chessboard. No, that was too calculated, more like litter caught in the wind. And man's eternal task was to wrestle with these coincidences whenever they arose, while resigning himself to the fact that they were just that: coincidences.

Leaning across the table, he rested his chin on the edge of the computer screen and looked at Lóa until she stopped writing and looked back.

'I'll make up for the damage,' she said, nodding in the direction of *Raven-Black Lola*. 'I was going to return it. And I'll pay for everything: the petrol costs, your loss of earnings, repairs if there's been any damage – no messing. If you want, I'll pay you the full value and you can still take it home with you. I don't want that thing in my house.'

He shook his head.

'What do you want then?' she asked. 'Are you hungry?'

'Yes,' he said. 'But it doesn't matter. I just want you to tell me what's going on here. I think you owe me that much.'

He'd been worried that she would go on the defensive, show her claws, bare her teeth. But the woman was unfathomable. She was sitting there, apparently in control of herself, although she was clearly upset. She seemed fair and sensible. He'd thought that by backing her into a corner he would force her to show her unpleasant side in all its fury. But no, she just looked blankly at the wall behind him and handed him the sheet of paper she'd been writing on. On it were names, addresses and telephone numbers – about ten in total.

'My elder daughter has run away,' she said. 'These are her friends' phone numbers, or her ex-friends, to be precise. They've all turned their backs on her. I know there's no point in ringing, but I can't just sit here waiting any longer.'

She avoided his eyes while she spoke. It was as if she was ashamed. And now he vaguely remembered something she had said the other evening. Her eldest daughter had mental health problems. How had she worded it? He couldn't remember; she'd not been clear about it. She'd been drunk but not enough to trust him, a stranger, with everything that was burdening her. Just drunk enough to mention something in passing, before changing the subject.

'Have you contacted the police?'

'They told me to come back tomorrow,' she replied, running her fingers through her hair repeatedly. Her cheeks were red, as if she'd been running. 'They also said she'd turn up this evening or tonight, but I'm not so sure. She's deadly earnest in everything she does. And yet I can't bring myself to go anywhere in case she does come home, knowing she doesn't have a key.'

Sveinn felt for her. She seemed so alone in the world. No-one had ever told her how to deal with situations like this. He wasn't entirely sure she was going the right way about it, but he didn't have a better way.

'Maybe I could let her in if she arrives while you're out,' he suggested. Although he really couldn't face being here on his own with his shoulder in pain, only two Tramadols and the unpleasant feeling that he was of no use to anyone.

'That's a kind thought,' said Lóa. 'But she's too sensitive even to be around people she knows, let alone with strangers. She hasn't always been like this. But how do you think she'd react to coming home only to be greeted by you at the door? I don't mean this unkindly, but you look like the wolf that's just eaten Little Red Riding Hood and her grandma — scruffy and unshaven and with all those bandages. What happened to you, anyway? You were as fit as a fiddle when I last saw you.'

'I clambered up onto the dirty laundry basket and threw myself down, just for fun,' he said.

She didn't show any reaction, and looking at her blank expression, he felt offended at the thought that maybe she'd switched off.

'I was, of course, preparing to face my own demise, which I understand awaits me in the near future. It's necessary to get me out of the way so that others can live a normal family life. Isn't that the idea?' he said staring at her.

She looked back at him for a long while before looking away and said, 'It's none of my business how you got hurt. But in any case, Margrét wouldn't want to meet you, and you would like meeting her even less.'

Toying with the cordless phone, she rubbed the small of her back before adding that it was nearly eleven o'clock and she should make a few more calls before it was too late. 'You can help yourself to something from the fridge before you go back to bed,' she said. 'You don't look like you're in a fit state to drive home.'

As soon as she'd spoken the words, he realized that was exactly what he wanted: to eat and sleep. Although this house was not exactly his idea of paradise. Never again was he going to be at the mercy of someone who despised him and wanted to see him dead.

He tried to put himself in her shoes, but couldn't. He would have felt better if she'd shown some sign of being deranged, but she didn't. He was filled with unease that she should behave so normally after falling asleep at a stranger's house, threatening him, stealing from him and stalking him. As if she was only crazy in her spare time, a Sunday nutcase. Hidden madness was more dangerous than overt – wasn't that a well-known fact?

Obviously he could ring Kjartan or Lárus and ask them to come and fetch him. But he couldn't stand being around Lárus, he could cope with Kjartan for an hour or two at the most, and besides, he didn't feel up to being alone at home when he couldn't work.

He'd once heard it said that people could seek refuge in their own heads, find a peaceful place there where they could relax when they were alone with nothing to do. He didn't understand what that meant. He found no such place of refuge, and having nothing to do was akin to suffering from cold or hunger to him: something that needed to be resolved immediately. Boredom was worse than death, to his way of thinking.

Lóa turned away with the phone pressed up against her ear. 'I'm sorry to ring so late,' she said. 'This is Lóa, Margrét's mum. Could I have a word with Agla Steinunn?'

Sveinn noticed a pile of scientific magazines in a basket on the floor. He picked up the top one and took it into the kitchen, where he made himself a sandwich with some leftover goulash and red cabbage. While he ate he read articles about the surface of Mars, grave looters in South America and a new medicine which was said to sharpen attention and improve memory.

From the living room, Lóa's voice blended with the hum of the fridge and the quiet plop of water dripping into the steel sink. Except once, when she swore loudly and he heard a loud crack followed by a dull tinkling sound. He closed his eyes and looked for a foothold, a handhold, to a peaceful place in his mind, or to anywhere he could blot out the feeling that he controlled nothing and understood still less.

## 12

When Ína had finally reconciled herself to going with her Grandma and Björg had gone to work, anger and fear erupted in Lóa with such an unfamiliar vehemence that she couldn't even think clearly. She tried to shake it off by pacing the floor – up and down the living room, into the kitchen and back again – but the sound of her slippers on the floor tormented her, and the apartment, which previously she had felt was constricting her, now seemed oppressively open and exposed. Her home was no longer the place of refuge which Lóa, in her innocence, had imagined it to be. People and things slipped in and out without so much as a by your leave.

But over and above all this, a sort of peace reigned within her; a blessedly rational strength which reminded her not to lose sight of herself, not to overreact. So in response she drew the curtains in both rooms and lit the candles, hoping that the candlelight would have a calming effect on her.

The phone rang and Lóa's hand was trembling as she lifted the handset from the base.

'How are you feeling?' asked Björg.

*I feel as though someone's trampling on my innards,* thought Lóa, but replied, 'I'm keeping it together, somehow.'

'It's manic here,' said Björg. 'But if you don't want to be alone tonight I can pull a sickie and come over . . .'

'There's no need,' replied Lóa. 'Just get some rest in the

morning when your shift's over and ring me when you wake up.'

'Are you sure?' asked Björg.

'Of course.'

'Is he still there?' whispered Björg.

Lóa glanced over to where Sveinn was lying in the flickering candlelight, his head on the doll's arm, his mouth open, his jaw relaxed and lopsided. He kept catching his breath as though he was seeing something terrifying in his dreams. 'He's still asleep,' she said. 'Do you think he might be ill?'

'Not necessarily,' answered Björg. 'People get tired when they've broken something. He's probably taken too many painkillers. Do you think he's harmless?'

'He doesn't look like he's up to causing much harm,' replied Lóa.

'Just ring me if you need me,' said Björg hurriedly. 'I've got to dash now. See you tomorrow, OK.'

Lóa carried on looking at Sveinn: his dark hair was beginning to go grey and looked oily with either hair gel or grease and his slim body had the beginnings of a paunch. His pot belly was the most likeable thing about him, along with his bushy eyebrows, which reminded her of the farmers in the countryside where she'd grown up, until she was six, when her father had decided to become a taxi driver in Reykjavík.

She couldn't help thinking of her grandfather who, bent over with hard work, had worn a belt to keep his trousers up which, as the years went by, had slowly crept higher over his belly until it had almost reached the knot of his tie. Why hadn't it been the same for her father? She couldn't understand why he'd had to follow his parents so quickly to the grave.

Suddenly she couldn't bear looking at Sveinn any more. He looked like innocence personified when asleep, and yet was so crude and debauched when it came to his doll, which lay half under him. One arm dangled over the edge of the sofa, the other lay inert on the doll's stomach, his hand resting between her unnaturally firm breasts which bulged under the flannel pyjamas, his fingers hidden by her hair.

Standing up slowly, Lóa called his name a few times, but he lay there, dead to the world. So she put her hand on his good shoulder and shook him slightly; gently at first and then more firmly.

He winced and peered at her in fright.

'You are welcome to go and lie down in the bedroom,' she said, but he appeared not to understand her, so she offered him her arm and led him out of the living room. She hesitated in the hallway, unsure where to take him. Ína's bed was too small, and she didn't think it was appropriate to offer him her own bed, so she showed him into Margrét's room and fetched the duvet Björg used when she slept on the sofa.

She asked him whether he needed anything, but he didn't seem to hear her. So she decided to leave him be.

She went back to her computer in the dining room and carried on looking up phone numbers. Lóa hadn't intended to get in touch with Margrét's old friends because she was sure Margrét wouldn't be with them, but the past few hours had taken their toll on her and she thought it was better to do something than sit idle.

A little while later, Sveinn was up and about. He limped past without speaking to her and she heard him running the tap in the bathroom for ages. Then he sat himself down opposite her at the table and seemed to be angling for some kind of a fight.

She couldn't remember if she had apologized. She probably had, and it would be ridiculous to do so again. He would take it that she was looking for absolution, for him to wipe the slate clean and tell her all was well.

In fact, that was exactly what she wanted, if she was honest with herself.

Leaning across the table, he looked at her over the computer screen and said, 'Lóa, is your surname Hansdóttir?'

She couldn't understand what he was driving at. It seemed like a totally random question and couldn't be meant literally.

His presence was oppressive, it prevented her from getting on with what she needed to do, and she felt relieved when he agreed to go and get himself something to eat from the kitchen.

There was no reply from Nadia, Margrét's old best friend, so Lóa turned to the next name on the list, Agla Steinunn. For a while she and Margrét had been joined at the hip, like giggling Siamese twins.

Her father answered. 'She's gone to bed already.'

'It's about Margrét,' explained Lóa. 'She hasn't come home from school yet.'

'Do you want me to wake her?' he asked in a harsh tone. The man sounded as if he thought Margrét was a bad influence on his early-to-bed daughter.

'No, no, don't wake her,' replied Lóa. 'But I would be grateful if you would have a look and see if Margrét is with her.'

'I think we would have noticed if someone was in her room,' he said.

'Yes,' said Lóa, making an effort to breathe calmly. 'I'm sure you would. But you understand that I must explore every avenue, no matter how unlikely.'

After thinking it over for a moment the man answered, 'Wait a second.'

She heard him put the phone down and the sound of his footsteps fading into the distance. Then silence, while Lóa stared blankly at Margrét's denim jacket hanging over the back of the chair next to her. Margrét's phone had been in the pocket. Of course. It would contain the names and numbers of her friends and acquaintances which Lóa might not have heard her mention.

The voice of Agla Steinunn's father interrupted her thoughts, 'Now we know for sure – your daughter is not hiding under the covers with Agla. She says she hasn't seen her since last Wednesday. She was awake anyway. Do you want to talk to her? Maybe you want me to have a look under her bed?'

'No, thank you,' said Lóa, wanting to end the conversation quickly before she said something she might regret.

She rang two more numbers from her list – and spoke to perplexed but helpful parents, who probably thanked their lucky stars that their own daughters were sitting in the warm in front of the TV – before scanning through the numbers on Margrét's phone. She decided to copy the numbers out before giving the phone to the police the next day. They would undoubtedly have a better idea what to do with any information they could retrieve from a phone.

Then her eyes fell upon a strange looking name, if you could call it a name: *Nexusboy*. When she put the phone to her ear it was almost as if it wasn't Margrét's mobile but her cold hand which lay against Lóa's flushed cheek. And obviously it was only her imagination, but she thought she detected a faint hint of the *White Musk* perfume Margrét had worn since she was twelve years old.

'Hiya, Marge,' a cheerful young man's voice answered.

'Who is this?' asked Lóa.

There was a brief silence, and when the lad started speaking again he sounded awkward and unsure of himself. 'Isn't that you, Margrét?' he said.

'No, this is her mother,' replied Lóa. 'I'm trying to find her. If you know where she is you have to tell me. You won't help her by covering up for her.'

His mouth had clearly gone dry when he answered, 'I've never met her; we got to know each other over the Internet.'

'Didn't she tell you she was planning to run away then?' asked Lóa.

'No, I've not heard from her for a long while,' said the lad.

'How long?'

'I'm not sure, maybe three or four months.'

'How old are you?' asked Lóa. Maybe it wasn't relevant, but she felt she needed to know.

'Twenty-one,' replied the lad. 'We just chatted a few times. I have no idea where she is.' Then he put the phone down.

The thought of Margrét having a secret life turned Lóa's world upside down. 'Bloody hell!' she exclaimed aloud, slamming the phone so hard onto the table that a crack appeared on the screen, and the back of the phone came off and clattered to the floor.

She bent down slowly to pick up the back and fixed it on again. The phone had turned itself off, so she turned it back on again and checked to see if it was still working.

It was long past eleven and she didn't feel up to phoning anyone else, but she stayed sitting there, staring up into the gaping darkness of the loft. She'd intended to set up her office there, but when it came to it she had realized that the loft would be an accident black spot and would have to wait until Ína was old enough to go up there safely.

A Jewish saying, which she had come across once and then used for an insurance advert, came to mind: *God cannot be everywhere, that's why he made mothers.*

She had also intended to block up the doorway into the loft area, but had made do with locking the door, spraying glue into the keyhole and leaving it as a decorative feature above the living room. When her life was pedestrian enough for the word *poetic* to have a positive ring to it, she'd thought it would look striking to have a door suspended in mid-air.

Sveinn appeared in the doorway, tipping pills into his hand from a glass bottle. He swallowed without bothering to fetch himself any water. Staring at the wall behind her, Sveinn announced that he was sorry that Margrét hadn't returned home, coolly said goodnight and disappeared into Margrét's bedroom.

Lóa went into the kitchen and filled a tall glass with apple juice. Her desire for wine had disappeared for the moment. In fact, all her desires had disappeared, apart from one – to find Margrét alive and have her put away where she would in some way be out of danger.

Back at the dining room table with her glass in front of her, Lóa's heart lurched for the hundredth time at the thought of Margrét being out in the biting wind, so inadequately dressed. Though Lóa knew this couldn't be true: Margrét didn't have the stamina to wander the streets for hours on end. She would have been found unconscious somewhere long before. But Lóa had already rung the hospitals, as well as calling the police twice.

Margrét would never entertain the thought of drowning herself in the sea or stepping out in front of a car – that was out of the question. She was too considerate to take her own life directly. Her rebellion was passive. In that respect she was a bit like a follower of Gandhi. Except that Gandhi's rebellion had been against the oppressive forces in life, while Margrét was rebelling against life itself.

It had taken Lóa a long time to realize how fascinated Margrét was by death. How was she meant to comprehend this longing of her daughter's? A longing which was nothing but a misconception. A wrong opinion, if that was not a contradiction in terms.

Death was not a redeeming power or a healing of this pathological condition called life. It was a punishing, crushing, harsh affliction, which toyed with life like a cat with a mouse. A meaningless and unpredictable higher force – an uncomplicated force, unable to see the complex sensitivities which constitute life. Margrét couldn't see that there was no beauty in death. No more than in a vomiting football hooligan with a bloodied nose brandishing a broken bottle. Death was nothing more than violence, and Lóa despised the deceitfulness of those who tried to convince themselves or others that this was not the case. She took death personally, rather like the Roman general – what was his name again? – who, at death's door, had wanted the world to perish with him. His last words had been: *I wish that the world had but one neck and that my hands were locked around it.*

No, Lóa saw no reason to be as meek as a lamb when Death, with a cold gleam in his eye, was trying to get his claws into her daughter. Her heart thumped with crippling rage. Not at Margrét. Not any more. Margrét was so weak that it was unthinkable to direct such a devastating force at her as Lóa's rage had become. The storm which raged within her, clouded her vision and whipped up a pungent taste of salty earth in her mouth.

Time crawled on, and by four in the morning Lóa's eyelids were feeling like sandpaper and beginning to drop. She got up, intending to lie down on the sofa for a while, but the doll was sitting there and she didn't feel up to moving it. She felt even less like lying down in her own bed. To allow herself a proper rest would be like throwing in the towel and neglecting Margrét.

Sveinn was sleeping in Margrét's room, holding his hand in the sling, his forehead and one leg hard up against the wall, snoring softly. He wouldn't stir if she stood over him and sang the national anthem at the top of her voice. Most men seemed to have one thing in common – this ability to sleep so deeply – and Lóa couldn't help envying him for it. The girls' father had always said he slept so well because he had such a clear conscience. If that was true then she must have a lot on her conscience because she woke at the slightest noise or movement.

She only hesitated for a moment before lying down fully dressed next to Sveinn and covering herself with a corner of the duvet. He swallowed in mid-snore, but was clearly in a deep sleep and gradually Lóa's heartbeat calmed. The warmth of the duvet had a soothing effect and there was a strong body odour coming from Sveinn which wasn't entirely unpleasant: a smell of dirty hair, fresh sweat and something bitter which she couldn't quite put her finger on.

Sleep washed over her and the last thing she remembered was her head lolling over onto Sveinn's warm shoulder and thinking that he was someone else.

# 13

*Monday Night*

A vibration near his groin caused him to knock his damaged knee against the wall in front of him in his half-awake state, and a pain shot right up into his hip. 'What the . . .?' he muttered, pulling the phone up out of his trouser pocket.

The vibrating stopped and the screen went blank.

He was chiding himself for not answering the phone when it began to vibrate once more.

'Well now, my voluble, articulate friend, what have you got to say for yourself this time?' he said wearily into the handset.

'*Killer,*' said a man's hollow voice, evidently recorded from the television. '*Murderer. Motherfucker. I am going to fuck you over and fuck you good.*'

'No, you just listen to me . . .' Sveinn began, but the line had already gone dead.

He sat up in bed, his mind clearer than it had been for a long time, and the pain in his shoulder becoming more acute as he came to. He would have to get some more of those painkillers; that was an absolute priority. But his immediate priority was to get out of there, to drive home with *Raven-Black Lola.* But first he must make Lóa understand that he was flesh and blood as she was, not some instrument of evil.

When he went into the living room the computer was still humming on the dining room table, as it had been the evening before, and although Lóa was nowhere to be seen he could hear her rushing about the apartment. Now she'd stopped in the entrance hall and was opening and closing the drawers in the chest there. Maybe this was her odd way of pulling herself together after making the abusive phone call. Or maybe she was searching the cupboards and drawers for her daughter's frozen corpse.

Feeling his face to make sure that after a night's sleep there was no drool on his chin, and glancing down to check that his flies weren't open, he went to ask her straight out how she imagined she was going to 'fuck him over' and what he had actually done to her. But when he saw her he couldn't bring himself to. He couldn't face being hard on her, this picture of terror, her hair plastered to her head, her lips bluish with worry, her stooping shoulders seeming slenderer than the day before.

'Good morning,' he said.

'Did you sleep well?' she asked, staring through him as she closed the top drawer.

He gave a snort and went straight into the bathroom, locking the door behind him. He went to the toilet and while he was washing his hands he stared at his face in the gilt-framed mirror. In the harsh light, he noticed for the first time the signs of ageing on his forehead and around his eyes, and it gave him a start. There were also deep lines running from his nose down either side of his mouth.

He was in his forties, so it was natural and to be expected. But he had never noticed it before. Not like this – an image in a mirror reflecting the ominous promise of an unhappy end approaching.

In the cupboard next to the mirror were thick jars of expensive cream. He vaguely recognized the names on some of them – 'Clarins', 'Lancôme', 'Shiseido' – and suspected that most of them were to put on your face. It seemed Lóa hadn't let age creep up on her as he had.

Maybe he should follow her example, wander up to the beauty counter in some department store and ask for face cream. How would he go about it? What would he say to the sales assistant? *'I don't want to get old and I'm frightened of dying, but I'm too stingy to spend more than ten thousand krónur. What can you offer me?'*

Laughing out loud, he dried his hands on a soft, pale-pink hand towel and went out, armed with the sense that he had nothing to lose and that none of this mattered as much as he'd imagined a short while ago.

Lóa was sitting at the dining room table with her head in her hands; the tips of her ring fingers met in the middle of her forehead.

'What are you doing?' Sveinn asked.

She looked at him without answering.

'I think I'd better be off now. Could you just help me out to the car with this?' he asked, pointing at *Raven-Black Lola*.

'Absolutely. No problem,' said Lóa. 'But I'm not so sure you'll make it all the way home. There are gusts of wind of up to 100 miles per hour on Kjalarnes.'

Sveinn sighed. He didn't know what to do, and the pain made it difficult to make decisions.

He opened his mouth and was about to say, *'I don't understand what it is you want with me . . .'*

Lóa looked at him with a frown on her face.

Before he managed to get the words out, the phone in his trouser pocket started ringing and his mouth went dry. What if he was wrong? Lóa was still looking at him as if he was the deranged one, and not her.

'I'm sorry,' he muttered, turning away with the phone in his hand. It was Lárus.

'Hello,' Sveinn answered in an unusually friendly tone. He was so relieved to hear Lárus and not his stalker. He didn't want to have to rethink his original assumption: that his stalker was Lóa.

'Hi there,' said Lárus, speaking fast as if he was afraid Sveinn would cut him off in mid-flow. 'I'm in Reykjavík and was wondering whether you needed anything, since I'm in town anyway.'

'I'm also in town,' said Sveinn. 'Held up by the weather. So are you, as you'd know if you kept your eyes and ears open a bit more.'

'Hang on a second,' said Lárus, and Sveinn heard him hitting buttons, clearly trying to extract some useful information from his flashy phone. 'Yep, you're right. Wild weather out on the peninsula. Cars getting blown off the road and all sorts. So you don't need anything?' he added, too young to know how to disguise his longing.

'If you can get hold of a dose of something strong, preferably morphine or heroin, and drop it round to me, I'd be eternally grateful,' replied Sveinn, laughing.

'Absolutely no problem,' said Lárus. 'Are you at her place? Was it her who . . .?' He seemed ready to take the blame if his tip-off had proved wrong.

'Yes,' replied Sveinn, looking at Lóa. 'She was the one who borrowed the doll. If you speak to Kjartan you can tell him he can rest easy – the goods have turned up. And thanks for your help and all that. I could never have found her without you. Be careful not to get blown away in the wind. We'll catch up maybe, when Kjartan has his birthday party.'

Sveinn walked slowly through the dining room, into the living room and sank down carefully onto the sofa where the previous day he'd fallen asleep. The rooms were separated by a section of wall where the windows were, so Lóa wasn't in his line of sight.

'Are you in a lot of pain?' she asked.

'I finished the pills yesterday evening,' he replied, amazed at how high the ceiling was. He felt almost giddy gazing up to the loft.

Lóa went into the kitchen and came back with a glass of water and two white, oblong tablets.

'What's this?' he asked.

'Ibuprofen,' she answered. 'It's all I've got.'

He gulped half the water and hesitated slightly, looking at the tablets in her hand.

'What's the matter?' asked Lóa. 'Ibuprofen is totally harmless – Iceland's favourite painkiller. No-one has died so far from taking it.'

Was she playing with him? Testing his reaction by offering him unmarked pills half an hour after threatening to take his life?

He downed them in one.

'Don't you find it a bit odd having me hanging around here?' asked Sveinn.

'You're welcome to stay here until the wind dies down,' she replied, her tone oddly gentle. 'You're good company compared to me.'

He burst out laughing. 'You can say that again,' he chuckled. 'Your behaviour hasn't exactly been exemplary, if you don't mind me saying so.'

'I know it's inexcusable,' she said. 'But I just wasn't myself. I admit I didn't think much about how it would affect you, but I've been under a lot of pressure recently and I . . .'

She went quiet and looked cautiously at him, as though he had her fate in his hands, and added. 'Is there any reason we need to involve anyone else in this?'

'Well, I don't know,' he said, snorting with surprise. 'Like who?'

'Like the police,' she replied. 'Don't you think the best way to resolve this would be for me to pay you damages? Name your price, within reason, and I'll pay you.'

She was unbelievable, this woman. Totally hardened on the phone, as if she couldn't care less about her reputation, and now she was standing there, humble and defenceless, pleading with him to keep quiet about it. This certainly supported the argument that people were capable of anything if they believed no-one would find out.

'It's not easy to put a value on the emotional upset you've caused me, madam,' he said, and laughed drily. He wasn't being totally serious, but couldn't resist scolding her a little.

'Yes, of course,' she responded.

'How am I meant to sleep easy at night? How can I concentrate on my work when I'm being persecuted like this? You inevitably become wary and anxious when someone intrudes on your private life in this way.'

'I understand,' said Lóa, though she looked as if she didn't understand a word.

'I don't know what you think you stand to gain by this,' said Sveinn.

'I didn't intend to gain anything,' replied Lóa.

'Shall we draw a line under it, then?' he said.

She nodded and took his outstretched hand. 'Thank you for being so understanding,' she said, with a questioning tone in her voice which threw him. It was as if she didn't mean what she said. As if she really thought he was being unnecessarily touchy.

'My condolences on the death of your father,' he said, half surprised at himself for agreeing to drop the matter.

She looked at him for a second and the furrows between her eyes noticeably deepened. Then she replied, 'Thank you.' And she walked away. She took the phone into the kitchen and began to speak into it, but he wasn't able to make out the words.

He thought the way to understand Lóa was probably through her complex feelings towards her father. Was she furious he had done away with himself in such a grotesque manner, while still feeling a fondness for him? But what had made her become fixated on an unknown doll-maker? It was highly unlikely that the old man had left a letter blaming the poor doll for his desperate unhappiness.

No, Lóa must be one of those daddy's girls who worshipped their father like a god and couldn't allow a shadow to fall on that perfect image. She couldn't direct her anger at her father/God, because that would mean admitting he was less than perfect. So she took it all out on Sveinn. It was rather an honour for him, if he thought about it, to be a substitute for the Almighty Father.

*Thank you for being so understanding?* It was nothing, my friend. It was nothing.

# 14

*Tuesday Morning*

Lóa woke to find her arm draped across Sveinn's side and the tip of her nose pressed against his back, and for a split second she felt good. Or at least she was in a neutral state, like a puppy in a basket full of puppies, who hadn't yet learnt to differentiate between its own furry warmth and that of its siblings.

But it only lasted a moment before the harsh hand of reality brought her round and rubbed her nose in the piss-puddle that her life had become. She jerked her arm off Sveinn's side and nearly fell out of bed in her desperation to get well away from him before he became aware of her.

Her jeans were clammy with sweat, her blouse damp and crumpled, and she had a metallic taste in her mouth as she rushed from room to room, looking in every corner, as if she imagined that Margrét might have squeezed in through the keyhole or through the window panes with the sun's first rays.

*What am I looking for?* she thought, stopping in the kitchen doorway as bands tightened across her chest and numbness overtook her hands. Turning on the radio, she dropped onto the nearest chair and tried to breathe deeply, but the air felt like treacle.

The news jingle sounded in her ears and she listened disinterestedly to a report of severe winds on the Vesturland road with gusts of up to 100 miles per hour making it impassable and blowing five cars off the road. Residents on Kjalarnes were advised to stay indoors and Reykjavík residents were asked to batten everything down because the wind was predicted to worsen in the metropolitan area.

The next news item had more impact on Lóa. It was about some stolen goods found in a basement flat in a Reykjavík suburb. The thought came to her that maybe Margrét had hidden something in the apartment which might give a clue to her whereabouts.

Leaping to her feet, she went to Margrét's room and began searching. Sveinn was still lying in the same position and there wasn't a sound from him while Lóa went through the contents of every cupboard and drawer. She was about to shift the chest of drawers away from the wall when he whimpered so miserably in his sleep that her back stiffened and she decided to finish the job when he was up. Then she could also move the wardrobe and look under the mattress.

She went through Ína's room with an equally fine-tooth comb, tidying up as she went, because it soothed her to see each object back in its place.

Lóa even started to look in her own bedroom, before deciding that Margrét wasn't cheeky enough to hide anything in there, then went into the store cupboard, where she rummaged around cases of old crockery, schoolbooks, magazines, clothes and toys. There was a tent there which they never used, sleeping bags, fishing rods, a Primus and a coolbox. Tools, screwdrivers and nails, left-over old paint, a food mixer and a massive fruit press, which hadn't pressed anything other than the surface it was sitting on.

On the bottom shelf, nearest the door, was a box full of her father's possessions, which her mother had handed her after the funeral. She hadn't felt up to opening the box and couldn't understand why his grieving widow had been in such a hurry to get rid of it. Perhaps it was out of mistaken thoughtfulness towards Lóa – maybe she'd thought that Lóa wanted to get over her loss by touching the mementos her father had handled so many times. But that kind of ancestor worship was alien to Lóa, and besides, the thought that a person's memory lay in objects filled her with disgust.

Margrét, however, had shown an interest in the box. Margrét, who had long since stopped showing interest in anything at all. Lóa had told her she was welcome to look at whatever was in the box, but that she mustn't take anything without asking permission first.

Lóa felt as if her fingers were trembling, though they looked steady enough, and seeing a letter lying at the top of the box her heart started racing: ink on thick paper, black words on a beige background.

But it wasn't from Margrét; it was from Copenhagen, from her father's childhood friend, and looking more closely she saw there were at least twenty old letters, mostly from friends in Denmark.

Sitting down on the living room sofa with the box on her lap, she took out the contents one by one and laid them out on the coffee table. A pipe in a leather case. When had her father smoked a pipe? Maybe when he was a young man and wanted to act the part, convinced that to be a real farmer you had to behave like one. Thick leather straps which he had used to protect his wrists when he was pumping iron, tattered and softened from rubbing against sweaty skin. A Parker pen. Pills for his heart.

What had her mother been thinking? What was Lóa meant to do with her dead father's pills? They hadn't helped him much. They had conceivably extended his life by a few months, but surely she hadn't been expecting Lóa to take them. No, her mother clearly hadn't been herself when she filled the box. She hadn't been able to face throwing anything away, but hadn't wanted any of it around either, so she'd passed it all on to Lóa instead.

A large, heavy Hasselblad camera which he had promised Lóa thirty years ago that she would inherit. A half-full pot of Vaseline. Her father had been a devotee of Vaseline: Vaseline on a cow's painful udders; Vaseline on dry lips; Vaseline to soften leather; Vaseline for sunburn, eczema, dandruff and corns.

There was also a silver hip flask engraved with the name *Muggur.* And then all the letters, which she would read one day and perhaps discover something unexpected about the man her father had been. Perhaps he had had a wilder side which he never revealed within the four walls of their home. And maybe he had enjoyed a rare type of humour which he only shared in his letters to his friends, or when they were out drinking. She longed to be wrong in thinking that her father had been devoid of a sense of humour.

Putting his things tidily back into the box, she returned it to the store cupboard and continued her search for something, though she didn't know what.

In the kitchen, under a big pile of cloths and tea-towels in a drawer, she found a little, lilac-coloured plastic horse with a beautiful, thick mane. It was clearly Ína's, but it was strange that she should have taken such trouble to hide it. Lóa hoped she hadn't stolen it. And in the gap between the fridge and the shelf above, lying in the dust, she found a gold ring with tiny diamonds, which she thought she'd lost on a picnic many years ago.

Lóa had been over everything in both rooms and was

rummaging round in the entrance hall when Sveinn emerged with a wounded expression on his face, as if she had done something unspeakably awful to him. Maybe he had been aware of her in the bed next to him earlier in the morning and was feeling totally indignant.

'Did you sleep well?' she asked, and his only answer was a snort as he stormed past her into the bathroom.

She tried to ignore his rudeness and went straight into Margrét's bedroom to look under the mattress.

By midday she had managed to summon up a smidgen of empathy and hospitality. She asked him how he was feeling and gave him something to take the edge off his pain.

He gave himself a good while to think about whether to accept this harmless olive branch, staring hard at Lóa as he gulped the tablets down. She thought he was rather aggressive and his manner rather strange, but it was better to keep an eye on him here and hear what he said on the phone than to imagine what trouble he might get her into in town because of that blasted doll. While he was here with her, there was the chance that she might manage to negotiate some kind of agreement.

'Don't you find it a bit odd having me hanging around here?' he asked.

'I should consider myself lucky that you're not raising hell, given how I behaved at your house,' she replied, smiling flatly.

'Well, that's true,' he said drily. 'You certainly haven't shown me the best side of your nature.'

There it was. He didn't think it enough that she should ask for forgiveness, no, he wanted to see grovelling remorse. But she was pleased that at least he assumed she did have a better side.

'You didn't need to invite me into your home,' she said. 'You weren't under any obligation to help me change the tyre, but you did it anyway. And in return I behaved like a spoilt brat. But I've been under a lot of pressure recently and, whether you believe it or not, I did intend to return the doll.'

She was silent for a moment before adding, 'Is there really any need to get the police involved in this? I'm willing to pay in full for the doll and to compensate you for your trouble and the unpleasantness this has caused.'

'Some unpleasantness simply cannot be measured in monetary terms,' he replied, and although he laughed coldly he was clearly deadly serious. 'I have no wish to get the police involved in this. But if you keep on harassing me then I don't know what else I can do, to be honest with you.'

'I understand,' said Lóa, even though she couldn't begin to understand why he had taken it so personally or why he would dream of calling this little moral hiccup of hers harassment.

'I don't know what you think you stand to gain by this,' he said.

Gain had been the last thing on her mind that morning, which was already hazy in her memory, but Sveinn had a habit of expressing himself oddly. Perhaps he had some kind of dyspraxia or a mild form of Tourettes.

Now he was all smiles, and extended his hand to her in an amiable fashion.

She shook the proffered hand. 'Thank you for being so understanding,' she said.

'My condolences on the death of your father,' he responded.

She looked at him quizzically, trying to fathom the train of thought which had led him from the theft of the doll to the death of her father. 'Thank you,' she said eventually. Then she went into the kitchen with the phone and a large recent photo of Margrét which she had printed out.

The sun shone straight in through the kitchen window and showed up every speck of dust and every grubby fingermark on the units. The window rattled on the latch and Lóa closed it, before sitting down with her back to the sun and studying the picture, which had been taken on Ína's birthday the year before. It showed Margrét in mid-air, trying to turn away from the camera. She'd come running into the room, but when she saw the lens pointing at her she'd tried to stop in mid-stride. She looked like a cat twisting itself around in the air so it could land on all fours. To be more exact, like a scrawny alley-cat, with lifeless hair and protruding bones.

Lóa dialled the number for the police station and was asked to hold the line. It seemed like ages before she was put through to the duty sergeant. Speaking fast, he introduced himself as Tómas, and from his voice she felt he sounded more like a delivery boy than a sergeant.

'You'll need to come and file a missing persons report and bring a recent full-face picture,' he said.

'I can't actually leave the house,' said Lóa. 'I was rather hoping you might send someone round. And I can email you the photo.'

The line went quiet and Lóa could hear quick, rhythmical tapping sounds in the background. She imagined him keeping time with his pulse or continually twanging the elastic on his underpants. Her suspicion knew no bounds.

'Well, we can do it this way,' he said eventually. 'I'll ask you some questions now, you send us a photo as soon as you can and ring back if anything comes to light, or if you remember anything else.'

Lóa had no alternative but to accept, since she had no clear idea of how she wanted to deal with this.

Tómas then began firing questions about Margrét: height, weight, eye colour, hair colour, where she'd last been seen and what she'd been wearing.

'Has she been getting drunk? Does she mix with older kids? Has she recently got in with a new crowd? Is she in a relationship with someone? Are there any problems at home?'

While Lóa talked he took down everything she said – she could hear his fingers flying over the keyboard.

'Have we got this right? Do you want to add anything?' he asked, when he'd read out what he'd written.

'I'm not sure what I could add,' she responded, the sweat beginning to trickle down her sun-baked back. 'Other than what I told the woman in reception yesterday – that my daughter urgently needs medical attention. Oh, and yes, I've got her mobile. I assume you need it for your investigation?'

The line went quiet once more and Lóa sensed that he thought the word *investigation* was too formal under the circumstances. She was filled with a desperate fear that her report would be left lying around somewhere, just to provide the illusion that the matter was being dealt with.

'OK, send it over to us,' he said. 'Does she have a computer? Bring that as well. If she doesn't turn up today or tomorrow we'll put out a public announcement. But these kids always turn up.'

Lóa gave a short laugh.

'We'll ring if we hear anything. Goodbye, dear.'

'OK, goodbye, *dear*,' said Lóa, with sarcastic emphasis on the last word. She disliked being called *dear* by strangers.

Once she'd emailed the photo, she switched on the kettle,

arranged the thermal coffee jug, filter and filter paper, and while she was waiting for the kettle to boil she weighed up whether it would be all right to ask Sveinn to drive to the police station with the laptop and mobile. She thought that he would either refuse point-blank or carry the task out conscientiously.

On the other hand, he was hardly presentable as her messenger – unshaven as he was and generally in bad shape. And who knew, he might suddenly get the notion to file a charge against her, if he was there anyway.

No, it would be better to wait for Björg or send them by taxi.

She spooned coffee into the filter paper, poured boiling water up to the rim, and watching the soft froth spread out, she breathed in the rich aroma as she listened for the first drops to drip into the coffee jug.

For a few seconds, her taut nerves relaxed. For a brief moment, she was able to forget herself and her surroundings as she stared unconsciously at the dark surface of the liquid gradually sinking down the filter.

When the doorbell rang she was so startled that she spun around, knocking her hand into the coffee jug, which fell with a crash, spilling the coffee grounds and newly filtered coffee all over the floor. Lóa rushed out, her socks and trouser legs spattered with coffee. She tore down the stairs and, opening the door, stood blinking at a young fair-haired man she vaguely recognized but couldn't place. Though he looked so ordinary that she could easily be confusing him with someone else.

Different possibilities kaleidoscoped across her brain at the speed of light. Was this Nexusboy? A plain-clothes police officer? A friend or acquaintance of Margrét's with a message from her?

'Lóa?' he asked. His voice was thin, like a child's, and when he shifted uneasily his black leather pilot's jacket creaked.

She nodded.

'Is Sveinn here? I've got something for him,' he said.

Her lungs deflated like a balloon. 'Come in,' she said, unable to hide her disappointment, and he followed her up the stairs.

'You've got a visitor,' she called.

Sveinn came towards her, wide-eyed, and his amazement didn't seem to diminish when he saw who it was.

'Lárus?' he said.

'You asked me to get hold of some painkillers and I had nothing better to do,' said the lad. He was so humble it was verging on the obsequious, though he tried unsuccessfully to appear laid back.

Lóa was horrified at the thought that Sveinn was such a hero and role model for young men that they couldn't address him without being crippled with embarrassment. Did they think so much of the fact that he was a puppet master of the female body? That he produced his own pussies? Was he some kind of porn king in their minds?

She'd never been particularly sensitive about such issues, but now she suddenly saw red. All her anger towards the world channelled into a vehement disgust for the two men standing opposite each other in her hallway.

She leant against the chest of drawers, the anger boiling inside her.

'I didn't mean it literally,' she heard Sveinn say. 'I know you need a prescription for this. How did you get hold of it?'

'It wasn't a problem. I just went to A & E and said I had

dreadful toothache and couldn't get an appointment for a week,' replied the lad. 'Which isn't entirely true. But the end justifies the means, doesn't it. Ha, ha, ha!' he added. His anticipation seemed to increase as Sveinn's frown deepened.

'Certainly,' said Sveinn, 'and it was kind of you to think of me. But I find it hard to understand why a young man like you has nothing better to do than run around after me.'

They glanced at Lóa simultaneously, as if they were both thinking the same thing. Curiosity glittered like a sparkling crystal in the lad's eyes and all at once she thought she knew the real purpose of his visit: what else could he want here than to take a look at her? The woman who appeared boringly normal and middle class, yet turned out to be a thieving habitual drinker. Sveinn's friends and neighbours must be having a good laugh about his adventures in the big city. Some of them clearly couldn't wait until he made it home with the damn doll and tales of his travels.

'Would you like to sit down?' she asked, totally contrary to what was going on in her mind, pointing in the direction of the dining room. Oh, how she despised that inner voice which compelled her to *make a good impression* even while the world was crashing down around her.

Sveinn gave her a dark look, which she pretended not to see.

'Well, no, I ought to be getting on ...' said the lad, but he evidently wanted someone to talk him out of it.

Lóa nodded.

'Then again, maybe I'll just have one cup, if that's not too much trouble,' he added, looking timorously at Sveinn.

The laughter which welled up unexpectedly inside Lóa alarmed her. She invited them into the kitchen, where she threw up her hands in despair, as if she was blessing the coffee spattered over the floor, or as if she wanted to flatly deny the uncharacteristic lack of self-control which was fast taking hold of her thoughts and behaviour.

'As you can see, I was just about to pour out,' she said, and her voice sounded as unfamiliar as the laughter.

Sveinn looked as if he had no idea what was expected of him, and the lad laughed politely, before staring intently at the photo of Margrét lying on the kitchen table.

'Go and sit in the dining room,' said Lóa. 'You can have instant as soon as I've finished mopping the floor and boiling the kettle.'

She didn't understand what it was in her that made her want everything to appear normal when everyone around her knew that was far from true.


'How do you two know each other?' she asked, when she had put down the tray with three coffee mugs, a milk jug and a dish of cinnamon buns.

'We met at a birthday party,' said Sveinn glumly.

She looked enquiringly at the lad, but he didn't seem to have the courage to add anything to that terse explanation.

'Have you lived here long?' he asked, looking around with artistic interest.

Lóa nodded, tight-lipped. She'd got stomach pains from no more than a taste of the coffee.

'It's pure genius. I mean, to open up the attic and make the most of the sloping sides,' said the lad. 'I helped my uncle on a similar project once. We had to rip out rotten beams, replace them with new ones and reinsulate the whole loft. This isn't exactly first-class workmanship. You must let me know if you'd like me to help you with anything.'

He seemed sincere and there was no doubt he thought he owed the world something or simply longed to be of use to someone.

'You don't say,' said Lóa, getting to her feet, the pain like a cold blade in her stomach. She went and poured the coffee down the sink, found a large, brown envelope in the cupboard and put Margrét's mobile in it, then fetched her laptop from her bedroom and placed them both on the table in front of the lad.

'What was your name again?' she asked.

'Lárus.'

'Lárus, will you take these to the police station at Hlemmur?' she asked. 'The duty sergeant is called Tómas and he's expecting them. Don't hand them over to anyone else. Will you do that for me?'

The lad looked so excited. He ran his fingers over the envelope containing the phone and glanced hesitantly at Sveinn, who nodded his head in agreement.

Gulping down his burning-hot coffee, Lárus stood up, rather flushed. He looked round the room, as if memorizing its layout and contents; when he spotted the doll on the sofa he couldn't take his eyes off it.

Sveinn hooted with laughter and bit into his cinnamon bun. 'Go and have a look,' he said. 'There's no rush. The police won't bust a gut over a youngster who's been missing for less than twenty-four hours.'

Lóa knew he was right, but in her frenzied state she'd come to believe that Sveinn was *responsible*, almost in a metaphysical sense. He had no right to talk so lightly about Margrét. It would be better if he *did* something.

'What youngster?' asked Lárus.

'I'll tell you later,' said Sveinn.

Lárus hesitated a moment before going out into the entrance hall, where they heard his jacket creak as he struggled into it. He reappeared in the doorway to say, 'Just let me know if you need anything.'

# 15

About two hours had passed since Lárus rang to say he'd done the job. Sveinn killed time playing patience and Lóa shut herself in her bedroom with the phone. The muffled sound of her voice reminded him slightly of whale song, which went well with the cards with their pictures of trawlers.

The Queen of Hearts resembled Lóa, and her friend Björg was the Queen of Spades. The other two queens were total strangers, but in his head Sveinn christened them Móa and Örg.

A searing anxiety shot through him when the phone rang; he must remember to change his ringtone as soon as he was sure these threatening calls had stopped.

'I thought you were my friend, but it turns out you're a wolf in lamb's clothing,' said Kjartan, sounding out of breath from running.

Sveinn chuckled. 'What do you mean?' he asked. 'What have I done?'

'Only lied to your friends about staying at home, and then set off alone on a perilous journey without so much as a word about how it's all going. Do you think that's what I deserve? Me, who's supported you through thick and thin all these years. Then I get word that you're in the enemy's lair – and then what? Did you manage to overpower her? Has she confessed and shown remorse?'

'In a way,' said Sveinn. 'At least she's not threatened me with a sticky end since early this morning.'

Kjartan burst out laughing. His coarse, loud laughter sounded as if it would scar his throat. 'You're a riot,' he said, when he was finally able to speak. 'You set off yesterday, didn't you? And what are you up to there now? Sniffing around her tail, I'll bet. Even though I advised you to steer clear.'

Then he burst into song, and Sveinn couldn't help admiring how musical he was – he had a beautiful quality to his voice.

> *Wee Lóa from Brú,*
> *She's as pretty as a wren.*
> *With her lovely blue eyes,*
> *She attracts the men . . .'*

'You never listen to me, my old friend,' he added, when the song was finished.

'Do you think I should listen to you?' said Sveinn. 'Would you listen to someone like you?'

'I certainly would if there was no-one better around.'

'You don't say,' said Sveinn, and they carried on bantering about nothing until it dawned on Sveinn that Kjartan's only reason for calling was to extract some juicy bit of information to gossip about.

'Well then,' said Sveinn. 'I'm sorry, but I have to go now and part the thief from her doll. They're at each other's throats like two drunken tarts the minute I lower my guard.'

Kjartan let out a strange sound which was meant to convey satisfaction. Sveinn's imagery had of course hit the mark. Some years before Kjartan hadn't stopped going on about a competition at some club, involving women wrestling in a trough full of chocolate Angel Delight.

Sveinn had barely put the phone down when it rang again. It was his mother, the rehab volunteer.

'Hello, Svenni dear. How are you doing?' she asked.

'Not too bad,' he replied.

'I was thinking of dropping by. Are you at home?'

'No, and you ought to stay indoors. There's a storm warning.'

'You're not at home? Where are you then?' she asked, sounding genuinely surprised that he should be anywhere else. How bad can things get, when your mother reckons she can be sure of your whereabouts? What did that say about his social life, let alone his love life?

'I'm visiting this woman, a friend,' he said.

'I seeee,' said his mother, doubtless imagining a potential, permanently-pregnant daughter-in-law who she could exchange recipes and plant cuttings with.

Sveinn contemplated the withered pot plants all around him and thought that his life was even sadder and more impoverished than his mother imagined.

'I'll catch up with you at the weekend,' he said.

'All right then, dear,' she replied.

He returned to his game of patience and managed to move a few trawlers before the phone rang for the third time.

The screen showed *Unknown*.

'Yes,' he answered, his heart in his mouth.

A woman's soft voice spoke his name, 'Sveinn Guðmundsson?'

'Yes?'

'My name's Ásdís and I'm from *House and Home* magazine . . .'

'Don't waste your energy trying to sell me something,' he said.

'I'm not trying to sell you anything . . .'

'Really?'

'. . . that you don't want,' she said.

He admired her determination, but put the phone down on her anyway. She only had herself to blame if she chose to bother strangers for a living.

The game of patience ended in deadlock. Sveinn reckoned that it would work out roughly once every three games. In any case, he doubted there was a more stupid activity.

He collected up the cards and watched the wind angrily whip the trees, stripping them of the remnants of the previous year's leaves and tossing them way out to sea.

The pile of science magazines was still there, so he took some into the bedroom with him. Folding the duvet up against the headboard, he leant against it carefully, so as not to upset the hornets' nest in his shoulder, downed two Tramadols and opened one of the magazines at random. The article was entitled 'The Power of the Mirror', and before he fell asleep he learned that the Japanese had started to line the sides of railway platforms with mirrors, in the hope that it will put people off throwing themselves under a train. The theory was that people would find it more difficult to do away with themselves if their own bodies were reflected back at them in all their fragile vitality, that people would be less likely to end their lives whilst looking themselves in the eye.

Sveinn woke feeling parched. There was an uneasy throbbing in his head, which seemed to stem from his knee, and surliness gnawed at his innards. It was getting dark, which meant that it must be getting on for ten in the evening.

He would have given an arm and a leg to be back at home. But he didn't feel up to the journey. Maybe he should take some more Tramadol and doze until the morning? No, he had left the bottle in the living room, and besides, he wouldn't keep them down on an empty stomach.

His lower back protested loudly when he got up. Wonderful. Was any part of his body in good working order?

Easing his back with his good hand, he hobbled out of the bedroom, and the first thing he saw was Lóa putting his phone down. She was barefoot, wearing a turquoise, knee-length woollen dress with sleeves down to her knuckles, her hair was soaking wet and her face had a frightened expression, which awoke a dormant ghost from his past. This sight, this event, this *moment*, reminded Sveinn of something he didn't care to remember. Indeed, he only remembered it as a sensation – like a horror film which leaves no conscious trace but a feeling of emotional exhaustion and an image you can't quite place.

His gruff voice rumbled right up from his stomach, 'What do you think you're doing?'

Why was she so frightened? Did he look the dangerous type? Or was her conscience beginning to get to her?

'The phone had rung a few times and in the end I answered,' she said in a shaky voice.

'And in the end you answered,' he repeated with exaggerated emphasis, and immediately realized he sounded as if he was hiding some dirty secret. He, who had nothing to hide except his darkest thoughts, and they definitely couldn't be seen on his mobile.

'Forgive me,' he said. 'But you can understand that I have difficulty trusting you, can't you?'

'I don't know,' she said, and now he finally caught a glimpse of what he had known all along: that she was mentally disturbed, on the verge of a breakdown. Her expression looked as if she was in free fall, like she had just lost her footing and fallen over the precipice.

'You have to go now. I want you to leave,' she said.

There was no way he was going to be ordered around like that; he didn't appreciate being spoken to like he was a dog with muddy paws.

'All right then,' he said. 'But before I go, I need to eat something so I can take my painkillers, so that I can focus on driving. Do you understand?'

'No,' she said. 'No. Get out of here and take that disgusting thing with you.'

She pointed at the doll lying innocently on the sofa.

'That disgusting thing is only here because you dragged it here without asking permission,' he retorted, his voice raised.

'Forgive me! Forgive me! Forgive me!' she cried. 'How many times do I have to say it? What do you want me to do? Go down on my knees? Crawl over broken glass? I've offered to pay compensation and you make out you've not heard me. No, you like getting on your high horse and lecturing me on morality, as if you were an expert in that field!'

'Now, you listen here, my friend . . .'

'I'm no bloody friend of yours!'

'I can fully understand that this is difficult for you, but it's not my fault your dad is no longer alive,' said Sveinn, nevertheless trying not to sound guilty about it.

'Stop going on about Dad. You didn't even know him!' she screamed.

'You raised the subject,' he said, trying to give a sarcastic smirk. But the truth was, he no longer felt blameless. Lóa was so convincing in her righteous anger that he was beginning to feel like the guilty party. As if he was the big bad wolf who'd just huffed and puffed and blown everything apart.

'Look here,' he said. 'I'm not prepared to go just yet. I mean, I don't want to be here a moment longer than I have to, but I need to wake up properly, have some food and take my pills before I can start driving. And we should discuss your little activities. How can I be sure you won't harass me in future?'

Lóa threw back her head and guffawed in a way that Sveinn found sinister, and his antipathy returned. She sat down and put her hands over her eyes. Her dress rode up over her bare knees and moisture glistened between her damp toes.

'I've no doubt you have your eager admirers, but I'm not one of them,' she said, and not only was her voice raised, it was so shrill that Sveinn's eardrums hurt. 'I didn't take the doll because I thought it was a priceless work of art.'

Sveinn didn't like to give himself away by saying what came immediately to mind: that although *Raven-Black Lola* was not a priceless work of art, she was still the best doll he had produced so far, and in the eyes of many Sveinn was the most talented in his sphere. Which meant that *Raven-Black Lola* was probably the best of her type in the world and *mirror, mirror on the wall* . . .

'No, it's not a priceless work of art,' he said, 'but it is very valuable and I must honour the commitments I've made.'

'Very valuable,' parroted Lóa. 'Valuable,' she repeated with that same sinister laugh.

What did she mean? Was he not allowed to mention the doll's value because her daughter was missing? As if the two were in some way comparable.

This wasn't the first time he'd noticed that women found it more difficult than men to differentiate between a woman and a doll. His customers were constantly comparing the dolls with real live women, invariably to the advantage of the doll, but then life had been hard on them and they were hurting from constant rebuffs. Still, in their minds women and dolls were totally different.

Yet women were exceptionally sensitive to such comparisons. As if they just didn't see that it was like comparing chalk and cheese rather than peaches and nectarines.

'I'm not the one you're after,' he said. 'I ended up doing this by accident. I was messing around putting a price tag on the female form and realized that I could make a living from it – even though they're expensive and the body is made out of plastic. That's why I own an expensive 4x4 and a house and have more than a few grand in the bank. You must know what I'm saying? At any rate, it looks to me like you've done rather well for yourself.' He looked around pointedly.

He didn't know why he said what he said next. It wasn't pure villainy. He was hungry, which in his case meant in a foul mood. The pain dulled his judgement and supressed his sympathy. And Sveinn saw red when he was ordered around like a dog. Besides, Lóa had provoked him enough over the past few days that he didn't feel he owed her anything.

'Was it a hefty divorce settlement then?' he said. 'Is the girls' daddy some fat-cat tycoon?'

Lóa blinked rapidly, as if someone had knocked her legs from under her. Sveinn was already feeling ashamed of himself, but his shame wasn't sufficient to stop him from digging himself in deeper.

*Wee Lóa from Brú, she's as pretty as a wren,* he carolled.

*And tumpty da dumm, ta tumpty da dumm.*
*And slowly their story, is just like the others,*
*They make their children a home in Reykjavík.*
*He works like a doggie, he's rarely at home,*
*As pretty wee Lóa, loves a shopping spree.*

Her face crumpled, and he thought she was going to burst into tears. He could only assume he'd really hit the nail on the head. He hadn't noticed her getting up for work, that was for sure.

Lóa had begun to breathe abnormally fast, and she let out a suppressed whimpering noise.

His conscience – or fear – cut him to the quick, and for a moment he felt as if his hands were bloodied from some brutal atrocity. What was wrong with a mother of two being supported financially by the children's father? Who was he to reproach her as though it was something to be awfully ashamed of? What was he thinking, anyway, having a go at someone who was clearly a whisker away from losing her mind?

'I'm sorry, I –' he began. But her scream silenced him – a scream which sounded like a bitter, viscous concentrate made up of thousands of years of deep-felt hatred – and she pulled her dress up onto her chest. Her humanity seemed to have fled in the face of her enormous rage and all that was left was the animal in her, caged in a human body. Sveinn hadn't felt so frightened since a dog attacked him when he was twelve years old and bit him on the thigh. The scar was still there: white-and-red and raised.

He gave a hoot of laughter, as he always did when he was very scared, as he'd done when the dog came charging towards him with a cruel glint in its eye and its teeth bared.

Either his hearing was distorted by fear or Lóa's voice had dramatically changed. 'You care bugger all for those around you, don't you?' she yelled. 'Who the hell are you, anyway? What kind of life is it you lead surrounded by nothing but bits of plastic?'

'I don't know exactly . . .' he began.

'You know exactly what I mean!' she screamed, so that he was almost deafened. Then she ripped off her knickers with a vehemence which was like oil on the flames of the turmoil in his head, and lifting up the hem of her dress, she exposed her breasts and genitals.

'N–no,' he said, his hands fumbling wildly in the air. Lóa could say whatever was on her mind. He could take it. He was strong enough to be a punchbag for a desperate woman. But why couldn't she show just a bit of dignity? Why did she have to humiliate herself like this?

'What am I to you?' she cried, in a hoarse and rasping voice. 'Am I a B cup with a hairy bush? Not quite past my sell-by date even though my boobs have begun to sag?'

Her underwear lay on the floor like a bird's skin, like the skin of the dove of peace: white knickers trimmed with a creamy yellow lace. Touchingly lifeless, as if they'd been deprived of something. And now Lóa was on all fours, her dress still with the wrong side facing out, the turquoise dress which hid her face and hair but nothing else. Her hands and shins were pressing on the dusty floor, her bare behind sticking up into the air, her breasts quivering. The fact that her face was hidden in the folds of her dress made it all the more poignant.

'Shall we just shag like dogs, then call it a day and you piss off home?' she howled.

The indignity, her posture and her piercing voice penetrated

Sveinn to the core. It wounded his perception of female beauty, his sense of what was refined and civilized. He couldn't remember ever having witnessed this kind of emotional pain, and in that instant he recognized how deeply shocked he felt.

'Just screw me and you can cough up before you go,' said Lóa. 'No, what am I thinking? It's me who owes you! You can have the fuck for what I owe you, then we're all happy, right?'

Her voice cracked in mid-sentence and became choked with sobs which sliced the words apart: *theh-en we-'re a-all ha-appy, ri-hight?*

She crawled away sobbing and yelped when she caught her knee hard on the threshold of the living room.

Sveinn rested his eyes and calmed his mind by gazing at *Raven-Black Lola* and what little he could see of the floor and the walls in the entrance hall. If he squinted he could make out a narrow strip of the front door.

Then he bit the bullet and followed Lóa, along the hallway and into the bedroom where he had slept earlier in the day. She was lying face down on the single bed, her back still heaving with sobs. He covered her with the duvet – carefully, as if he feared she might bite if he made any sudden movements.

He eased the dress from under her leaden head, and as he was supporting her neck and shoulders with his arm he felt her skin burning to the touch.

He flung the dress over onto the chest of drawers under the window.

'Shall I phone for a doctor?' he asked.

'No,' she moaned.

'Shall I go?'

She didn't reply but turned her head so he could see her face.

He sat down in the armchair by the bed and watched her cry: her cheeks and temples streaked with black mascara, the whites of her eyes reddened and her hair like a damp veil over her face.

# 16

*Tuesday Evening*

For a long time, Lóa had felt that her life was sadly insignificant. But what do people consider significant? Politics? Money? If her life wasn't significant whose was?

She didn't know exactly what *a significant life* entailed, but she sensed more than ever before that her existence didn't come into that category – especially now it seemed she wasn't equal to the task of providing for her family, or even of being a mother.

She'd never actually felt guilty about what she did for a living until then. If she'd longed for a noble vocation she wouldn't have been able to focus on putting food on the table and bringing up the children, and only in that respect could it be said that she was invaluable. There was nothing noble or worthwhile about conning people into constantly desiring more luxury items they don't need, and although her bosses hadn't wanted her to take unpaid leave, everyone knows that no-one is indispensable in that line of work.

She knew that her longing for a sense of purpose was nothing more than a pretension, permitted by the assurance of a full stomach today, tomorrow and for the foreseeable future. That was why she'd never been able to take these thoughts too seriously, and now she longed for her old life: going to work in the mornings – where she would try to think laterally – doing the shopping on the way home, making dinner, helping Ína with her homework, doing the laundry, watching TV and feeling slightly guilty.

It was still light outside, but the day was drawing to a close and the light was turning an ochre-yellow. Björg had looked in and left a hip flask of cognac, which was now half empty and the last couple of hours had been wasted on countless phone calls which had amounted to nothing, most of them to the police in Reykjavík. Every officer who'd picked up the phone had known about her case, and she wasn't sure whether she should be pleased or worried that at last she was being taken seriously.

She sat on the end of the bed, a tormented shadow of her former self, staring at the untidy mess through the open wardrobe door, when she heard a muffled ringtone. The phone lay half-buried in the duvet next to her. It was her mother on the line.

'Yes?' Lóa answered.

'Your line's permanently engaged, Lóa dear.'

'Yes.'

'No news of her then?'

'No, Mum. I promised I'd let you know, remember?'

'Lóa dear,' said her mother. 'Ína is at her dad's. I rang him like you asked and he insisted on fetching her at once.'

Lóa felt a chill within, without fully knowing why. Ína was best off with her dad until Margrét was found. The little mite took everything that was going on around her so much to heart.

'Why didn't you let him know straightaway, yesterday,' her mother continued. 'You mustn't always think the worst of him. I promised you'd be in touch when you had a moment's peace and quiet, and he accepted that in the end. Give him a call, my love. You two need to support one another.'

'I know,' replied Lóa. 'Of course. I'll ring him after this.'

'Good for you, dear,' said her mother, and in the silence that followed Lóa sensed some incomprehensible embarrassment.

'I've been meaning to ask you ... How are things between you financially?'

'Don't worry about that, Mum. I can get an overdraft until I go back to work.'

'Are you sure the job will be held open for you?' asked her mother, unable to conceal her anxiety. She clearly found it hard to believe that Lóa's bosses were so understanding.

'I don't know why you're worrying about this now, but yes, the job's being kept open for me,' responded Lóa.

'Can't Hjálmar help out until then? He is their father after all.'

'By giving me money? It was my decision to take a leave of absence. He's running a large household and doesn't have much more income than I do. Don't be so old fashioned, Mum, for heaven's sake, and what the hell does it matter right now anyway?'

Lóa knew it was just one of her mother's coping mechanisms: to whip up a sandstorm of minor details to block out the real threat which was looming. But right now, Lóa didn't have the patience for such games.

'I just don't want you to be worrying about money on top of everything else,' said her mother. 'And there are two of them, whereas you're on your own ...'

Lóa was seething. Sometimes she hated her mother more than all the evil in the world put together. 'I've got enough money,' she said. 'So just stop creating problems when I've got enough to deal with already.'

There was a short silence and then her mother said, 'Did you sort everything out together, you and your friend, what's his name again?'

'Sveinn,' replied Lóa. 'And there was nothing to sort out. I'll be in touch later or in the morning,' she added, before her mother could summon up the courage to ask about the doll.

She forced herself to call the girls' father, even though he was the last man on earth she wanted to talk to right then. She could hear a deafening racket going on in the background, and he sounded out of breath, as if he'd been running. 'What happened?' he asked. 'Why didn't you let me know? What were you thinking?'

'Nothing happened,' she replied. 'She just disappeared. I don't know whether she'd planned to run away or not. Where are you anyway?'

'At A & E. Ína needed stitches. She'd hardly walked through the door before she changed into her nightie, which was far too big for her, and started running round the house, tripped on the hem and headbutted a radiator. Where did she get that nightie from, anyway? Are you into high fashion these days?'

'No,' said Lóa. 'How is she? Should I talk to her?'

'The doctor gave her a prize – a dark-brown horse in four bits which she can put together. Don't worry about it. Has there been no word from Margrét since Monday? Have you spoken to her friends?'

'What do you think?' asked Lóa.

'All right,' he replied. 'I'll contact the police and the school and you let me know as soon as you hear anything, OK?'

'Yes, of course,' said Lóa. 'And I'm sorry I didn't ring you earlier. I was just hoping that she would turn up that evening or at least by night-time. I was hoping that she'd finally decided to behave like a normal teenager. And besides, I feel guilty.' Her voice cracked as she held back the tears. 'I feel guilty for not keeping a proper eye on her and I feel guilty about the state she's in. I must have made some terrible mistakes and I'm scared it's too late to make up for that now.'

The other end of the line was totally silent and Lóa had to summon every ounce of strength not to lose what little control she still had. 'Are you there?' she asked.

'Yes,' he replied.

As she was drying herself after her bath, putting on clean clothes and applying some eye make-up, Lóa could hear Sveinn's phone ringing constantly. The sound reminded her of the phone at her parents' house before the old man invested in a cordless wonder with a disco ringtone.

Amazing how Sveinn could sleep thought it, and not be disturbed by that awful ringtone.

She thought about waking him, but decided to put the phone on silent instead. But when it was in her hands it was as if something took over; her mind was taken up with Margrét – her face, her body, her voice – and Lóa was hardly in control of herself when she pressed her burning fingertip to the button and allowed this tenacious caller into her house on Framnesvegur.

'*Damn you. I'm going to fill a glass bottle with horse shit and stuff it up your arse until it breaks,*' said a cold, harsh, synthesized voice. '*Death is too good for you. Your insides deserve to roast in eternal agony, you scumbag. When I hack off your fingers one by one maybe you'll realize you aren't God. When I flay you alive with a lash maybe you'll regret using your precious life for evil.*'

Lóa jerked the phone away from her ear. She was standing frozen to the spot, her stomach churning, the phone still in her hands when Sveinn came out of Margrét's bedroom, scowling like a direct continuation of the threats.

'What are you doing?' he asked.

Her brain froze still further.

'I'm sorry,' he said. 'But you can understand that I find it rather hard to trust you, can't you?'

'I don't know,' she heard herself say, and knew immediately that it was true. She found it hard to understand all this suspicion. But now she realized that she couldn't have Sveinn with all his animosity and his abusive enemies under her roof any longer.

'You have to go now,' she said. 'The road is open to traffic again.'

'I have no desire to remain in your company any longer than I have to,' he said, and the suppressed tension in this voice amplified Lóa's fear. 'But I can't leave until I've had something to eat. I'll black out before I get halfway to the car. Do you understand?'

'No,' she said. 'No. Just get out.'

'What's got into you?' he asked.

'I'm just trying to make you understand that I want you to take your phone and your bimbo and get out of here. I'll say it again – I'm sorry for taking the doll – but now I want to be rid of it. You'll have to make up your own mind whether you believe that I didn't take it because I thought it was a priceless work of art and I couldn't imagine life without it.'

'I know it's not a priceless work of art,' said Sveinn, 'but it's worth a lot.'

Lóa was at the end of her tether. No-one knew whether Margrét was alive or dead and Sveinn was standing there like a buffoon, waxing lyrical over a ridiculous bit of plastic which did nothing but create arguments and abnormal behaviour.

'Yes,' he said, 'it's worth seven hundred thousand krónur.'

His hand waved in the air as if he was losing control and spittle sprayed from his mouth.

'I'm fed up with the priggish attitude you lot have to my work,' he said.

'What do you mean, you lot?'

'You women,' he replied in such a strident voice that Lóa's head hurt. 'I'm fed up with your stupid jealousy. Your average bloke is ashamed of having sex with a doll, let alone keeping one at home, like a mummy's boy who can't go to sleep without his teddy. It's not macho to have it off with lifeless conquests. There's no excitement in it. So you don't have to worry that one day no man will look twice at a living, breathing woman because we've all got a *Raven-Black Lola* sharing our bed. At least you can stop giving me such a hard time. I produce the dolls, not the demand for them. It's intimidating women like you who create the demand by driving easily scared wimps into my shop. But I'm not so easily scared, I'll have you know.'

The fury erupted in Lóa creating a wound deep in her bowels. That he should have the gall to write off the torment she was going through in this way! He obviously wasn't right in the head, judging by the frequency with which he made random comments, and Lóa's desperate need for a logical context in which to make sense of everything now exploded with a vengeance.

'I couldn't give a toss about your stupid doll. I just want you out of my sight,' she screamed. 'And I don't understand why you put so much time and effort into something you're ashamed of!'

'No particular reason – I ended up doing this by coincidence. If you could only see that life is made up of a string of coincidences, then maybe you wouldn't be so controlling and full of spite. Try to go with the flow. Try to chill out.'

'Chill out? Like her, you mean?' said Lóa, pointing at the doll, which was lying prostrate on the sofa, her eyes staring through the roof and out into space in lifeless ecstasy. Her face was peaceful, as if in death. Her black hair, a stream rippling down the side of the sofa.

'Well, maybe not exactly like her,' he replied. 'But, yes, you could perhaps learn something from her, such as taking it easy.'

Lóa's overwrought muscles tensed in agitation which she tried to suppress, but that only added fuel to the fire, making her stomach churn. She was on the verge of throwing up.

'It's not my fault your dad killed himself,' said Sveinn.

'Just what kind of mental problems do you have?' she said. 'I can barely understand half of what you say. Your brain just doesn't make normal logical connections.'

'Oh, really?' he said.

'Yes, really,' she replied. 'Connections are the glue that builds thoughts into a chain so they're not just a random pile of rubbish. Do you see? This is the second time you've mentioned Dad completely out of the blue.'

'You raised the subject,' he said. 'Were you a bit of a daddy's girl? It doesn't take a psychologist to see that you're unnaturally obsessed with the old guy and particularly the fact he did away with himself in such style.'

She looked down at the hip flask and was surprised to see there was only a little left. She couldn't remember having drunk so much. She stared at the few remaining drops.

Sveinn continued talking, and then he began to sing, taunting Lóa mercilessly. His singing cut through the few threads that still tied her to a sense of reality, and the non-reality which had beckoned her before now took hold of her. Everything became shrouded in mist, and she no longer had control over her tormented body, which convulsed with sobs. She felt she couldn't catch her breath properly, although her chest was heaving so hard she must be taking in enough oxygen. She tried to breathe slowly but without success.

*With her lovely blue eyes, she attracts the men,* sang Sveinn.

> *And tumpty da dumm, ta tumpty da dumm.*
> *And slowly their story, is just like the others,*
> *They make their children a home in Reykjavík.*

Lóa tasted cognac-tainted bile in her mouth, and then was barely aware of what she was doing. From somewhere in the distance, she heard herself screeching, a rasping version of her own voice surrounding the abject victim within. Maybe she wasn't even speaking for herself but in the universal female voice, echoing bitterly across the ages, choked with suppressed pain and passive aggression.

It couldn't be described as speaking. She screamed, she sobbed and words spewed out of her which, in her frenzied state, she wasn't able to understand. And that was only the beginning: soon words weren't enough, and then her body took over in a grotesque fit of rage which could never have happened had she not lost all her self-awareness. Lóa was no longer Lóa. She was a nameless vent, a tiny drop of bile in the oesophagus of the universe. This experience could be called an anti-nirvana, because although it was followed by a kind of ecstasy and a merging with the infinite, it gave her no peace or feeling of wellbeing. It was a relief to kick over the traces, to permit herself to plunge into the mire, but it was also harrowing and harmful.

'You can have a fuck on account and then everyone's happy, aren't they?' she heard herself say, and that word, *fuck* – a word she never used – brought it cruelly home to her that she was no longer in control, and that she should crawl into her hole before she shamed herself still further. But perhaps it was already too late. Perhaps she had already relinquished her right to be counted as a civilized human being.

She cried out when she banged her knee on the threshold, and her hands were shaking as she pulled herself with difficulty up onto Margrét's bed. The world had become a merry-go-round, spinning out of control, and sickness overwhelmed Lóa until nothing else penetrated her swirling thoughts, which were like muddy water spiralling down a drain.

The doll-maker came into the room and murmured something.

She thought she might understand him if she looked at him while he spoke, but when she turned towards him all she could see was his hair gleaming with grease, his rough stubble, his plastered arm in a sling and his embarrassed manner – all of which made him seem even more distant and incomprehensible.

Why did he find her so unbearable? The thought crossed her mind that it might not only be her behaviour which aroused his antipathy but her very being: her memories, her thoughts and her body. Why did she long for acknowledgement and approval from someone who meant nothing to her?

'I can't go on,' she said.

He looked away quickly.

Her eyes were burning and she couldn't keep them open. And yet she was filled with dread at the thought of falling asleep. 'Don't go,' she said. 'Don't leave without waking me if I fall asleep. Answer the phone if it rings or the doorbell and wake me, whatever it is.'

She heard him walk out of the room and close the door behind him.

# PART THREE

PART EIGHT

## 17

*Tuesday Night*

It was going on for midnight when Sveinn dragged himself past the entrance hall and into the kitchen, where he soon discovered that there was precious little in the fridge.

It was an effort to keep steady. No matter how he tried, he shook all over, and he had a bitter taste in his mouth, his jaw felt stiff and his cheeks were burning hot.

At the very least, people should be able to determine what they do and don't want, he thought. But Lóa was behaving like an archetypal woman: I want to kill you – help me. Leave – stay with me.

He thought about grabbing a bite to eat, downing two painkillers and driving home, with or without *Raven-Black Lola*. Maybe he could phone Lárus and ask him to help get the doll out to the car.

No, that wasn't on. He couldn't leave Lóa in this state. She was probably a danger to herself and others. Wasn't it illegal to leave someone alone when they were not compos mentis?

How come he was suddenly responsible for this woman? Where were her mother, her family, her friends?

There was nothing for it – he would have to delay any decision, slip into the living room and fetch some more science magazines. He investigated the contents of the fridge more thoroughly. Yes, there was a jar stuffed full of marinated herring, strong mustard, some blue cheese and pineapple juice. Switching on the light, Sveinn began looking for some crackers or crispbread, when his eye caught some old photo albums on a shelf in amongst the cookery books. He picked one and found himself looking into the eyes of children with varying shades of blonde hair, all wearing dungarees and machine-knitted woollen jumpers. Children with lambs in their arms, leaning on rakes with handles twice as long as they were tall, or riding bareback around rusty-corrugated-iron barns and rickety fences. Children with milk moustaches, children in a bathtub and several camera-shy adults with stiff smiles and tensed shoulders. Men leaning in towards the camera as if they didn't quite believe it would reach that far. Women, invariably carrying some kind of food, or with their arms folded under their bosoms.

Pushing the magazines to one side, he piled the albums up next to his glass and the carton of juice. He speared three pieces of sweet herring onto his fork and, putting them into his mouth, he began to flick through the pages. Yes, that was definitely Lóa, maybe six years old, golden-white, wavy hair and serious eyes. An innocent little child, with a lop-sided smile and a distinctive dimple. Just as well she didn't know then what the future held in store for her when she grew up. And there was some bruiser with Lóa on his lap, probably her father. Hadn't she mentioned that he'd been the European Bench Press Champion? What incredible shoulders and arms, like a giant's thigh.

Was this Hans Sigurjónsson from Hlíð in Svarfaðardalur? How had he looked in the picture from the obituaries column? Grey-haired, broad-shouldered, not particularly remarkable. Definitely not as solid as in this picture. He'd probably shrunk with age. But there again . . . Lóa had said something about him pumping iron right up to his dying day.

Sveinn peered at the features and tried to see in them those of a potential suicide. But he couldn't. There was nothing to see there other than a picture of work-worn health and masculine simplicity.

They sat there, the bruiser and Lóa, on the bonnet of a dark-blue Mercedes Benz. Or rather, she was sitting and he was just leaning nonchalantly against the boot. She was slightly older, her hair was cut short and she had a little money pouch round her neck. In the background was a tree in leaf, a well-tended flower bed and her mother standing in the doorway: the same woman he'd met when he first got caught up in this, only she was twenty-five years younger and smiled considerably more.

He gave a start when his phone rang.

It was Kjartan and while he was getting to his point Sveinn finally found a packet of oatcakes in one of the kitchen cupboards, smothered one in mustard, placed two chunks of herring on top and a slice of blue cheese.

'Am I to suppose you're still down South?' asked Kjartan.

'I am indeed,' replied Sveinn stuffing the biscuit into his mouth.

'Is she wild in the sack, then? That's what you expect of these criminal types. They do nothing but get laid and multiply. It's no wonder mankind is going to the dogs. But it's different for you. I wouldn't tar you with the same brush, you old crock, and you badly injured into the bargain.'

'Well it's not . . .' began Sveinn.

'No need to apologize. I'm not criticizing you. You're an artist, after all, and need to nurture your artistic spirit. It'll shrivel up without an active sex-life. Just as your loins dry up, so does your soul,' said Kjartan, husky with sermonizing zeal. 'The soul is not driven by dry logic; it's no Aristotle. The soul is Socrates, who dared to die!'

Sveinn couldn't help laughing, even though he disliked such insinuations which could easily end up with crossed wires.

'Shouldn't you be asleep, old man? What do you want?' he asked.

'Just checking how things are with you, checking whether the woman has sucked the life-force out of you,' replied Kjartan.

'You can be sure of that,' said Sveinn. 'And by the way, do you think old Hans from Hlíð was into weightlifting? Was he as broad as a truck?'

'I'm not sure about that; I didn't know him any better than you,' answered Kjartan.

'You followed all the gossip about it much more closely than I did,' said Sveinn. 'I wasn't interested in getting involved, as you know.'

Kjartan was quiet for a moment, apart from a few hummings and hawings, and then said, 'Judging from the photo of him which appeared in the papers, he was only average build. Why do you ask?'

Sveinn felt the air whistling out of his lungs like a punctured tyre.

'Are you still there?' asked Kjartan.

'Yes.'

'I don't see what the build of a dead man has got to do with anything,' said Kjartan.

'I'm just trying to piece the picture together,' replied Sveinn. 'We're always being told that the purpose of life is to search for the big picture. That's why they say that things which are apparently unrelated are in fact connected; we just need to look for the connections and then we feel so much better.'

'I think you're making this up,' said Kjartan, hiccupping with laughter, as though a weight was compressing his chest. 'When, if ever, are you thinking about coming home?'

'Tonight, or at the latest tomorrow morning,' replied Sveinn. 'I'll drop by later tomorrow with *Raven-Black Lola*.'

He carried on flicking through the albums, without paying attention to the details. He was thinking about Lóa. The deceased Hans Sigurjónsson almost certainly wasn't her father, judging from Kjartan's description of him.

*So what's she doing hassling me then?* he wondered. *She really is deranged if she lets tabloid gossip get her so wound up.*

The phone rang.

*Unknown.*

This was his chance to catch her red-handed so she had to admit that she was the one behind the abusive calls which were robbing him of any peace of mind.

He hurried as fast as he could manage, through the living room and into the hallway, but the ringing stopped just as he reached the bedroom where Lóa was. He opened the door carefully and peeped in. Lóa looked as if she was asleep. In fact, she looked as if she was dead. He couldn't hear her breathing and couldn't see her chest moving.

He closed the door again and was going to go back into the kitchen, but an uneasy feeling grew with every step, making him think again. Creeping back into the bedroom, he put his hand close to Lóa's mouth and nose.

He wasn't sure if he could feel any warmth or dampness, or anything else which might indicate she was breathing, and his heart began to beat faster. The hairs on the back of his neck stood up and he became aware of an unfamiliar sensation down his spine.

Without thinking, he bent down towards her, supporting

himself with his good arm on the headboard, and laid his cheek close to her slack mouth. He stood there half doubled over and held his breath until the muscles in his upper arm began to tremble. And then finally he felt it: a tiny difference in temperature when she breathed in and out, a hint of cognac and dampness which tickled his skin, as if millions of minuscule insects were dancing all over it.

Standing up again, he sighed with relief. What had made him think she was dead? His nerves must really be on edge thanks to his stay in this hysterical household.

No, it wasn't fair to call her reaction to her daughter's disappearance hysteria. He obviously couldn't put himself in her shoes, since he hadn't had children, nor had to sit by and watch them become ill or run away from home. Even so, it wasn't an adequate excuse for her behaviour.

The thought of leaving before he had managed to talk her round made him feel almost physically unwell. He didn't want to have to put up with any more emails or phone calls.

Whenever a problem raised its ugly head in life, he was accustomed to confronting the issue and resolving it. He had always thanked his lucky stars that he was neither work-shy nor acquisitive, as most people were inclined to be. But Lóa wasn't like anything he'd encountered before. As a problem, she was in a category of her own. He felt as if he'd been strung up by the ankles and the more he kicked the more his feet got tangled in the rope. Was it best to lay low then and wait for further developments? If he stopped fighting the inevitable maybe a timid little mouse would emerge and gnaw through the rope, setting him free?

For some reason, he imagined Margrét as that mouse. Margrét, who he'd never set eyes on, except in a framed picture on the wall. There, at twelve years old or thereabouts, she was doing a handstand against the wall of a barn, smiling an upside-down smile at the camera, screwing her eyes against the sun, her T-shirt carefully tucked into her shorts so as not to reveal the open secret of her pubescent chest.

He decided to go back into the kitchen, have some more to eat, take some Tramadols and read up a little on the latest technological and scientific discoveries. Then he would shift *Raven-Black Lola* onto the floor and lie down on the sofa until Lóa was up and about in the morning.

If she appeared reasonably clear-headed when she woke then he would attempt to reason with her. And if that didn't work then he would take himself off home with the doll, buy an Alsatian, get an ex-directory number and give it out to friends and relatives only, with strict instructions to keep it to themselves.

# 18

*Wednesday Morning*

Sometimes Lóa thought she could hear the distant sound of everything going on in her mind. It wasn't like the chatter at a cocktail party, more like the sounds God would hear if he laid his ear a little closer to earth: a voice here and a voice there, music, a vibration, the movement of the waves, of planets and meteorites whistling past at high speed, unbearable shame bursting out in piercing wails of regret, and so it would go on. That was how she was feeling as she washed her face in the bathroom, applied face cream and wandered into the kitchen, where photograph albums and magazines lay strewn amongst biscuit crumbs on the table. From there, she made her way into the living room and found Sveinn sleeping under a blanket on the sofa, the doll bent in a fireman's lift over the arm of a chair, and it dawned on her that she didn't know where to go or what to do.

Pausing, she looked at them, these unfamiliar sleeping forms: Sveinn with a severe, half-frightened look on his face, breathing unevenly, the doll looking so peaceful, with her pyjamas buttoned up to the neck and a saintly expression reminiscent of a Renaissance painting. And for the first time Lóa experienced a pang of the jealousy towards the doll which Sveinn had accused her of feeling the day before. Jealousy not only for the obvious reasons: for having beauty which time cannot touch; for basking in admiration without having to work for it; for not even having to catch a man's eye, despite being designed specifically to be the apple of his eye.

No, not only for these reasons; the doll had something which meant more to Lóa at that moment than anything else: oblivion.

Fear gripped her as she realized that maybe she'd never been so close to understanding Margrét and her desire to disengage from life, to be unable to face playing the game, which played on regardless.

More than that, she understood that she too could do as Margrét was doing – throw everything aside, lie down and wait for death to come.

She wandered aimlessly out into the entrance hall, the centre of the apartment and the most natural place to pause if you didn't know where you were going or why. There, a picture looked down at her which had been taken by the wall of the cowshed at Jaðar, the farm where Lóa had spent her early years. Margrét was eleven in the photograph, with a Prince Valiant haircut, doing a handstand and absolutely bursting with life. Her sturdy arms had no difficulty supporting her firm, young body. Anyone looking at this photograph would assume that this girl would sail into the promising future which lay ahead of her.

But when puberty hit she had seemed to stop *doing* and start *waiting*. As if her passion for life had been replaced by a fear of doing something wrong and being rejected as a result. It was as though she'd been told: *You will prick yourself on a spindle and sleep for a hundred years.* Just when she'd perfected the role of the Prince she'd been transformed into the Sleeping Beauty. Why? Lóa didn't know the answer, but in her time she'd been guilty of the same thing, although not in quite such a decisive manner as Margrét.

An old memory came to the surface: of her mum arranging

green tomatoes on the window sill where the sun would shine on them and turn them a beautiful red. Lóa remembered the boundless wonder and admiration she'd had for her mother's ability to make things ripen, to create food from the inedible. Back then, sitting on a stool, when her feet still didn't reach the floor, she'd longed more than anything to grow up and become like her mum – with the power to make things happen. But when that longed-for change began to take place her focus had shifted.

'What are you doing?' asked Sveinn, who was standing in the doorway, looking like he'd just woken. It was the second day in a row he'd begun by greeting her that way, except the day before he'd been agitated and sharp with her, whereas now he seemed hesitant, almost apologetic.

'I'm on my way up to Akranes. I'm going to meet the woman I was going to see that day when I accidentally ended up at your place,' she replied. 'You can come along if you want. I'll give you a hand with the doll.'

She hadn't thought the plan through, but as she heard herself put it into words she knew that this was the nearest she would get to doing something, to making things ripen instead of hanging about behind her hedge of thorns, making a list of her own doll-like virtues and silently asking, '*Why me?*'

The road up to Akranes seemed longer than Lóa remembered, and she felt as if a band was tied round her chest, stretching tauter the more the city diminished in her rear-view mirror. She had phoned Björg and asked her to be around in case Margrét turned up while she was away. Björg had promised to stay awake, even though she'd been on night shift, and to use physical force if Margrét tried to leave again. But the thought of not being there to greet her prodigal daughter made the tarmac seem tacky under the wheels. Mount Esja appeared bathed in melancholy but at the same time looked menacing; a column of white clouds towered up out of the sea, like a tsunami, and the crashing waves made Lóa feel nauseous – they seemed to eddy around something deep within her in a place safest left alone. She tried constantly to convince herself that she wasn't rushing into this rashly, that there was a rational reason for her actions. If anyone had any idea of Margrét's whereabouts it must be Marta. The gentle old soul Margrét had trusted more than her own mother.

Lóa switched on the radio and listened to the obituaries and funeral; in the presenter's voice she heard confirmation that she'd been right all along: life was a victim and death its attacker.

A brief news report followed, coloured by the sufferings of everyday life, and at the end there was an announcement about Margrét: *Police in Reykjavík are looking for a sixteen-year-old girl. She is 174 centimetres tall, extremely thin with light-brown, shoulder-length hair. She was last seen wearing jeans and a long-sleeved, red cotton T-shirt with a stencil of a laughing sheep and the words DON'T BE SHEEP-ISH.*

Tómas, the duty sergeant, had rung Lóa as she was on her way out the door and run the description by her. He had sounded apologetic that he'd initially made light of Lóa's concerns, and made a point of stressing that radio announcements like this for youngsters who'd run away from home invariably produced good results. In his years in the force, numerous young people had been found as a result of a missing persons announcement on the radio.

She tried hard to trust what he said, but the fear refused to let go of her and it knotted her stomach even more when she turned into the car park at the care home.

Sveinn hadn't gone straight home, as she'd expected, but followed close behind her all the way to the care home. He parked the truck crab-wise across two spaces, got out and began rummaging in the back seat.

His manner had changed since the day before. Suspicion seemed to have given way to a bad conscience; his harshness had mellowed into apologetic gentleness and overbearing helpfulness. You might almost think he'd had a revelation in his dreams. God only knew what went on in his head.

Lóa paused on the pavement, forcing herself to breathe calmly. A black-haired young woman sat waiting in the front seat of the red pickup truck. The longer you looked, the more her utter stillness seemed rather sinister and after a short while she no longer looked as if she was waiting, but as though she was in a deep trance-like sleep.

Suddenly Lóa saw herself not only as a failed mother, breaking down under the weight of the task, but also as the hero in a fairy tale, whose role was to awaken the girl in the checked pyjamas. She imagined everything she had to contend with as dragons she must kill to win half the kingdom, treasure chests she must fill, riddles she must solve.

And now Sveinn had turned up, looking as if he thought his role was to keep an eye on her. To offer absolution. Frowning, he pulled on the green waxed anorak she remembered seeing on a hook in his porch, and limped towards her. One sleeve hung loose, blown by the wind.

Lóa had regained just enough clarity of mind to be able to stand up and talk reasonably clearly. Running her fingers through her hair to collect her thoughts, she walked quickly into the light, airy building. Down a corridor she soon found a member of staff – a woman in a blue apron, busily folding laundry from a large basket on wheels.

'Excuse me,' said Lóa, ignoring the tremor in her voice. 'Does Marta Jónasdóttir live here?'

The woman nodded.

'May I have a word with her? It's an urgent matter but it won't take long.'

'I don't know if she's in her room,' answered the woman, laying down a half-folded sheet.

Lóa saw Sveinn standing like a dope in the corridor and, from his expression, clearly wishing he was elsewhere. Nevertheless, he hobbled towards them and showed no signs of leaving.

The woman led them up the stairs and down a long passage, and pointed to a door halfway along. She made as if to leave then, thinking better of it, knocked gently on the door, before scurrying back downstairs without saying goodbye.

'Who is it?' A wavery voice came from within and Lóa was shocked because this wasn't how she remembered Marta's voice. Then there was Marta, standing stooped in the doorway, looking at Lóa as if she'd never seen her before. A patient smile played on her lips, and her eyes were gently questioning, as if she had no will of her own, and Lóa sensed the old aversion rising within her. She made an effort to suppress the menacing growl deep in her soul, but it was not to be quieted. Marta had this effect on her and there was nothing to be done about it.

Marta sat down in a big armchair decorated with embroidered roses, and Lóa couldn't help noticing that her feet didn't reach the ground, but hung limply over the ornate stitching. She was wearing flesh-coloured, knee-high nylon socks and white, breathable, orthopaedic shoes. Her dress, which was beige with a dark-brown leaf pattern, was two sizes too big.

'Do you want to see my watch?' she asked coyly, and showed them an old, scuffed watch face.

Lóa's mouth was dry. 'How beautiful,' she said. 'Who gave it to you?'

Whipping her hand away, with a fearful look on her face, Marta hid the treasured object behind her back and refused to meet Lóa's gaze. It was as though she wanted to forget they were there, to convince herself that she was alone in the room, as she hummed to herself, tapping her tiny foot to an internal beat and peering all around her but never in the direction of Lóa or Sveinn.

Lóa was just about ready to give up, not only on Marta, but on the whole thing, to jump in the car and drive off. But where would she go? Round the country on the ring road? Take the Norræna ferry to the Faroes? This sort of dramatic gesture becomes farcical when you live on an island; a bit like not finding the door in a fit of rage, storming into a cupboard and slamming the door behind you.

She smiled wryly at the thought until she felt Sveinn looking at her.

'Would you mind waiting outside for a minute?' she asked.

In the corner behind the door stood a small dark-wood writing desk and chair. Lóa pulled the chair out into the room and sat down.

'Ína sends her love,' said Lóa. It was only a white lie. Ína would definitely have insisted on coming along if she'd known about the visit.

Marta scratched hard at the crease of her elbow.

'You remember her, don't you?' said Lóa. 'And Margrét? You remember them? Ína's always asking after you.'

'Have they got married yet, the little dears?' asked Marta.

'No,' replied Lóa. 'No. But Margrét's gone missing and I don't think she wants us to find her. Do you know where she might have gone?'

Marta fiddled with the watch in her pocket and swung her feet, banging her shoes together with soft thuds.

'Do you know where she might think to hide?' asked Lóa.

'Shouldn't she be marrying a nice, young doctor?' said Marta, looking enquiringly at Lóa.

Lóa shook her head, and grimaced to stop her tears.

'Thank you for coming. You're welcome to come again tomorrow. Do come again tomorrow, my dear,' said Marta, patting the back of Lóa's hand gently.

The shiver which shot up Lóa's spine, melted just as quickly, as she realized Marta's hand was not weak and clammy, as she'd imagined, but firm and warm.

# 19

*Wednesday Morning*

'We'll go in convoy out to Akranes,' said Sveinn. 'You don't have a spare tyre and you're in no fit state to be driving around on your own on the moorland out there.'

He was sure she was thinking *that's the blind leading the blind*, or something along those lines. He must look a joke in her eyes: he had a broken collarbone and a limp, he was coming down with some bug and was tetchy, and he'd slept like a little child more or less non-stop since he'd arrived.

She didn't laugh, though, just looked at him, wracked with worry. Strained, and shrivelled like an autumn leaf barely clinging to the tree, she brushed her hair from her face and said, 'Shall I give you a hand with the doll then?'

As he drove behind her into the Hvalfjörður Tunnel, it was as if everything shifted, as if a layer of reality was peeled away, or a veil was lifted from his eyes – he wasn't sure which. All of a sudden he didn't know what the point was of Lóa and him being there, or even what the point was of any living creature being anywhere.

Lying on the sofa earlier that morning, his first thought as he opened his eyes had been that there was no way Lóa could have rung him as the unknown caller the previous evening and fallen into such a deep sleep the next moment.

His shame ran so deep that he wasn't able to find the right words in his own head, let alone voice his feelings. His whole manner towards Lóa had been based on the assumption that she was his stalker. Although he couldn't remember exactly what he'd said the previous evening, he remembered all too well that he'd given vent to his rage towards this stalker-woman and the society which had produced her and towards the world in general.

Lóa drove straight past his house and into the centre of town, where she parked the car outside the care home.

Two Tramadols. A slurp of flat orangeade, which he found on the back seat buried under a pile of assorted outdoor clothes and other bits and pieces. Buffeted by the wind, Lóa stood waiting for him outside the entrance.

They stood together for a while in the lobby. There were no signs of life other than distant clattering noises and the buzz of voices. Carefully opening the nearest door, Sveinn glanced into a long and spotlessly clean kitchen. There was no-one there, only the reassuring sound of swooshing water coming from a large dishwasher.

He turned back to Lóa to ask whether he should go in search of a member of staff, but she had already set off down the corridor. From behind, she looked so sad and depressed that his heart went out to her.

Now she was standing in a doorway, talking to someone inside the room, then she beckoned to him, and the three of them – Sveinn, Lóa and a young woman with mousy hair, wearing a blue nurse's uniform – walked up the stairs and along another corridor, before stopping in front of a closed door. The woman knocked on the door then walked away. She had already turned the corner when they heard a quavering voice on the other side of the door, asking who was there.

'Lóa,' said Lóa, and when she got no response she added in a slightly louder voice, 'Lóa – Margrét and Ína's mum.'

Then the door opened and Sveinn could hardly hide his surprise, because the person standing before him was not the kindly old soul he'd imagined when Lóa told him about the girls' old childminder – more than anything, she reminded him of a wrinkled child. She smiled up at them subserviently, a diminutive figure, with tiny hands and a hunched back.

'May we come in?' asked Lóa.

'Yes,' replied the woman in an almost questioning tone, and she went and sat down in an armchair embroidered with roses. The hump on her back meant she couldn't sit upright properly and Sveinn thought she looked rather like a tortoise, sitting staring at them with her head jutting forward and her arms firmly by her sides.

One hand crept slowly into her dress pocket. She pulled something out, which she then hid behind her back.

'Are you happy here?' Lóa asked gently, and when he looked at her he realized to his surprise that she'd put her own concerns aside for the moment and was doing her utmost to win the trust of this strange little woman.

'Yes, I am,' answered the woman. She grimaced as if struggling with some internal battle, then added, 'Do you want to see my watch?'

Hesitantly, she showed it to them. It was as if she expected them to snatch it from her, this token of her sorrow which almost filled her tiny palm: a man's watch, scratched and strapless.

'What a beautiful watch. Who gave it to you?' asked Lóa, leaning in. But the old lady was quick to close her fingers round it once more, whipping it behind her back.

Lóa's disappointment showed clearly in her face, but she

obviously hadn't given up all hope, because she asked Sveinn to wait outside.

He hadn't been waiting long in the dim light of the corridor when a girl with a lazy eye appeared, pushing a hospital trolley in front of her. On it were various items he didn't recognize and a familiar white bottle with a blue lid.

Stopping in the middle of the corridor, the girl left the trolley and turned back; maybe she'd forgotten something.

Sveinn looked around and listened for footsteps then, sidling up to the trolley, he looked at the label on the bottle: Tramadol with the bright-red triangle. He was in luck! He tipped half the contents into the pocket of his anorak. They must have plenty of this stuff here. Going by what the doctor had told him, he shouldn't still be using this medication, but the pain was not easing up and Sveinn had no intention of suffering any more than was absolutely necessary.

Lóa came out of the room and closed the door carefully behind her. She looked drained of colour. Even her lips looked pale. Sveinn didn't think he'd ever seen someone blanch with emotion before. He'd heard about it and read about it, but never seen it with his own eyes.

'You're welcome to go home if you want, but I need to talk to whoever's in charge here,' said Lóa.

Sveinn shook his head. He couldn't leave.

'Can we have a word with the manager here?' he asked the girl with the lazy eye, who had now returned and was busily concentrating on pushing her trolley.

She looked at him for a second as she registered what he'd said, then pointed to a door at the end of the corridor. Heavily accented words tumbled from her tongue, 'There manager inside,' she said.

Lóa seemed to have lost her manners. She knocked briefly, opened the door without waiting to be invited, sat down on the first chair she saw, and propping up her forehead, gazed blankly at nothing. Embarrassed, Sveinn stood in the middle of the room and smiled awkwardly at the woman of about sixty who was talking in grave tones into the phone. She was grey-haired with a boyish haircut and was wearing a silk blouse and pink lipstick.

'No, that won't be possible,' she said. 'No, tomorrow. Yes, let me know tomorrow.'

She put the phone down and, indicating for Sveinn to take a seat, she asked, 'What can I do for you?'

'I came here to meet Marta Jónasdóttir,' announced Lóa.

'She's in room 219,' said the manager.

'Yes, I've seen her,' replied Lóa, who looked as if she was cold, even though the room was quite warm. 'I just want to know how she landed up here and when she became like she is now.'

The manager leant back in her chair. 'Are you a relative?' she asked, seeming unperturbed by Lóa's rudeness.

'No,' answered Lóa, 'she's a friend of the family.'

The manager paused to think, touched the keyboard in front of her and straightened a picture frame and a glass full of pens, before answering, 'I'd only just started here myself when she was sent here, thirty years ago.'

'That can't be her,' said Lóa. 'It's not long since she minded my two daughters and she was seventy-two then. Or so she told me. I thought she looked older.'

'We're talking about the same woman, my dear,' said the manager. 'She was only about forty when they brought her here. It was probably the best option after her mother died. It's a sad story. Her mother was well known around here. I remember her well. As children we were all scared of her and she had a habit of bursting into tears on the rare occasions anyone spoke to her. She never took off her full-length coat even though she worked in a fish factory and it was completely spattered in fish-slime. She never got over her fiancé breaking off their engagement.'

Sveinn listened uncomfortably as the manager told the story of how their love child, Marta, had been shut up inside her mother's foul-smelling house for years, as if to punish her for her father's betrayal.

It was all a bit too much like a wicked stepmother fairy tale for his liking, and he regretted not having left when Lóa suggested it. He could have been home by now, could have cleaned up *Raven-Black Lola*, put her into a new dress and laid her back in her box. Well no, that wasn't really true. He couldn't do any of that with his left arm flopping uselessly across his chest. He might as well sit there and listen as these two traded miseries, as only women knew how.

'I was told that she'd been strapped to her bed while her mother was at work,' said the manager. 'That was when she was a young child, but as time went on that was no longer possible, of course. She wasn't allowed to meet anyone except on one occasion, when the doctor was called. He wrote out a prescription for penicillin and gave her his watch. I don't know how her mother got away with not sending her to school. I don't know why it was allowed to happen, in such a small village where everyone knows everything about everyone else. But that's how it was.'

She fiddled with a blue ball-point pen and added, 'I saw her once when I was little. A face as white as a sheet at the window.'

Sveinn glanced at Lóa to see the look on her face. It couldn't be easy to listen to this account of the story of the woman who had minded her children. He fidgeted in his seat, fiddling with his numb finger. The pain in his shoulder was becoming unbearable, but he couldn't very well take the stolen pills in front of this woman. He rather admired her because she obviously put her heart into her work. As he did.

'It took three of us to bath her when she first arrived,' the manager said. 'She was infested with lice and fleas. I saw them jumping. I couldn't bear it. When we tried to take the watch from her, she clung to it like grim death and the straps got torn off.'

The manager bit her lip, without disturbing her lipstick, and continued, 'She was scared of draughts for the first few weeks and she couldn't even step over the threshold without support. We had to hold her hands and lead her from room to room. She was allowed to eat in her own room because she couldn't cope with eating in the dining room with the other residents. She was frightened of people she didn't know, of large rooms, the radio, sudden movements, running water, children, animals and she was wary of most food.'

*The poor woman,* thought Sveinn. *The poor miserable wretch.*

'Her mother taught her to read and brought her books from the library,' continued the manager. 'She still loves to read, and that's really all she does. Other than going for walks if someone will accompany her, but she never strays far from the building.'

Lóa stood up and sat straight back down again. 'What was she doing out in the world on her own?' she asked. 'Did she run away from the home?'

The manager shook her head. 'After sixteen or seventeen years with us she was much more able to look after herself than most of our other residents, and we were delighted when her uncle came forward and offered to take her to live with him. No-one knows why his name hadn't cropped up earlier. He was often at sea and perhaps he hadn't wanted any more to do with his sister and her daughter than the rest of the family. Some of the staff here were worried that he just wanted a cheap housekeeper and they continued to believe that until he died. He left Marta his flat in his will, but she came back here when he died. So she has outright ownership of a flat in the capital which has been standing empty since then, because she has no-one to help her rent it out. She has no-one to advise her financially and I don't have the authority to get involved in these matters.'

'Where is this flat?' asked Lóa.

'On Ránargata,' replied the manager. 'I've tried to get her to make a will, because it would be much better if she could dispose of her assets herself rather than the state acquiring them. But she's not bothered. She doesn't believe in death and has no interest in money or property.'

Her pink lips curled into a smile as she added, 'But she's fascinated by weddings, especially when celebrities are involved! She has a vast collection of gossip magazines with wedding photos. Anka, one of the staff here, had the brilliant idea of bringing her a Polish catalogue full of fluffy, white meringue wedding dresses. Her favourite books are romances with a happy ending, especially hospital romances. She also enjoys looking at the shells and jellyfish on Langisandur beach. If you want to make her happy, you should buy her the newest novel from the "Loving Hearts" series or offer to take her down to the beach.'

Lóa cleared her throat, rubbed her forehead distractedly,

stood up and sat back down again. Tears were streaming down her cheeks, and when she tried to speak her voice was falsetto.

'We live just a few yards from Ránargata,' she said. 'I had no idea she lived so near. Maybe I would have looked in on her occasionally or invited her over for a meal some evenings. If only I'd known . . .'

'What . . .?' began Sveinn.

But Lóa interrupted him, 'No, you don't understand. I couldn't even force myself to like her. I was often cold towards her. It's too late to fret about that now, but I can't just . . .'

She fell silent and looked out of the window behind the manager. At the grass, the buildings, the sky and the blue-tinged mountains.

'It's not too late at all, my dear,' said the manager, and her warm, genuine manner touched Sveinn like the aroma of Christmas baking. 'Marta doesn't have many friends and even though she isn't talkative she does appreciate having visitors from time to time. And little presents: books, sweets, jewellery. I don't know anyone who delights so much in such small things as Marta. If someone gives her something she's aglow for days afterwards.'

# 20

*Wednesday Afternoon and Evening*

When she pulled up outside Sveinn's house he'd already got out of the truck and was standing by the open passenger door, looking confused. She walked over to him and saw that he'd undone the safety belt but the effort of it seemed to have proved too much and he'd given up. He stood there, glued to the spot, and all at once he looked drawn, his shoulders sagging. He was holding his bad arm in its sling and appeared not to notice Lóa, even though she was standing right next to him.

'Would you like me to help you?' she asked.

'I suppose so,' he answered eventually, as if it hadn't occurred to him until then to feel sorry for himself.

'How did you manage to hurt yourself so badly?' she asked.

He answered with a loud sigh, like the whicker of a sturdy workhorse on the verge of collapse, and moved so Lóa could get to the doll.

The doll's bosom rested comfortably on Lóa's arm as she used the Heimlich manoeuvre to pull her out of the car. She was about to drag her towards the house when Sveinn barked loudly, 'Mind her feet!' and slammed the car door shut, before bending down to lift the doll by the ankles with his good arm. He limped after Lóa, who stumbled backwards with her burden as far as the door. Sveinn then laid the doll's bare feet carefully down on the step and, fumbling for his keys in his anorak pocket, he opened the door for them.

They laid the doll down on a clean sheet of plastic on the workshop floor and then went back into the kitchen. Lóa sat down at the kitchen table while Sveinn emptied the fridge of bread and fillings, fried a couple of eggs and held up a bottle of port.

'Just one measure,' said Lóa.

'Pah,' said Sveinn. 'When I was seventeen my gran said to me, "Aren't you ever going to start drinking? Are you really going to turn out to be a temperance man like your scoundrel of a grandad? Teetotalism is for people who don't have the courage to look unreality in the eye. The road to unhappiness and faint-heartedness. Just look at your twit of a grandfather, sober as a judge. Every day is the same to him and he is the same each day – dull as ditchwater."'

With the taste of the port on her tongue like a bed of honey-sweet flowers, Lóa burst out laughing. The laughter vibrated against the fear and grief deep within her, channelling a path for her emotions, and she felt a lump rise in her throat once more. She stood up, pushing away her slice of bread. Her eyes were welling up.

'Where's the bathroom?' she asked, swallowing hard. 'I was looking for it the other day, but couldn't find it.'

'Just off the hallway – first on the right,' replied Sveinn.

'I tried the handle – it was locked,' she said.

'No, not locked. Just swollen with the damp. You have to give the door a shove and then lean hard against it to close it. Or there's another toilet off the entrance here, opposite the front door.'

She rushed into the toilet off the entrance hall and, locking the door behind her, she looked around: a worn, but clean hand towel hanging on a bent nail, a white-tiled wall, a pale-green toilet and matching handbasin. She must have come in here, probably more than once, the evening she'd had the puncture, but she'd been too drunk and full of despair to remember it the next day.

Leaning on the basin, she looked in the mirror. The muscles in her face were rigid, her eyes cold and hard. She didn't recognize the woman in the mirror and a shudder of revulsion ran up her spine. The lump in her throat was choking her, but the tears would not come to release it. But there was no use staying locked in there with the strong smell of cleaning fluid irritating her nose and eyes.

She sat back down at the table and made a second attempt at her slice of bread and the port. The coffee machine spat the last few drops into the filter and Sveinn set a brimming cup of black coffee down in front of her. She gulped half of it down, despite the protests from her stomach.

A muted ringtone could be heard from the coat rack in the porch. Pushing his coffee cup away, Sveinn got up and came back with the phone still ringing in his hands, an anxious expression on his face.

'Aren't you going to answer it?' asked Lóa.

'It doesn't matter,' he replied, rubbing his little finger vigorously – a strange habit of his. 'It's my ladyfriend who I've never met, and her expressions of friendship make me rather uneasy.'

Lóa felt queasy at the memory of the stream of abuse which had assaulted her ears when she'd answered his phone the evening before.

Sveinn opened the drawer under the sink and, pulling out a card, handed it to Lóa.

*Our creator and father in crime, Sveinn Guðmundsson, who died suddenly at his home on Friday 13th June.*

*The Used Innocents*

'This dropped through my letterbox the morning you took *Raven-Black Lola*, and the abusive calls began in earnest the same day,' he said. 'Up until then I'd just had a few prank calls where the caller hung up as soon as I answered.'

He went silent and looked down before adding, 'I thought it was you.'

It took Lóa a while before the meaning of these words sank in.

The computerized voice echoed in her head: *'When I hack off your fingers one by one maybe you'll realize you aren't God. When I flay you alive with a lash maybe you'll regret using your precious life for evil.'*

She turned the card over and saw the cutting, the obituary of Hans Sigurjónsson from Svarfaðardalur.

'Who is this Hans?' she asked.

Sveinn shrugged. 'An old customer.'

'How do you know that your pen pal and this abusive caller are the same person and how do you know it's a woman?'

'I just know,' he replied.

'And what does she want?'

'As I understand it, for me to kick the bucket so that humankind can survive,' he said, picking up the dishcloth from the sink and wiping down the table between the cups and glasses. Then he rinsed the cloth carefully, before dropping it back in the sink. 'She's still generally silent on the phone,' he added, as he sat down wearily at the table opposite Lóa.

Her thoughts wandered to a painting which used to hang at Björg and her boyfriend's flat, before they went their separate ways. It was a picture of a man and a woman at a kitchen table, and below their feet in black letters were the words: *You only get on with me when there's a table between us*.

For a while, they ate and drank in silence.

'When she next rings why don't you just tell her what she needs to hear? Speak on behalf of the world, no, the disgraceful state of the world, and ask for forgiveness.'

He stared at her. 'You're not right in the head,' he said. 'You don't know what you're talking about.'

She poured herself another drink, then when it came to downing it, thought better of it, and poured it into Sveinn's glass, even though it hurt her to do so.

'Are you worried she might leave the country?' asked Sveinn.

'Margrét? She can't,' said Lóa. 'She's under age and has no money.'

'Does she have a passport?' asked Sveinn.

Lóa's shoulders tensed as she realized that Margrét had had her passport with her. She'd needed to show it as proof of identity for her exam.

'She wants to go to New York,' said Lóa.

The thought that Margrét might have got that far terrified her like a nightmare from the darkest folk tale.

'But they've put out an announcement for her on the radio, and it'll be on the TV this evening and in the papers tomorrow,' she added.

Sveinn nodded slowly.

Lóa grabbed her phone and, rushing into the living room where she'd fallen asleep a few days earlier, she closed the door and rang Tómas, the duty sergeant.

'Margrét has got her passport with her,' she said. 'She'll be stopped if she tries to leave the country, won't she?'

He was silent for a moment then said, 'What makes you think she'll try to leave the country?'

'We've no idea where she is,' said Lóa. 'She could be on her way out to the airport.'

'I can let them know,' Tómas replied. 'But I think it's unlikely that she'd have such elaborate plans.'

'Unlikely isn't enough,' responded Lóa and felt her primal instincts taking over. 'The odds are against fifty per cent of what happens,' she said. 'Wake up, man! Have a strong coffee or something. Life isn't that predictable. According to your optimistic prediction, my daughter should have come home days ago, shouldn't she?'

'I understand that you're upset—' he began, but Lóa ended the call before she screamed something at him which she would later regret.

When she returned to the kitchen Sveinn was waiting for her with a surprised look on his face, as if he could hardly believe a person could move as fast as Lóa, darting between rooms like she did.

'You should go to bed,' said Lóa. 'And maybe you shouldn't take so many painkillers. Besides, they don't mix too well with this.' She pointed to the bottle of port.

'Look who's talking! I saw you working your way through a hip flask of cognac yesterday evening,' he retorted. But no sooner were the words out of his mouth, than he was all of a fluster, as if he feared he'd gone too far again.

He tried to make amends with a smile, which almost made him look handsome.

# 21

*Thursday Afternoon*

Before Lóa left, Sveinn got her to help him change *Raven-Black Lola* out of her pyjamas and into a new silky dress, wipe the dirt off her, brush her hair and wrap her in a clean sheet. They packed the doll carefully in the white linen so that nothing could be seen of her, from her toes to the crown of her head. They struggled back out to the car with her and Lóa secured the seatbelt, before getting into her own bright-green Renault. The tyres threw up gravel from the driveway as she waved goodbye.

'Your coat!' he yelled into the wind, while Lóa was still within shouting distance, and he hobbled back in to fetch it.

'Thank you,' said Lóa.

There was something not quite right about saying goodbye without knowing what had happened to her daughter. Now he might never know.

It was long past two o'clock. Kjartan would surely have got back from work by now, so Sveinn decided to make his way over with *Raven-Black Lola*.

He picked up his anorak and car keys and got in next to her.

'More hassle from you, old thing,' he said to the white-linen chrysalis which hid his work of art.

She nodded briefly as the car jerked into reverse, but otherwise was as quiet and demure as ever.

★

Kjartan was standing out on the driveway, stretching, as they drove up.

'What's this? Are you here already? I haven't even had a bath or changed my clothes.'

'Just take her in with you. I'm not your slave,' said Sveinn.

'No,' chuckled Kjartan. 'Take it easy. I need a bath first, and clean clothes.'

'As you can see, she's well wrapped up.'

'Forgive me, but I wouldn't dream of touching her before washing and splashing on some aftershave, whether she's wrapped up or not,' said Kjartan. 'Consider it a compliment, master-craftsman!'

'Then I'll just wait here while you smarten up for your date.'

'In this awful weather?' said Kjartan. 'Wouldn't you rather sit down indoors?'

'It's eased off a lot since yesterday. A few gusts of wind in my face won't hurt,' replied Sveinn, turning his face towards the sun, his eyes tightly shut. Although his shoulder still hurt, he felt as if he was waking from a bad dream.

He heard the soft purring of a car engine as it drove by, and then pulled over and reversed into the driveway. Sveinn opened his eyes and saw exactly what he'd imagined: Lárus in his flashy, silver-grey car.

'Lárus!' he called, the laughter bubbling up inside him. He now found the lad's intense expression endearingly familiar, even comical, rather than unbearably irritating. 'Well, hello there, my friend. Everything's OK. I'm just waiting for Kjartan.'

The lad darted a glance towards the white bundle in the front seat of the pickup truck. 'Right then,' he said. 'I won't hold you up.'

'Not at all, we're just chilling out,' said Sveinn. 'Do you want to hang about and help us get this awkward little bundle into the house? Knowing Kjartan, he'll definitely have a few beers in the fridge.'

Lárus glowed like he'd just been given the whole world. As if he'd been given *Raven-Black Lola* who'd then magically come to life in his arms.

'How long have you had it?' asked Sveinn, nodding towards the silver-grey number.

'I bought it brand new last year, on credit. It eats up nearly half my wages, but I don't mind,' said Lárus. His voice was warm with fondness for the vehicle.

'Right,' said Sveinn. 'And what have you thought about doing with your life when you no longer feel like sitting in a booth at the mouth of the tunnel?'

'I'm thinking of going to technical college in the autumn,' replied Lárus. 'Maybe become an electrician or a brickie.'

'That sounds good,' said Sveinn. 'But whatever you do, don't study Art.'

'I'd never do that,' replied Lárus, and they both laughed unnecessarily loudly. Lárus especially had difficulty controlling himself. He looked as if he was about to dissolve with sheer happiness.

'Who was the youngster you were talking about, you and the woman who stole from you?' he asked, once he'd managed to suppress his laughter.

'Her daughter,' replied Sveinn. 'Her name's Margrét. She's still missing. Her mother's obviously frantic with worry and to be honest, I'm worried too.'

'Margrét,' Lárus repeated.

'Do you know her?' asked Sveinn.

'I don't know if it's the same one, but my friend Nexi knows someone called Margrét. Actually, I didn't know she was called Margrét until the other day. He always called her Marge. He said her mum had called him the other day and was mad at him even though he hadn't done anything and had no idea that she'd run away.'

When Kjartan emerged, straight from a steaming-hot bath, flushed with heat and with a generous dollop of gel in his damp hair, Lárus had already carried the bundle into the living room. Sveinn had made himself at home by pouring out three beers from the fridge and putting them on the coffee table.

'Are we having a party?' asked Kjartan.

'Of course we are,' said Sveinn. 'Open your parcel.'

'The master-craftsman is more excited than me,' said Kjartan, winking at Lárus.

Lárus contented himself with giving Kjartan an indulgent smile. His devotion was clearly directed entirely at Sveinn.

'Can't I just open the parcel later?' said Kjartan.

'Are you shy about meeting her?' asked Sveinn.

Lárus laughed.

'Well, if you really want a round of applause for a job well done, then I suppose I'd better get on with it,' said Kjartan, sounding very uncomfortable.

*He feels ashamed,* thought Sveinn. *But what for?*

Kjartan unwrapped the sheet from around *Raven-Black Lola.* 'She's magnificent,' he said awkwardly. 'Such a fine outfit, and not a scratch on her, despite her trip to the city.'

'Her hair is a bit ruffled,' said Sveinn. 'It'll never be as shiny and smooth as it was. You can have her for half price. I insist.'

'I think the sunshine's put you in a good mood,' replied Kjartan, covering the doll's body up with the cloth again.

Sveinn looked at Lárus and saw that the lad was relieved *Raven-Black Lola* was no longer on display. What was the matter with these two? Were men no better than women when it came to understanding the difference between a woman and a doll after all?

'What's the difference between an apple and a Christmas bauble?' asked Sveinn.

'What?' chorused Kjartan and Lárus. 'What did you say?'

'Nothing,' replied Sveinn.

The phone rang in his anorak pocket.

*Unknown.*

'I need to get going,' he said. 'See you later.'

He hurried out and switched on the ignition before answering, 'Hello?' But he got no response, just a deafening silence.

'Aren't you going to say anything?' he asked. 'No hooligan insults today?'

Silence.

'You're probably right, Hansdóttir,' continued Sveinn, into the emptiness. 'The world would be a better place if it wasn't for men like me. I've just realized that even my most regular customers are ashamed of what I do.'

He had the phone clamped between his ear and his good shoulder, and while he was talking he'd driven down to the football pitch, where he parked the car and looked out over Langisandur beach and out to sea.

'I've no excuse other than that there seems to be something missing from my brain. Self-respect, perhaps? Reverence for God? I don't know. Modern life is a bitch and I've played my part in that. For which I'm sorry. But for your own sake and mine, try to forgive me. Just for the record, I have a shitty life. I have few friends, no girlfriend, I do nothing but work, and I've broken my collarbone, so I can't even do that at the moment.'

Hansdóttir cleared her throat and Sveinn was surprised at the bass sounds emanating from the phone, reminding him of Louis Armstrong. This woman certainly had a deep, powerful, whisky voice. How many packets of unfiltered cigarettes did she smoke a day?

The quality of the silence changed, and when Sveinn looked at the screen he saw that Hansdóttir had put the phone down.

The speech he had given had a strange effect on him. While he'd been speaking his body had worked like a lie detector, his nerves alternately tensing and relaxing depending on how much he exaggerated or told the truth. There was a grain of truth in some of what he'd said and other things were totally absurd. He couldn't help laughing with relief that his life wasn't quite as pathetic, his guilt as weighty or his sense of responsibility as absolute as he'd given her to believe.

He had never been able to make up his mind whether it was wise or exceptionally stupid to live in fear, considering how unpredictable life was and how much of the time people spent feeling anxious about it.

He shut his eyes, filled his lungs with air and breathed out again, in a sigh which spread out across the earth, and innumerable minuscule thunderclaps from the cloudless sky vibrated against his numb finger. It wasn't quite like acupuncture – more like what Pinocchio might have experienced when his wooden limbs became flesh and blood.

Sveinn gently bit his finger and felt the pressure, the warmth and the moisture of his mouth. He wiggled his finger and laughed quietly to himself. He stared into the distance, to the mist on the horizon where the sea met the sky, merging in a seamless blue, one into the other.

## 22

*Thursday Afternoon to Friday Morning*

Akrafjall mountain, the sky, the grass, the fence posts: Lóa felt as though she was trapped in a nightmare that was repeating itself. Driving this same route, the taste of bile in her mouth and a feeling of being hunted down by life, misfortune and her own mistakes.

The gaping mouth of the tunnel awaited her. She didn't want to go down into that black hole, into the darkness under the sea. Something inside screamed at her not to drive down there. She slowed down involuntarily then, stamping on the brakes, she turned off to the side of the road. The car behind just managed to swerve past her, honking all the way to the tollbooth.

How could she be so out of it when so much was at stake? Why could she hear words spoken to her but be unable to make out their meaning?

The tyres squealed as she spun the car around and, instead of going home, headed off for a third time towards Akranes, towards the sunlit building facing the sea.

The manager was standing in the middle of her office, putting on her grey woollen coat. She looked up in surprise as Lóa appeared in the door.

'Who's got the key?' asked Lóa. 'Do you have the key?'

'The key?' repeated the manager.

Anxiety held her in an iron grip as the doors of the care home closed behind her and she walked out into the sunshine holding a key ring with three keys and a tiny portrait of Saint Therese of Lisieux.

Now that she had a suspicion of where Margrét might be, the ball of fear ballooned in her gut. She was frightened of hounding Margrét out of her shelter into the unknown. Or of being wrong, and this last straw just turning to dust. She feared that Margrét's disappearance was divine punishment for not only letting Marta down, but adding to her unhappiness.

The thought had become like crystals stuck fast in her head. Their razor-sharp edges cut her and the harsh ringing of the phone in her pocket jarred them, making her feel that her eyes or ears might begin to bleed at any moment.

It was the girls' father on the phone. 'Ína wants to go home,' he said. 'She's been in tears for hours. Are you up to . . .?'

'Of course,' said Lóa. 'Björg is at home. I'll let her know you're on your way.'


Parking the car on Ránargata, the thump of her heartbeat echoing round her chest, she looked for Marta's house. It was a wooden-clad building, red with a black roof. The flat was on the ground floor. The window sills were covered with ornaments, and long, white lace curtains hung at the windows.

Closing the car door quietly, she crept up the concrete steps and picked a key at random. But it only went halfway into the keyhole. The next one slid in easily and she stepped into the dimly lit entrance hall, from where she could see into a carpeted living room and a little kitchen.

There was a smell of wool and sheep fat, like on an old country farm.

The silence in the living room was made even more deathly by the presence of the large grandfather clock which stood silent in one corner. There was a brown, yellow and orange striped three-piece suite. The coffee table, sideboard and bookshelves were all covered in a layer of dust, and behind the curtains Lóa could make out the ornaments: a brown grouse, a sleeping kitten, an African woman with rings round her neck, children in dresses and sailor suits, a crouching frog, an old babushka, a girl with an umbrella, a bearded man in yellow oilskins and sou'wester.

Lóa walked over to the bookshelves and glanced along the spines: the collected works of Þórbergur and Laxness, numerous editions of *Bóndi er bústólpi*, and even collections of interviews with farmers, and fishermen's accounts of their lives at sea. On the bottom shelf were recently translated novels, and what was that? Holding her breath, she knelt down and studied the traces in the dust. Her heart was in her mouth.

She looked under the sofa and the sideboard before jumping up and going into the kitchen.

One chair, by the window, had been slightly pulled back from the kitchen table. It had a thick, embroidered cushion on it: lilac pansies on a red background. The table top was entirely covered in dust, apart from in front of the chair.

Lóa pictured Margrét with a book open in front of her, her elbows propped on the table, staring out of the window, biting the skin round her nails. Her shoulders drooping and her eyes full of sorrow.

There was a single glass on the draining board. It looked clean and dry, but when she turned it over a drop of water ran down the surface, stopping at the rim. She opened all the cupboards, but found nothing except rice and an open packet of sugar cubes.

The bathroom was empty: no toiletries round the edge of

the basin or in the cupboard behind the mirror, and the shower tray was dry. Over the toilet was a window which looked out onto the back garden. A tattered curtain with pink-and-white roses hung down in front of the window. And were those foot-prints on the toilet lid, or just signs of age on the cracked, white plastic?

She pulled a small hand towel from its hook and wiped the lid, which became whiter.

A loud noise made her run out onto the landing with the towel in her hands, but it had only been a car door slamming, and she heard the sound of fading footsteps.

There were two bedrooms in the house, each with a single bed, bedside table, lamp and wardrobe. The curtains were drawn shut. Lóa went into one of the rooms and opened the wardrobe. The shelves were empty, but on the other side, below the empty wire hangers, duvets, pillows and rugs were stacked high. She looked under the bed, then went into the second bedroom and opened the wardrobe. There, the duvets and rugs were not carefully folded, but had been shoved in together in a bundle which almost reached the hanger rail.

Her phone rang.

'How are you feeling? Where are you?' asked Björg.

'I'm at Marta's flat,' replied Lóa. 'I found out she has a flat which has been standing empty all winter.'

'Really?' said Björg.

The optimism in her voice made Lóa uneasy. She didn't want to count her chickens too soon.

'I'm sure Margrét has been here, but she's not here now,' said Lóa. 'I need to wait and see if she comes back. So I may need to stay until this evening or tomorrow morning.'

'Don't worry,' replied Björg. 'I'll stay around until you come home. And Ína's fine. She's doing some colouring in front of the TV.'

Lóa sat down at the kitchen table, on the chair by the window – the seat Margrét had chosen for herself, judging from the signs – and tried to think as she would, to imagine where she might have gone. The silence pressed in on her from all sides, broken only by the sound of the occasional car driving down the street. It was nearly five o'clock. She decided to ring Tómas, the duty sergeant, her mother and the girls' father.

It was nearly midday and Lóa had been lying on the sofa for a few hours, dozing on and off. Shafts of sunlight pierced the net curtains and penetrated her eyelids, preventing her from dropping off to sleep properly. She thought she heard a phone ringing somewhere in the flat. But she couldn't have because her phone was lying on the table next to her. She was too hot under the blanket, but shivered if she took it off.

The previous evening had been like watching a never-ending scene of violence on TV. The rapid thump of her heartbeat had been at odds with the agonizingly slow passage of time, and everything had seemed disjointed and disconnected from reality. Lóa's mother had rushed over after she'd rung her, and had stayed with her, only laying down to sleep when it was almost morning. They hadn't talked much: both had been listening out for Margrét, and Lóa had been too tense to follow a conversation for more than a few minutes at a time. She had tried to look at a book but hadn't understood a word of what she'd read.

Her clothes felt damp with bitter-smelling sweat as the daylight pummelled her weary body. It was the fourth day since

Margrét's disappearance. She felt cold, her back was stiff and there was a shooting pain in her hip.

She got up carefully, as if worried about breaking something, put on her shoes and went through into the kitchen. The food her mother had brought with her lay virtually untouched on the table. Food she'd grabbed from the fridge: bread, cheese, cucumber, orange juice. Lóa drank tepid juice straight from the carton then looked in on her mother, who was lying half curled up under the coverless feather duvet with a stained pillow under her head.

It felt strange coming out into the fresh air, as if she'd feared she would never get out of that abandoned flat. The wind had died down a little from the day before, so Lóa left the car where it was and walked home. The trees were beginning to blossom, despite the wind's onslaught.

Framnesvegur 19. The house seemed unfamiliar. Lóa didn't feel like it was her home, even the staircase smelled different.

Björg and Ína were sitting at the dining room table playing snap. Turning towards Lóa, they both pushed their cards aside, but Lóa went straight to the bookshelves and ran her finger along the spines. There it was: *Hollywood Weddings*. A coffee-table book with a gilded cover which Björg had once given her. Inside were photographs of Monroe, Hepburn and other stars, dressed in white on the arms of handsome men in black dinner jackets. She went into the kitchen, found a little clear-plastic bag to wrap the book in and stood in the doorway ready to leave.

'Are you going immediately?' asked Björg, getting to her feet.

'I must return the keys to the care home,' replied Lóa, dangling Saint Therese in the air. 'Mum is still in the flat.'

The last she saw of them was Ína staring after her with a wounded look in her eyes.

Lóa didn't exactly drive the car – she was more of a passenger in her own body, which seemed to know where to go. Just like horses in the old days who would find their own way home with a half-frozen or exhausted rider on their backs.

She silently reminded herself not to raise her hopes and certainly not to presume that her pilgrimage with a shabby book would mean the Almighty would have Margrét appear out of thin air, rosy-cheeked and healthy.

She parked the car, did up her coat buttons and made for the entrance lobby.

A loud clattering from the dining room indicated that the staff were clearing up after dinner. Lóa ran up the stairs, hurried along the corridor, knocked on Marta's door and waited.

She knocked again, but nothing happened.

Putting her ear to the door, she listened.

Nothing.

She tried the handle and went in. The room was deathly silent and there was a faint smell of dusty cushions and old-fashioned eau de cologne.

Everything was clean and tidy, the bed carefully made, no mess or unnecessary objects, not even ornaments – other than a deer with her two fawns, one on either side, and a framed picture of a young Asian woman holding a bonsai tree in a clay pot.

She went over to the window, put the bag with the book in it on the window sill next to the Asian woman and looked out over the back garden, and beyond to the still, blue sea with its little, sparkling waves. Her eyes strayed back to the garden and then she saw them: two hunched forms on a bench. One had such thin, fine grey hair that you could make out her scalp; the other had dull, straggly, mousy brown hair. One was wearing a light-blue coat, buttoned up; the other was in a black, quilted anorak, with a fur-trimmed hood. One was rather small; the other was of average height.

Lóa put both hands to her chest to try to calm her heart, which was beating for all it was worth. She tore back down the stairs, out of the main doors and round to the back of the building, and in through the half-open garden gate.

It was her! It was Margrét! Pale and panic-stricken, she looked at her mother as if she'd been caught red-handed. Then she looked away. More from shame than antipathy, judging from the bewildered look in her eyes.

Lóa grasped Margrét's arm, just to reassure herself she really was there, squeezing until she yelped, then she flung her arms around her daughter.

It was like hugging a bag of feathers around a handful of bones, or a gust of wind. It was almost like hugging nothingness, and a breathy cry escaped from Lóa's lips. She expected Margrét to push her away, but instead she began to quiver in her arms, and it took Lóa a while to realize that the child was sobbing her heart out. She held her there in her arms, half giddy with relief, until the sobs gave way to tearful breathing.

All the while, Marta smiled dreamily into the distance, as if nothing unusual was going on. She stared at the budding green trees, the bulbs and the moss, which were coming back to life as though that was where life's real drama was to be found.

'She's going to get married, the little darling,' she said. 'Of course, I'll lend her what she needs. You have to rent a hall and book the caterer, get the invitations printed and, as you can imagine, the dress won't be cheap. You can't expect young people to manage all this without some help.'

Margrét started to sob again, and the realization flashed into Lóa's mind that Margrét had planned to trick Marta into giving her money.

For some reason, the heavy burden of guilt suddenly did not weigh so heavily on her own shoulders.

'Where's this anorak from, darling?' she asked, and realized she was speaking too loud. The anorak didn't matter – she just longed to hear Margrét's voice.

'I nicked it at school,' she answered. Her voice was thick with emotion and tears.

'And where were you last night?' asked Lóa, even though she didn't expect to get an answer. 'I waited for you at Marta's flat.'

'At my friend's place,' Margrét sobbed into her shoulder. 'You don't know him.'

'You're not getting married, are you?' said Lóa, her voice softer now.

Margrét shook her head.

# 23

*Friday Afternoon*

Sveinn was sitting at his computer in the workshop, trying to focus on printing out the orders he would accept and deciding how to politely refuse the others. He thought he'd noticed a greater demand for male dolls and wasn't sure how he should respond. Should he throw himself into the business and see it as a natural expansion? Could he face grappling with naked male dolls with hard ons?

There was so much he didn't know how to respond to. When he tried to imagine the future he could only see a hazy shade of grey and an endless cycle of hard grind. It couldn't go on like that. The time had come for some kind of sea change, whether he liked it or not. He'd never liked changes; they just happened, made their demands on him like the taxman, felled him like a field of ripe wheat.

He looked around and knew that his life there was over. He should have woken up to the fact long ago. Why should he carry out every stage of the process himself when from the beginning he'd planned it for mass production? Admittedly, rather complex mass production, but nevertheless he should view each stage as a clock-maker sees his clock movements: carefully line up the cog-wheels, then set the machinery going and not think any more about it. He should focus his intellect on creating even more beautiful and complex machinery, which would develop in the future and flourish. That was what he did best: uncurl his fingers and feel the cool, smooth weight of something coming into being from nothing. His role was to bend his mind around plump, ripe ideas, then leave time to give them weight and shape. He wasn't made to be a drone, as he had been these past years since he started wearing himself out to keep up with the demand.

All that time, he'd been thanking his lucky stars that he wasn't a student any more – an experience only marginally better than the fires of hell. But now he saw his life in an entirely different light. Now it seemed comparable to Pinocchio turning from a lifeless wooden doll into a lifeless little boy. Surely that wasn't the sort of fairy-tale life his mother had wished for him when she brought him into this world?

But it wasn't enough to know what you didn't want. He shuddered at the thought of the path some of his colleagues around the world had taken to develop what they called *the ultimate product*: the next generation of dolls, with sensors under the skin and little speakers in the neck. These weren't beautiful pieces of craftsmanship – they were a pretentious embarrassment. A mockery of beauty. A deception taken one step too far, so far that any man with an ounce of sense or imagination would be appalled.

For a long time, he'd toyed with the idea without actually intending to do it, but now he would make it happen: set up a proper factory, have a workshop installed; employ a production manager, a sales manager, a bookkeeper and a secretary. No, there was no need for him to work his fingers to the bone. He would make sure that the apprentices did a good job and didn't damage his reputation. Their work would be of as high a quality as if he'd guided their hands himself. Of course, he would pay them a decent wage so that there was a good atmosphere on the shop floor and he retained a good workforce. He was no immoral capitalist.

*I really do have a sense of decency, despite what other people may think*, he said to himself, and that comforted him, because he knew in his heart that it was true. The self-doubt which had thrived in the last few days while he'd been holed up at Lóa's now released its grip.

He turned back to the computer and ran his eyes down his inbox, looking for an email from Athena, but she appeared to have lost interest. Her malice had only been a harmless dog, nosing around here, sniffing about there, until it got distracted and the mangy animal trotted off again.

His phone buzzed, telling him he had a text. Maybe he'd thanked his lucky stars too soon?

*The lost sheep has been found. A little the worse for wear, but safe and sound.*

The phone buzzed again and a second envelope appeared on the screen.

*Thanks for your company these last few ghastly days. Not sure I would have kept it together if it hadn't been for a twit with a broken arm.*

He was startled. Why should Lóa thank him? If this was meant to be sarcasm then it was a type he'd not encountered before. His heart thumped. How should he reply? What did she really mean?

He aimed his thumb at the keys and responded: *You didn't keep it together and my arm's no more broken than yours is, but thank you anyway.*

*Lóa sat with her legs stretched out on a checked rug, the sun shining on her bare limbs, white after the winter, even though it was late June. Yellow sand was all around her. Nearby some jellyfish that had been washed ashore lay dying in the sun, transparent and somehow beautiful in their suffering.*

*Ína was absorbed in filling her bucket with wet sand and building her own design of pyramids which were already half finished; each bucketful was tipped up to form a kind of platform, reminiscent of basalt columns, with a smaller platform rising above the previous one.*

*Marta was standing entranced on the shoreline, watching the waves gently lap at her wellies. She'd been standing like that for ages, without looking up, without giving a thought to the girls, the sky, the beach or the sea. Every time a wave ebbed away it drew the sand from under her feet and deposited it back onto them, so that she'd sunk down almost to her ankles.*

*'Be careful the sea doesn't splash over your boots!' called Lóa, more in the hope of arousing Marta from her trance than out of concern that she would get her feet wet.*

*Marta looked round slowly and smiled good-naturedly, the hem of her short-sleeved blue summer dress already darkened by the water. Then she resumed her earlier stance, staring down, her head hanging below her hunched shoulders and her hands clasped into tiny fists at her sides.*

*Standing up, Lóa dusted the sand off her shorts and, squinting against the sun, she subtly watched Margrét. She was talking on the* phone and drawing large letters in the sand with her foot. She was wearing red trainers, jeans and a long, white hoodie with blue stripes. Her hair was hidden by the hood and, with a sense of unease, Lóa saw that she looked like a nun; like an acolyte of Mother Theresa, with her blue-and-white bandeau. Margrét's psychiatrist had said that in earlier generations her illness would have been a nun's condition. The most devoted nuns dropped like flies in huge numbers, all from emaciation, because of their sincere desire to prove to the other nuns and to God, who was their Heavenly Father and husband, how faithful they were by denying themselves.

Snatches of Margrét's conversation carried on the breeze.

'Yes,' she said. 'I'm out on bail. I'm going back to the unit after-wards.'

And she laughed her tinkling laugh.

Keep in touch with
Portobello Books: